G000066170

POWERBORN

Shadows and Light

Leila Kotori

POWERBORN

Shadows & Light
By Leila Kotori

Editing/proofreading: Simon Oneill

Book Cover: Alix Kelman (@kelmanmedia)

Dedication

**This is for my beautiful little sister Chloe
'The bond of sisterhood forever remains strong'**

CHAPTER 1

<u>Rae</u>

I stand awaiting my death, looking into the eyes of my killer, the same eyes that have haunted me for the last year.

"Are you ready to die Rae?"

Within that second all my fear evaporates and is replaced with pure undeniable hatred and anger.

"Are you?" I whisper defiantly

****

Lurching awake, covered in sweat, my mind disconcertingly still half stuck in the nightmare, it takes a little time for me to realise the foggy haze surrounding me is actually a consequence of the tears in my eyes.

"Not again!" I shake my head to rid myself of the last remnants of the dream.

My clock beeps reading 6am. Typical! First day after finishing exams and this bloody nightmare wakes me again! This is seriously getting out of control.

Three months of the same dream; the initial darkness, no not darkness – a nothingness that stretches forever. I run, scrambling around the vast nothingness with only my heavy breathing for company. Always driven by the knowledge that there is something important to me trapped in this black

1

nothing. Though, in all the recurring dreams, I never can find what I am searching for because the moment I get close to it I hear and feel another presence. Something that makes me stop dead and my blood freeze. I never see it but I sense it or them circling me getting ever closer. Then directly in front of me appears a set of scorching red eyes aflame with evil and bloodlust.

I try to scream but nothing escapes, my terror catching in my throat. And just as the thought of running clocks into my frozen state, a warm breath blows down the back of my neck.

It is here that I always wake, never screaming, the terror still choking in my throat. Though the dream itself has never changed, the breath on the back of my neck is becoming more real and its effects linger for longer.

Tearing myself out of bed, I throw open the curtains and soothe myself in the morning sun. I love the summer months, the warmth of the sun always feels like it is healing me, it's as if I'm able to absorb its energy to burn out the last threads of the nightmare. I have never liked the night much, not that I am afraid of the dark, I just always prefer the warm glow of the sun.

A stark contrast to my younger sister, Sky, who has always been a creature of the night, one of our many differences.

Smelling my sweat stained body, I head to my bathroom and almost laugh out loud at my gigantic cookie monster hair, how come I always wake up looking like I've been dragged through a hedge backwards? I'm totally not a vain princess or anything, I mean I have never really been bothered by my deep brown-red hair regardless of the 'Ginga' comments, not like its proper carrot coloured. My hair has a natural wave that flows all the way down my back to the middle of my spine. It's just if I could wake up looking a little less dishevelled it would save me so much time trying to brush and tame the mane! I am pretty lucky though, I've got an olive complexion that tans easily, which is rare as most people who have red hair are cursed with super white skin that will burn even in the winter sun. Not me, though thank god and to top it off no freckles either.

My most prominent feature has to be my eyes, huge and emerald green, which contrasts nicely with my hair. Well most days, right now none of me is looking good! I never refer to myself as being beautiful or even pretty, but I am content I'm not a total loss.

Sky is the stunner in the family; porcelain skin, big midnight blue eyes, slender and with dark short-cropped hair that accentuates her beautifully structured face. From the moment she turned fifteen, Sky has had the attention of all the guys in school. I've kind of lost count how many boyfriends she has gone through. Not that any of them last long, Sky gets bored, quickly!

I, on the other hand have had no boyfriends, yes that's right, not one, Zero! I mean I have kissed guys before but other than a handful of dates it has never gone any further. I've never been officially asked to be someone's girlfriend, this of course has previously led to some at school thinking I was a lesbian, which is totally not true, if I could jump Thor I totally would. Unfortunately, when I'm on a date I end up a jabbering, incoherent mess and just altogether pretty bloody awkward. I'm usually perfectly comfortable talking to guys, hell my best friend is a guy, but as soon as I get on a date with a guy the nerves take over and let's be honest most guys like to date someone they can actually talk to. Mum says that maybe it is just my internal system letting me know that those guys hadn't been the right ones for me, it's a nice romantic thought that I just have to wait for Mr Right, but I'm eighteen and I want a date that will eventually go past the first kiss!

Looking again in the mirror, more frustrated than on first waking, I now sport a red face as well as bushy hair! Great, second thought probably best that I don't have a boyfriend staying overnight, I can just imagine the horror on their face at seeing me looking like this.

Stepping into the shower I let it run cold, cooling my skin and washing away the hot sweat from the night. What to do with my morning? Everyone will still be asleep, usually I would just curl up on the sofa downstairs and catch up on my latest TV series obsession. But I'm way too agitated, I need to get out of the house, maybe I'll head to the beach or something.

After towelling down, I open my wardrobe to pick an outfit! A highly complex decision! I admit I am a classic shopaholic and love all things fashion, always being up to date on latest styles and I enjoy switching them up. Unfortunately, this vast wardrobe means I spend a good half hour trying to put an outfit together. Today is no different, except that it just irritates me more. I grab the first few items at the front. Boho chic look it is, a pair of whitewashed, shredded looking shorts, with a gypsy style top. I then match it with some gladiator sandals. Grab a pair of sunnies and my small over-the-shoulder leather handbag. I don't even bother to put on makeup, just ram a hairbrush through my wet hair, I can never be bothered to try and do anything with it, my hair has a mind of its own. Right now, I just need to get out. Walking past my Mum's room I can hear her still snoring. Sky's room is silent too, no surprise there she will probably sleep until noon at least.

I silently make my way down the stairs, grabbing an apple from the kitchen before heading out the less noisy back door.

It's really warm this morning, quite unusual for England even in the summer. It has been the hottest on record for the last few weeks, the country is going into a panic over droughts. But I love this weather, it makes a nice change from the usual rain and cloud cover. Making my way round the back of our house and to our little street stopping momentarily to enjoy the sight before me. From the top of my road there is a clear view to the sea, and on a lush bright morning like this, it truly looks beautiful, the sea glistening in the early sunrise.

Me, Mum and Sky live in the small town of Doversham in the South West of England, in the little county of Devon. The place lacks general entertainment, it is no London, and this is one of the main reasons I am desperate to escape and explore the world. Devon is the place people come to bring up their kids away from the city, or to retire, very few young people actually stay. So, my best friend Danny and I have been planning our gap year, a round-the-world trip starting in Thailand. Well if my Mum actually gives in and lets me go. I have a suspicion that she will be against it. I mentioned it a few weeks ago when the discussion about our future had come up with Danny's Mum. My Mum had just gone silent and really rigid, unlike Danny's who thought it was a wonderful idea for us to grow and explore, she even suggested places we must visit. I love my Mum but she can be so overprotective sometimes and other times completely laid back. I don't get why something like going to a big party and drinking is ok but travelling the world and learning about different cultures is not. I know I am getting ahead of myself, assuming she will say no but Mum has really been on edge recently.

As I walk and think on when to broach the subject with Mum again, I suddenly get an unnerving feeling I am being watched, the hairs on the back of my arm stand up and a chill snakes its way up my spine. Turning, I see nothing and no one, the road is empty except for a couple of cats. But the feeling won't go away, maybe it is just the remnants of the dream causing an overactive imagination. I resume my stroll towards the beach this time at a slightly more hurried pace, glancing every so often over my shoulder, but there is still nothing, it is not until I get to the end of my road that the feeling disappears.

Ten minutes later and I am sitting on our beach, it is a two-mile-long stretch of sandy shores, and when the tide is out it connects with the neighbouring beaches on the other side of the cliffs. The sea always calms me whether I am sat by it or swimming, its energy is refreshing no matter what the weather. It's always quiet at this time in the morning which is what makes it so perfect. I could sit here for hours, lost in my own thoughts, the one place I really feel at peace as if the waves are washing away any worries in my life.

Dad and I used to come here every Saturday morning whilst Mum and Sky slept in, we were the early risers in our family. We would come and jog the length of the beach and then sit, watching the waves before racing each other back home. I miss him so much. Whether the dream had woken me or not every Saturday since Dad died, I still make my way down to the beach but I can't bring myself to jog it anymore, instead I usually grab a coffee, sit and read. Another thing we had both loved was reading, Dad and I hadn't had a huge amount in common, I was much closer to Mum. But the time we had spent together had been ours and I cherish those memories. Disturbing the peace, my tummy gives the biggest rumble which the people halfway up the beach probably heard. The apple I bought is no way going to sustain me, the last few days I have been so hungry I could eat anyone out of house and home.

One last glance back at the gentle waves and I get up to head into town. Danny will be opening the café and if I'm lucky I can get a free breakfast, so long as his boss isn't there.

I make my way through the park that sits between the Beach and the town. A place full of flowers and a couple of small play parks for the kids, it is also where the local festival is held, but it is mainly the place to be if you're an underage teenager and want to drink!

I feel the hairs on my neck stand on edge again and a chill that has nothing to do with the breeze races up my spine. Out of the corner of my eye I see some movement and spot something between the bushes. It is a hulking shadow but I can't really make out much more than these eyes that are so dark they pierce my soul. I stop and turn my body to get a better look, but in one blink they're gone. Did I imagine that?

I edge nearer, breath caught, as a shadow moves behind the bush I stop and just stare at the spot I had last seen the eyes. Suddenly, half knocking me to the floor, a Great Dane tears out of the bush.

"Oh my god, I am so sorry my dear." A little old lady comes trotting over as fast as her little legs can carry her. "Benny means no harm ... are you ok?"

"I'm fine.... just took me by surprise." I stand brushing any grass off me and drool, this dog is huge, like a bloody horse.

"Well I don't know what got into him, he just suddenly took off for the bushes almost sent me flying, not like him at all."

I turn my attention to the bush, maybe I didn't imagine it. I absently stroke the giant dog's head, sitting next to me, who is also staring at the same spot, only he is cocking his head from one side to the other. Weird!

"Well sorry again dear.... Are you sure you're ok?"

She must've noticed my glazed expression. "Yeah ...... yes, I am fine, have a good day."

I make my way quickly to town, every now and then peering over my shoulder. I can't shake the eerie image of those dark eyes, well if they were eyes at all, at this rate I'm starting to think I am going a little mad. But the dog, Benny, definitely sensed something and dogs have keener senses than humans, so how do you explain that?

****

I finally get to Café Gossip which is still fairly quiet seeing as it's only 8am. Danny's bustling around preparing food, he is moving so quickly it is obvious he turned up late this morning.

"Well, well if it isn't my so-called friend." Glaring at me through waves of bleach tousled blond hair.

"Hey now I told you I wasn't going to go."

"But as my friend of ten years you should have changed your mind." He grins.

"Oh come on, it couldn't have been that bad, good enough that you overslept."

"Yeah well I may not have drunk so much if my usually sober best mate had been there to keep an eye on me".

Yep that's right, I am the height of coolness, I don't drink either! "Ha like I could ever stop you."

"Well I am paying for it now," rubbing his already red eyes. "Want some brekkie?"

"Hell yeah, I am starved."

He strolls off to the kitchen to start breakfast, Danny is your typical surfer dude, always in boardie's or baggy jeans and flip flops. Mum had and still does hope we will get together but I just can't imagine it, there is nothing wrong with him, I just love our friendship too much to risk anything else. Not only that, but I don't get the overwhelming desire to ever jump his bones, something from all my teen romance books I know I totally want to feel someday.

"Breakfast a la one hungover Dan…Sorry, it's not up to my usual standards."

Danny pops a huge pile of bacon, eggs and beans in front of me, embarrassingly I'm actually drooling, I am that hungry.

"Thanks. You know you only have yourself to blame for this one."

"Nope still blaming you. You're my personal self-control coach."

"Oh ha-ha…So what was the party like?" Not that I really care, it's always the same douchebags and stuck-up bitches that attend these parties. At some point their little digs and mean stares stopped getting to me, I think the prospect of leaving this town soon has helped me ignore them.

"See you are a little interested really."

"Well of course I'm bloody interested it was our end-of-exams party."

"You would know if you came." Giving me an eyebrow wiggle. "But you didn't miss much, just the usual, same sluts sleeping with the same dickheads, Aaron was sick all over Chelsea… I literally thought she was going to kill him."

"Now that I wish I had seen."

Chelsea is the bitch's leader, she is truly horrendous and with no mercy, she thrives off causing pain. I really hope he puked on something expensive. She lives on Sunny Hill where all the big houses in this town are, her Dad is one of the big bosses of some computer company, so yeah, they can afford a lot, something the whole family likes reminding people. Chelsea had taken an instant dislike to me when she moved here five years ago, since then I have gone out of my way to avoid her. I am not the confrontational type but sometimes all I want to do is smack her in her plastic face.

"Yeah well she got even more pissed off because everyone was laughing at her, she stormed off with the bitch squad."

The Bitch Squad, I know, not very inventive but so true. Tiffany and Jazmine were never far from Chelsea's side, both equally as hideous yet not quite as rich, they were born and bred here which puts them a notch below Queen Chelsea. God just the potential of not having to see their faces for a whole year really brightens my day.

"I split not long after that, though not before I saw Sky sucking face with some Goth head … did you know she was at the party?"

"I'm not her keeper Danny, she's seventeen not twelve, and besides it's nothing you haven't done before."

"Er I have never sucked face with a Goth head thank you very much."

"Stop saying suck face, I don't need that mental image thank you…look she's my sister and I love her but I tell her not to do something and she will just go do it anyway."

"True, I just don't know what her obsession is with eyeliner-wearing leather clad, white skinned dickheads… she could do better."

He looks quite irritated at the memory of Sky and the Goth head, I have suspected for a while that Danny has a crush on my sister, if only she would go for him, it would save giving me and Mum repeated heart attacks with the type of guys she keeps going for. I am still hoping it is just a phase she's going through; death of a parent can make anyone change. Then again, she has always been a little dark-natured but just not quite as much as this. The day Dad died nearly three years ago Sky lost her softer side, she's more hardened and distant.

"The good thing is she loses interest quickly…huh take that back, that's not a good thing."

"You know you just called your sister a slut, right?"

Laughing I punch him in the ribs.

11

"Ouch that hurt." He grabs his ribs, mocking that he is pained.

"Oh shut up, what I meant was she just gets bored quickly, mainly because of her choice in guys, I think she does it on purpose so she doesn't get attached." Sky is really only mimicking what Mum does, she is less loving than she used to be and is often too hard on Sky. I mean I can relate, if you keep people away then you don't get hurt, exactly what Sky is doing! But then surely you miss out on the best parts of life?! Right?

"You finished with that?"

Danny gives me a small hug before he takes our plates to the kitchen, he's my best friend and knows exactly where my train of thought is going. I don't talk about my Dad often, I am sure a Therapist would say that it's better to talk it out, let all the emotions out. Unfortunately, talking about how I miss my Dad so much it hurts is not an option, the moment I do, Sky shuts down and Mum, well it's a mess I don't want to deal with for days on end.

So, I keep it to myself, except for the occasional outburst to Danny. My family needs me to be strong, they can't know that there are days I feel like falling apart or mornings I just sit by his grave, staring into nothing.

It still feels like yesterday; Mum rang us from the hospital saying Dad had been attacked. The fear in her voice was enough to shake me to my core, I knew it was serious. When we got to the hospital, I found Mum talking to the police, she was covered in blood and crying hysterically.

She said a man had followed them from the restaurant to the car, he demanded their wallets and when Dad tried to stop him, he went mental.

Stab wounds to the neck, one to the heart; he died before he even made it to surgery.

"Earth to Rae ...you still with me?"

"Yeah, sorry." Wow how long had I phased out for?

"So, what are your plans for today?"

"Think I am going to stop by the bookstore, pick up some travel books, maybe check out some flight prices and start really planning this trip."

"You really think your Mum's going to let you go?"

"She doesn't really have a choice. I'm eighteen, old enough to do what I want."

"I really hope so, I wouldn't want to go without you!"

"I'm coming, I just need to figure out the best way to tell her."

"Yeah, maybe it won't be as bad as you think! Anyway, better get on before the boss rips me a new one."

"Cool I will text you later."

Walking out of the cool café and back out into the scorching heat, I can feel eyes on me again, looking around I try to search for the source, but nothing. Danny is busy serving a table with his back to me. I start walking in the direction of the book shop, trying to shake this feeling. I mean with such disturbed sleep it is in fact possible that I am going a little mad or maybe talking to Mum about travelling is getting to me. Once I turn onto the small high street I lose the feeling of being watched, I look behind me but there is nothing. Of course there is nothing Rae! I shake it off and head towards the little old bookstore.

****

Walking into my house I am hit by the soft cool air of the fan; it is really nice. I should be covered in sweat from the walk in these temperatures, but I always seem to maintain a low core temperature even if it peaks over thirty degrees.

"Rae where have you been?" Mum suddenly rushes out.

She envelops me in a crushing hug. "Whoa Mum I was just in town, went to see Danny."

"Just let me know next time please, you may be eighteen but I still worry." Pulling away she walks off into the kitchen.

Weird! "Uh Mum is everything ok?"

"Yes darling...I just didn't know where you had gone that's all."

I don't believe her, yes is my mother a little over protective, who wouldn't be after what she had gone through. But I know she is hiding something from me, she's never been able to hide the truth from her eyes.

"Are you sure? You know if something is wrong, you can tell me. I'm old enough to take it."

Sighing she turns around, tears in her eyes.

Oh god I didn't mean to make her cry.

"I know my little sunshine, and I love you so much for that. But I am fine, I overreacted."

There it is again, in her eyes, there's fear or something, she is worried and I can't think why.

"Are you hungry?"

Nice change of subject Mum.

"What are you doing?"

"Just a chicken salad, you want to see if Sky wants any?"

"Is she even up yet?"

"I think I heard movement a while ago, she needs to get out of that pit sometime."

She yells up the stairs after me.

I knock on Sky's door and wait; I can hear rushed movement on the other side. No doubt she's having a fag out the window.

"It's me!" Save her throwing half a fag away. Not that I smoke, but Christ they are bloody expensive.

"One sec."

I wait for another minute. Maybe she's getting changed. Why is everyone being weird today?

The door opens and the stench of fag's wafts in my face. I swiftly move in closing the door behind me.

"If Mum smells this, she will throw a fit."

"Shit, I only had a couple." Sky grabs air freshener and sprays the shit out of her room. "Is Mum ok? I could hear her stomping around earlier."

"I don't know, she totally freaked out that I hadn't told her where I was going, she said sorry after but something is definitely up with her."

"Well add this to her weirdo behaviour, when I was on my way back from the beach party, I saw her with some guy by the church."

"What time was that?" Mum had been downstairs watching TV when I fell asleep at ten.

"Duno but it was well after midnight."

"So what, you reckon she's got a man?"

"Erm no, they were arguing, she did not look impressed. I tried to get closer but I didn't want her to see me. Any ideas who it could be?"

Mum hasn't really socialised since Dad, she has friends, but the only one we ever really see is Rhonda, our next-door neighbour who we've known for years.

"I don't have a clue. Maybe it was someone from work?"

"Well if it is, we need to pop in there more often cos he was hot-hot-hot!"

"Interesting. Well I can always do with some good eye candy."

"Yeah."

Sky looks tired, and sad.

"What's wrong?"

"Nothing, just not sleeping well."

I can tell there's more to what Sky is telling me, but I know not to push her.

She looks at me, desperate to tell me something but fighting it at the same time.

"Sky, what's wrong?"

She gets up and goes to the window, lighting another fag. "You're going to think I'm mad."

Laughing, "I think I am becoming a pro at madness at the moment."

"Okay," looking at me with confusion. "Well I have been having this really bizarre dream, it's been going on for like three months and is the same every night…."

I can't hear anything else; my mind is blank. How is this possible? The level of crazy shit for the day just went up a notch and it's not even midday.

"What happens in the dream," I demand

Sky is taken aback by the seriousness to my tone.

"Well it first started with just a black nothingness… but now I can feel something in the dark with me. Recently though I have seen red eyes and a voice whispering to me."

"A voice?" That is different from mine. "What does the voice say?"

"It says come to me Sky, your mine."

My hands are shaking, badly. What is going on? It is just not possible that we have both been having the same recurring dream! But it also can't be possible that we are both completely mental. Maybe we have both gone crazy?

"Rae…."

"I have been having the same dream too for the last three months, every night. Only without the voice"

"What do you think it means?"

Putting my arms around her I pull her in for a hug. "I have no idea."

****

Rosaline

I pull away from Sky's door, panic radiates through me, this can't be happening, it's too soon. They're too young, my daughters are too young to deal with this. I can't lose them. Not them.

I quietly make my way downstairs. I don't want to alert them to the fact that I have been listening. As I reach the kitchen, ice trickles down my spine as the phone rings. I know who it is, they know! Slowly I answer, my hand shakes uncontrollably.

"Rosaline, it's time." whispers the voice.

CHAPTER 2

<u>Rae</u>

The cinema is packed tonight, I did try to warn Mum but she insisted we all went tonight as a family. It's the latest blockbuster 'Stop to Kill' that both Sky and I are desperate to see, except we would have waited for a few days so we could actually sit comfortably in our seats. Now I'm sandwiched between Sky and some smelly emo whose constant loud munching is starting to make me rage. As much as I am enjoying the action, I have to get away from the stifling heat.

"I'm just going to the loo," I whisper to Sky who barely reacts, too absorbed by the high-speed car chase roaring across the screen.

I don't even bother to say excuse me and knock half stink boy's popcorn across the floor, though I do attempt to smother a giggle. Serves him right, chew with your bloody mouth shut next time.

I open the doors to a much cooler hallway, but it is still so hot. Sod it I will just come watch it again, I need air so decide to go outside for five. I notice someone else is out there too. He's tall, got to be well over six foot, with tanned, weathered skin, he has that Hispanic look. He turns so I can really see his face, and, well, dear god I am staring, actually I am pretty sure I am drooling. This guy is…well hot! Like hero god hot!

Stop staring Rae, stop bloody staring you loon.

"Can I help you?"

Apparently my vocal cords have abandoned me, as well as my senses. I am literally paralysed by his hotness.

"Are all you kids like this?" he says.

This time his harsh tone wakes me from my embarrassing trance.

"Sorry ...I just..." Think of something clever Rae. I notice he is smoking. "You know cigarettes kill."

Wow just wow. Straight A student and you would think I was a mental retard.

"No shit, you just figure that one out?" He laughs at me.

The Dick is actually laughing at me. "No need to be rude, you look like an intelligent man, so I can't figure out why you would be dumb enough to kill yourself in such a slow painful manner."

He laughs. Again! And an uncontrollable desire to kick this guy where it hurts springs to mind.

"Well aren't you a feisty little one."

"Call me little again and my feisty little foot will meet your ass."

He flicks his fag and leans in a little, the door light catches his eyes, they're the deepest amber-brown I have ever seen, hypnotic.

"Now that wasn't nice, it was you who was staring at me."

Lost for words again, what the hell is wrong with me, get a grip Rae. Who does this punk think he is? "Like I said...."

"Yes, smoking kills." He leans a little closer. "But there are far worse things that can kill you in this world."

I take a deep breath to spit back some obscene retort but instead I am flooded with his scent, it's distinctive and very alluring, like spice and fruit, I barely notice the smoke smell.

"Come on, better get inside before you miss the film's grand finale."

As if by command my body moves to walk in on total autopilot, as I get in, my senses return, along with my need to unleash my inner bitch, I turn, but he is gone. I look outside but no one is there. For a big guy he sure moves fast.

Shit. I've probably missed the best bits of the film. I slip as carefully as I can back into the screen trying not block anyone as I make my way to my seat. Stink boy is still picking popcorn off of him.

"That's the quickest piss ever."

"What?" I look at Sky and then at the screen, it's still the same car chase at the exact point I had left! Not possible, I must have been gone for at least ten minutes.

I look around to see if I can locate my mystery man, he had known I was watching this film so he must be in here somewhere, but I can't see shit in this dark. This is turning out to be one really weird day and I have a feeling it's not over yet.

****

Driving home I churn over what had happened with that guy, I hadn't been able to enjoy the film after that, and now I'm just annoyed and completely weirded out. As ridiculous as it sounds, I'm more focused on the shithead's comments than the fact that time had apparently stopped. And it was as if time had stopped, or at least slowed down. I know I had to have been outside for nearly ten minutes. Or was I? Well I think I was, it's not like I had actually checked the time. I must be suffering from sleep deprivation; three months of disturbed sleep must be giving me some kind of mild hallucinations. It's probably time I saw a doctor!

We round the corner just before our road and blue lights of the police and an ambulance block our way. Mum slows to wind down the window as an officer approaches the car.

"Hello Officer, what's happened here?"

"Mam. Unfortunately a young lady was attacked. This road will be taped off for the rest of the night."

"Oh my god, I hope the poor girl is ok."

He doesn't respond, but he doesn't need to, his look says it all. Whoever she is, she is dead.

"I can't allow you to pass through, where are you headed?"

Mum just stares ahead at the ambulance unable to respond.

"We're going to Olive road," Sky says leaning over to the Officer.

There is no other way to our road, we live in a cul-de-sac and this is the only way to get there.

"Ok please pull over and wait in the car, I need to go check with my superiors as to how we get you home."

He walks off towards a cluster of police and two men in suits, which must be the detectives.

At this moment in time I'm more worried about Mum, she is still staring blankly at the ambulance.

"Mum are you ok?" I know this must bring back some

awful memories for her. She hasn't heard me and her hand grips the steering wheel, closing her eyes she takes a deep breath. I look at Sky, she is equally as worried. Before I have a chance to ask again the Officer and a detective approach.

"Hello Ma'am, I'm detective…."

"Detective Wade," Mum cuts in.

Recognition dawns on the detective at the same time I recognise him. He was the detective who headed up our Dad's murder.

"Mrs Morrigan, I'm sorry I didn't recognise you in the dark."

"Not to worry, we are just a little stuck to get home."

"Yes, I can't let you come through with your car I'm afraid, but I can escort you on foot."

"Ok, thank you."

Mum parks well off to the side and we walk over to detective Wade.

"For obvious reasons try not to look, and stay close please."

We all nod and follow behind him, the officer who had originally approached the car brings up the rear.

Detective Wade leads us into the road avoiding the neighbours who are being questioned by the police. As we approach the back of the ambulance, I get a view of the blood on the street. There is a lot of blood, the girl must have totally bled out, it is thick and dark crimson against the concrete floor. A vision of my Mum covered in Dad's blood rushes to my mind. I glance at Sky and I can tell she is thinking the same thing. Off to the side are bloodied drag marks that lead to the other side of a car, the coroner stands with two people in hazmat suits, I assume are forensics taking photos. The officer behind us taps us in the back motioning us to move on quicker. I am glad, whatever state the girl is in on the other side I am sure it is something no one wants to see. Mum is slightly ahead with the Detective and they appear to be in deep conversation, but with all the noise I can't hear what they are saying.

We get to our house within minutes, all our neighbours are in their gardens, watching, gossiping. Does no one have anything better to do? A girl died tonight for Christ sake and by what we just saw pretty brutally too.

We head inside, but not before I hear the Detective telling Mum he will keep her updated.

My pulse spikes. They never found my Dad's killer. Is there a possibility this is the same killer? There has to be a link else why would the Detective Wade say he will keep Mum updated. More importantly if it is the same killer could it be pure coincidence that he's killed again so close to his previous victim's house?

****

Rosaline

I check on the girls to make sure they are in bed and asleep. Both are snoring soundly, they should be, I gave them a dose of Temazepam in their hot chocolate. That should stop the dreams and make sure they get a good night's sleep. I feel bad for spiking my daughters, but I know the dreams would've returned tonight and I want to spare them, even if it is for one night.

Heading downstairs I text Rhonda, I know she's been waiting for me to contact her.

Within seconds Rhonda is outside the kitchen door.

"Hey, you all ok?" She walks in hugging me.

I simply nod.

She rubs my arm and scans the area outside the window and shuts the curtains. "Right, tell me everything."

"The girls, they've started waking."

Unlike me, Rhonda isn't so shocked by this, she knew this would happen sooner rather than later. I just wish it could have been later.

She lets me talk.

"I overheard them this morning, they have both been having the same dream for the last three months."

"Did you hear them say what they saw?"

"No, they didn't realise I was listening."

"We're going to need to find out what they have been seeing…I know you don't want to, but it will help us if we know."

All I can do is nod. I know that, it's my duty. Standing a little straighter I gather some of my strength. "The girl who was killed tonight, that was no usual murder."

"You think it was one of them?"

"I know it was, Detective Wade pretty much confirmed it, he said he would keep me updated. He also said the girl killed had red hair, just like Rae." Rhonda lets out a heavy breath.

"Christ Rose, they know where you are. We need to

get them out, like now."

"They won't send someone back tonight, besides there is still a chance it was a rogue"

"Are you listening to yourself? Rose, they came this close to getting your daughter. Fortunately they got the wrong girl."

"Fortunately," I hiss back "That poor girl………." I can feel the tears working, I can't cry, I shouldn't cry. This is my job. My duty. But they are also my daughters.

Rhonda can see the effect this is having on me. "I'm sorry, that was callous of me. As much as I hate to say this, be thankful their intel was wrong."

I nod, wiping my eyes.

"As a friend I am here for you. I know how tough this is for you. But as a fellow guardian, you need to pull your shit together."

There is a smirk on her face as she says this.

"We need to get them out…. And we need to contact the rest."

Nodding, I push down the panic and unease unfurling in my stomach. Something bad is coming but I will do everything in my power to stop it. "Ok we move them tomorrow, ring the others and tell them to be on guard."

****

Skylar

It is different this time, no darkness, just thick fog. I can barely see my hands. I walk around, not knowing where I am going. I wonder if Rae is having the same dream too?

I don't hear anything; I also realise I can't feel the usual dread that I always get when I enter the dream.

I don't even know why I am moving around anymore, there is clearly nothing else here. Just as I think this, I walk right into a huge rock, well more like a boulder. It isn't grey like I would expect, it is smooth black with flecks of blue crystal. The boulder rises up, through the fog beyond my sight, maybe if I go up, I can get above the fog for a better view. Looking around at the fog I can't see anything else, grasping the smooth rock I battle to get myself up the first little bit, it is so smooth, but as I push up, I find small creases just big enough for me to get my hands and feet in.

I keep climbing, but after a while my body starts to ache, I feel like I have been climbing for ages and I stop to take a breath. I have no idea how far I have climbed; the fog blocks any view above or below. Well this was a fantastic idea Sky. No point going back down now, plus I would probably only fall to my death, if you can die in a dream anyway.

I return to the climb ahead of me, a few minutes pass and I realise the fog is lifting, I reach up with my hand and meet a flat surface, I feel around but all seems flat, hooking my foot into another a crease I push up and see that I have in fact reached the top. I pull myself up over a ledge and come up out of the fog, I lie there legs still dangling off the edge whilst I get my breath back, I turn and gasp.

The sight before me is beautiful, nothing but starry skies as far as my eyes can see, but what strikes me the most is the sheer size of the moon, it takes up half the sky. The air is so clear, I must be up very high but I don't feel cold, in fact I feel warmed by the moon's rays. I close my eyes and open my arms, soaking in the feeling of utter peace, forgetting this is just a dream. I have never felt such tranquillity, I don't want to wake up.

"But you have to Sky."

My eyes flash open, searching for the source of the voice. Just a little way away shrouded in darkness I see a figure.

"Who are you?" I should be fearful, but all I feel is calm and besides I am in a dream, he can't hurt me.

"Yes you're right, I won't hurt you," says the man.

His deep voice mirroring my exact thoughts

"What can you read my mind or something?" I laugh. Seriously who is this guy?

"In fact, I can, and my name's Theo." He steps forward out of the dark. He is tall, athletic build, jet black hair styled like a model, chiselled face and pale skin.

It's not until he gets closer that I realise his eyes are violet, like proper violet with a slight glow to them, is that possible? Gotta be contacts?

"I get that a lot."

"Hey stop doing that, it's rude to……. snoop in a girls mind." I should be afraid, he's dressed head to toe in black, fitted black trousers, a dark slate grey jumper that hugs every inch of a well-muscled body and a long leather jacket. He kind of reminds of a vampire!

He laughs, but stops when he sees my expression.

"Sorry, I can't help it, you are kind of yelling your thoughts at me."

"What?!"

"Yeah, I am not trying to pry, you're just very loud."

"Oh …well …Sorry." Well done Sky, apparently you're a

gob shite even in your mind.

He takes me by surprise and is suddenly right in front of me moving at an inhuman speed, touching my chin he stares right into my eyes. And his eyes are even more amazing up close, literally like swirling pools of violet liquid. This close he is more handsome than any man I have ever seen, heck he is damn near perfect.

"No you're not gob shite, you're amazing, even if a little loud."

He smiles and I find myself smiling back, I haven't moved and neither has his grip on me.

"You need to head back in a minute, they will know you're here."

"Who will know that I am here?"

A chill to the air that wasn't there before surrounds us.

Theo lets go of me and looks around, panic on his face. "Go now, quickly."

"How do I go; I don't even know how I got here?"

He looks at me, grabbing both sides of my face and kisses me. It's not a light kiss and I feel the tingle and heat of that kiss all the way to my toes. Electric pulses through me, warming every part of my body. This stranger who I know nothing about, is having more of an effect on me than any of the guys I have been with and then he pushes me, ever so gently and I am falling over the edge through the fog.

"Be careful Sky." I hear his words in my head as I plummet, a scream caught in my throat.

I wake with a sudden jolt in my bed, breathing deeply, I try to get my bearings. I can still feel the tingle of the kiss lingering on my lips. Impossible.

I reach to turn on the lamp and wince, my arms and legs ache like hell. Looking down at my hands I see they are dirty. Dirt from the climb covers my hands and feet, but how can this be possible, it was just a dream.

What the hell is happening to me?

CHAPTER 3

Rae

The mirror reveals that I'm looking much more refreshed, this was the first night in so long I haven't dreamt. I feel lighter, more energised, though the events of last night still puzzle me.

I am actually surprised I even managed to sleep, there is so much to think about, I was sure that it would have kept me up all night, but then I have probably been exhausted from not sleeping properly because of the dreams.

I wonder if Sky managed to have a dream free night too.

Again, another thing that does not make sense. I know we are sisters but could that make us dream the same dream endlessly for three months? I have heard of twins sharing stuff like that but there is a year between Sky and I, we have never had anything like this happen to us before. I know some say that dreams are a manifestation of things you have seen or heard whilst awake, like watching a scary film, but thinking back there is nothing that we have watched or done together that could make this happen.

Something is going on here and I know somehow all these events are related, I just don't know how. It is like the answer is there but just beyond my reach. Quite what it is, I don't have a clue, but too many things have happened over the last few days to just be coincidence.

Leaving my bathroom I go to investigate whether Sky dreamed again. It's still early so I sneak across the hallway to Sky's room, only I am stopped by the fact that Mum's door is a jar and through the gap I can see an open but fully packed suitcase.

Where the hell is she going?

I hear Mum talking, but her voice is muffled due to my distance from the door. I inch closer, keeping to the wall to avoid creaking the floorboards. As I get to the door, I can hear her a little more clearly.

"No I think they are still asleep ...I don't know what to say ok, I just......I know I KNOW ...by this afternoon, I just want them to sleep a little longer......they are my children Phoenix I suggest you remember that........duty yes I haven't forgotten my duty.... Be ready by fourteen hundred."

With that she hangs up, and I am left stunned. What in the mother of god is going on? Where is she going? Who the hell is Phoenix?

I suddenly hear her moving towards her door. As quickly as I can, I rush to Sky's room entering just in time, I slowly and quietly close the door.

Turning I expect to see Sky sprawled in bed but she is up, by the wall that is next to Mum's room with a glass held to her ear. She must have heard the same judging by her stunned face.

"Rae, what is going on?" she whispers.

"I don't know," I mouth back, as I can hear Mum outside in the hallway. Both me and Sky dash into her bed, pulling the covers up and feigning sleep.

Mum opens the door, I know she is standing there watching us, I don't need to take a peek, I can feel her watching. Then there is a sniff, as she breathes out a long slow sigh. Is she crying? And what for? My thoughts stray to her leaving us. She was talking about duty. Duty to what?

32

She wouldn't leave us, would she? I can't believe that, she loves us too much, we are her children. I am just about to open my eyes and question her when the door closes again.

Both Sky and I open our eyes and stare at each other for a long time. Sky's big blue eyes start to fill with tears, so I pull her in for a hug, wrapping her in the safety of a big sister's embrace.

"It's ok, we'll figure out what is going on, ok. I promise."

We lie there for a minute; I can feel a tear drop on my arm from Sky crying. I have always cuddled her when she's upset, from the moment she came into this world and I became a big sister. That is my job, to protect her and love her no matter what.

Pulling back I gently grab her face, I need to know.

"Did you have the dream again last night?"

She nods. "But it was different……did you dream too?"

"No and that's the first time in months." Now I am worried, why did I get a reprieve from the dream and not Sky? "How was it different?"

"There was fog everywhere, and then a mountain sort of thing I had to climb, when I got to the top though there was someone there."

"Who?"

"A guy who literally looked like some kind of vampire……. shit I can't remember his name."

Now that's an entirely different dream, to add to our endless stream of weird questions to puzzle over.

"That's not all, when I woke up my hands and feet were covered in dirt, as if I had just been climbing ...but it can't be real."

Shocked, I look at her hands and feet, there is still the faintest darkening of dirt and scratches on her finger tips. How the shitting hell can this be? Investigation is what is needed. I grab my phone out of my pocket.

"What are you doing?"

"We may be able to do a little research."

I google search 'dreams', of course a bunch of crap comes up first; how dreaming of cutting your hair means you are experiencing a loss in strength. Not what we are looking for. Delving deeper, I type dream realities, recurring dreams, sisters dreaming the same dream! Nothing of use, until I scroll to the bottom and find a website called 'Ascended Masters are here'. Probably another bullshit site but I feel a pull to look further.

Here it specifies that an 'Ascended Master is a spiritually enlightened being who can appear in human form, one who travels through the various planes surrounding Earth'.

What a load of.......

My thought process stops when I read on; 'Ascended Masters can enter these realms through what your average human calls a dream, they may partially enter thus appearing more like a dream state or fully pass through the plane. Vestiges of their experience may return with them to Earth's plane'.

My heart races, Sky is reading over my shoulder and a slight gasp escapes her.

"Do you think this is possible?"

It couldn't be, this stuff doesn't exist, it's all bull, scientists round the world scoff at this kind of shit. But then what is happening to us? We are probably going bat shit crazy. I mean we wouldn't know if we were actually going crazy, that's the point isn't it!?

"I really don't know, it sounds insane ...but then what has been happening to us is pretty nuts."

Sky just nods, taking my phone and reading more from the page. I can tell she believes she has found an answer, she has always gone straight in for the first answer, no real logical thinking with her. I'm the one to research, look down different avenues until I come to a reasonable answer.

"Hey let's research some more before we start making assumptions."

Still staring at the screen she just nods at me. I go to reach for the phone when Mum walks in.

"Hey you're up."

Sky closes the phone screen quickly handing it back to me. Subtle!

"Morning Mum." I jump and give her a hug, hoping she didn't note Sky's less than stellar secret agent skills.

"You girls ok?"

Dam it, apparently I suck too, I had wanted to compose myself a little before grilling her on where the hell she is going.

"Um yeah ...well no not really, we heard you speaking this morning and also I saw your packed suitcase, is everything ok?"

She is silent for way too long, I can see in her eyes she wants to tell us something, something big. But the moment I think she will, the barriers in her eyes shut.

"It's nothing serious, I just want us to get away for a bit, as a family.

Liar! "Who is Phoenix?" I ask.

"Oh, he's just a work colleague." She seems shocked that I heard so much.

Lies! I know she is lying and I'm fed up with it.

"Really Mum, so why were you yelling at him to remember we are your daughters?"

She doesn't answer, just stares dumb-founded. Usually I would feel somewhat bad for harassing her like this but nothing is making sense and I'm desperate for some answers.

"And what is going to be done by this afternoon?" Sky adds to the onslaught

She still doesn't answer, just stares from Sky to me, shocked!

"And why did Detective Wade say he would keep you updated?"

I cross my arms, much like she does when she wants answers from us.

She turns and looks out the window, I look at Sky and she just shrugs her shoulders.

"Mum please, just tell us what is going on," Sky begs.

She takes a breath and turns to face us, but it is not the face of the Mother I have always known. No this is a harsh, unmoving, impassive face, someone I don't recognise.

"Now is not the time for questions. Especially questions with answers you are not ready for. Now get ready, pack your things because we are leaving at 2pm."

I go to speak, angry at her lack of answers.

"Don't Rae, don't question me again. I mean it. I am your mother and you will do what I say. Now get ready."

With that she walks to the door and slams it shut behind her.

What the bloody hell? Mum has never ever done anything like this.

"What the shit was that…" Sky starts but I want answers, and I want them now.

I hear her downstairs and run down after her.

"You know what, you may be my mother but I am eighteen now, so I don't have to do what you say anymore, especially when I know you're lying."

I can feel my cheeks heating, I must resemble something close to a tomato with my red hair and face. But I don't care, and I don't even feel bad for yelling at her, all my frustration and pain bubbling to the surface.

"You think we are just going to pack up because you decide to go all militant on us for a few seconds, well think again."

She hasn't turned around yet, which is probably a good thing. We have never fought like this. But I feel so angry, hurt and fed up with all the crap going on at the moment.

Sky silently sidles up next to me, arms crossed. She wants her say too.

"Mum you can't just spring this bullshit on…."

That is as far as she gets, next thing I know Sky is sprawled on the floor clutching her face. I have never seen anyone move as fast as my mum did just then. Impossibly fast. It stuns me to silence. In fact, I think we are all shocked as to what just happened. Mum in all my life has never lost her temper, never struck out. Yes, she hates swearing but this…...this is bang out of order.

I go to Sky but Mum is there first.

"Oh baby I am so sorry…I didn't mean to."

Sky just looks at her like she doesn't know her, scooting

back away from her.

"Get off me."

She shrugs out of Mum's grasp, standing she has tears in her eyes, she looks at me and runs out the front door.

"Sky please…"

Mum goes to run after her but I grab her arm and haul her back with more strength than I thought I had. Mum kind of stumbles a little, but I don't have time to worry about if I just hurt her, I need to go after Sky.

"I don't know what is going on with you Mum, but I suggest you stay here, I will go get her."

"But you don't under…."

"UNDERSTAND? No shit I don't Mum, because you are telling us nothing!"
She looks at me, I can't tell what it is I am seeing in her eyes; pain, anger, love?

"Ok, please go find your sister and be quick, please! It is very important that we leave as soon as possible."

Still with this shit! "Are you kidding me Mum, we are going nowhere until you tell us exactly why we need to leave so desperately, so I suggest you plan on telling us the truth."

She goes to cut in but I hold a hand up to her face and just walk out, I don't even care that I am barefoot and essentially in my night wear.

I need to find Sky and I am pretty sure I know exactly where she has gone. I look over my shoulder and see Mum watching, she's crying again.

The overwhelming urge to run back and hug her keeps me rooted to the spot for a moment, but the thought of Sky and the look of betrayal on her face after Mum hit her makes me turn my back and run off after Sky.

****

Rosaline

What have I done?

I just hit my precious baby Sky, and now I have endangered them both, they are out there with danger everywhere.

Why couldn't I have just been honest?! Rhonda was right, they are old enough, I saw it in Rae just then.

Rhonda! I need to tell her, maybe she can go after them, I am pretty sure I know where Sky will head.

Before I even turn, I smell them! Too late, they are here. And then the worst pain I have ever felt vibrates through my body. Before the blackness claims me, I hear him.

"Where are they?"

My last thought is of my girls, have I failed?

CHAPTER 4

<u>Skylar</u>

The cemetery is always quiet in the morning which is why I love it, I can come see Dad and not be disturbed by others mourning their loss. The grass feels great on my sore feet, I hadn't been thinking about shoes when I ran out of the house, it wasn't until I got round the corner from ours that I really felt the dig of gravel and they hurt. Treading carefully amongst the graves, I make my way to Dad's spot. Blossom trees hang over most of the graves, creating a curtained shade from the sun, in the spring the blossoms carpet the floor in varying shades of pink, white and purple. It's a beautiful, almost ethereal, forest feel to the place, and sporadically throughout the small cemetery are a variety of plants and flowers seeking the sunlight from the shade of the blossom trees.

Though the place is full of the dead, it's also so full of life. I come here at night too, it's then if you're still and quiet enough the place really comes to life, all kinds of animals come out to play, foxes, badgers and the odd owl. It's fascinating to watch and the only moments of peace I truly feel. Before I know it I am standing in front of his grave, my Dad. I had been so much closer to him than Rae, she and Mum have always had a strong bond, but me; well I was Daddies girl!

We would go surfing, hiking, running, any kind of outdoor activity, we would do it! When he was murdered, I felt like a piece of me died, the young girl I once was vanished that night. The young girl Rae is so desperate to get back.

I love Rae, she's my big sister but I always feel like she is trying to take his place rather than just being what I need. A big sister!

I sit leaning up against his grave, people may see it as disrespectful, I see it as how I used to sit on his lap whilst we watched some cheesy sci-fi show. I laugh at the memory of our Stargate obsession. My eyes burn with tears and I pat the ground, grabbing at the grass in my anger, anger aimed towards her, Mum!

"Bloody bitch!"

Sniffing back tears, I inhale a big breath and exhale slowly, Dad always got me to do that whenever I lost my temper, which was quite a lot.

"Always learn control! Yeah…. that's what you used to say. Shame you couldn't have shown Mum some of that self-control too."

What was her problem? She totally overreacted, I mean I wasn't even the one yelling at her, but then she would never hit her precious Rae.

I bite my lip, instantly regretting that thought, it's not Rae's fault Mum prefers her. Rae has always done as she was told, whereas, since Dad died, Mum's had zero control over me. Sometimes I even think she is scared of me.

I hear someone approach, I don't even look up, I knew she would know where I had gone, we often bump into each other here.

Rae's bare feet break my view, dirty and also a bit red from walking over gravel. The cemetery isn't far from our house but the small road leading here is old skool gravel, not forgiving on bare feet.

"Hey?"

She sits in front of me, checking my face, concern etched in her eyes. I know she cares, but I am annoyed, she looks just like Mum when she does that.

"Hey yourself," I say in a flat tone.

She doesn't even react, but then she's used to my sudden temper fits having been the brunt of them many times.

"Look, what Mum did was not cool, I have no idea what is up with her, or what is going on with us, but she loves you, I know she did not mean to lash out."

I can feel it building, the anger. "You just stood there," I spit at her

"Sky...Don't start with me, I was in shock and if you haven't noticed I came right after you."

'Breathe Sky, breathe.' I hear Dad's voice in my head, or at least the memory of him. I stand up and grip the side of Dad's grave, steadying the unexpected increase in my heart rate. She doesn't move, but she is soft with her words.

"I am sorry Sky, and I know Mum is too. Whatever is going on is obviously bad enough that she struck out. She shouldn't have and she never has before. So that really begs the question, what the hell is going on that would push her this far?"

I feel calmer, like I am drawing calming energy from Dad's grave, the tears come again. Shit when did I become such a loser? "I know she may not have meant it but she would never have lashed out at you. She treats you differently and you know it. And just so you know, it's not the first time she's lashed out at me."

"What?"

"She's never hit me, but she's lashed out, almost like she was afraid of me or something. Ever since Dad died, she's watched me differently, spoken to me differently… like the other day I got back, ok so I was a little late, but she grabbed my arm and demanded to know what I had been doing and who I had been with. I have never seen her do that to you."

I can tell Rae is desperately trying to think of a time she may have done that to her, but she can't, she knows Mum treats us differently. Looking at me sadly, she glances down at Dad.

"Again, it's no excuse but it is probably partly to do with the close relationship you had with Dad. You two were always together, you did what he said. It's bad but she probably sees a lot of him in you and so resents that!"

I never thought of it that way, if that is the case, then I suppose I can sort of understand. Sort of!

"But you have never treated me differently, even though I was closer to Dad?"

"Trust me, sometimes I resented how close you guys were, but then I am really close to Mum so call it evens." Rae laughs.

I smile, it's weak, but somehow she always finds some way to make me feel better. Suppose that's what sisters do. "I still think it's something else though Rae, you should see the looks she gives me sometimes."

"Like what?" She inches closer

"I dunno, like… I am something bad…. evil. It's stupid but it's just a sense I get from her sometimes."

Rae chews her lip, like she always does when she's thinking.

"She loves you Sky, no matter what, don't doubt that. You're her child."

Sometimes I did wonder though, I look so different from Mum and Rae. Suppose I looked a little like Dad, he was dark-haired. But I have jet black hair, pale skin and deep blue eyes that in some light look almost purple. The complete opposite to Rae and Mum's olive skin, reddish hair and green eyes. It's not the first time since Dad died that I have doubted Mum being my actual mother, I even hunted through old photos, baby pictures etc. They all match up though. She is my Mum.

"Talk to me Sky." Rae taps my head "What's going on up there?"

"Nothing." She doesn't need to hear my outlandish doubts.

"Look we need answers and we're not going to get them here." She touches Dad's grave.

It triggers another doubt I have about Dad's death. Did he even die the way Mum described it to the police? "You ever think it's odd Mum wasn't injured when Dad was murdered?"

Rae stops, hands still on the grave.

"I mean Mum was covered in blood, but not a scratch on her, why didn't the psycho go for her?"

"Sky…"

I interrupt, two years of questions spilling out of me.

"Why couldn't we see his body after? I know I would

have liked one last goodbye. But more importantly why did Mum lie about where they had been that night?"

Rae looks at me, bewildered. "What do you mean? They had been on a date night, meal and cinema."

I shake my head. "No they weren't, I saw them on a few of their supposed date nights, in the window of that shithole bar down the beach. They were always with what looked like another couple. I didn't think anything of it until Mum lied to detective Wade. I had seen them that night at the same place, so why did she lie?"

Rae just stares at me, I'm ready for her to come back with something smart, like I had seen wrong or I'm lying because I've been hurt by Mum. But she doesn't. "We need to confront Mum, Now! I am fed up of being lied to."

I nod, secretly sighing in relief that she believes me. I move from Dad's grave, patting the top. "I love you Daddy," I say under my breath. Turning, I walk right into Rae's back, smacking my face on her shoulder blade. I grab my nose giving it a little rub.

"Dam it Rae!" I cuss

She's not moving, I poke my head round to look at her, she's shaking and I follow her gaze. Shit the bed!

Ahead are two of the biggest dudes I've ever seen, head to toe in leather, tattoos everywhere even on their faces, pale skin, shaved heads and all muscle. But what sends another terrifying shudder through my body is the fact their eyes are solid black, no whites!

Rae grabs my arm, pulling me behind her, protecting me. And for once I don't protest.

The biggest of the dudes scoffs a laugh at Rae's action, he probably sees it as pathetic.

We should run. We're young, lighter, shit I can outrun these mini hulks anytime. But Rae is standing her ground. Bloody nutter. The guys edge forward slightly and Rae whispers to me.

"Run!"

She grabs my hand squeezing hard.

"Run...Now!" screams Rae.

I turn and full sprint, jumping over graves, dodging roots and branches. I have no idea if they are following us or how far behind they are. I have one thought and one thought only 'Run'! I hit the open ground of the neighbouring field and drum up the excess energy to fully pelt it across, my feet hardly touch the ground, ahead are the woods that border the farmland on the other side.

"Rae," I yell over my shoulder. "We can lose them in the woods."

No reply. In fact, now I am paying attention, I don't hear anything other than my own breathing.

Still running I look behind. Nothing. No one is there. Oh my God where is Rae? Had I really run that fast? I stop immediately but at the speed I'm going I nearly topple over, kicking up dirt somewhat painfully with my bare feet. I manage to regain my footing, I look towards the back entrance of the cemetery, I wait for a heartbeat. Nothing

Maybe she ran a different way?

A scream reverberates through the field, freezing my blood. Rae!

I race back.

****

<u>Rae</u>

"Run!" I tell Sky.

I squeeze her hand tightly, for all I know this maybe the last time I see her.

"Run...now!"

I hear her bolt behind me, she's a fast runner, much faster than me.

I look towards the two menacing men as they shift to move forward, but I am not running. I stand rigid, a barrier between me and my sister. The sound of Sky's foot falls disappear, relief floods me, at least she is safe! I would have held her back; I can run but I am more long distance than a sprinter. My relief is quickly replaced by fear as the men stalk towards me, sneering, almost growling.

"Lookie here Ryzlar, this one thinks she can protect the other."

There is a twang to his accent, one I can't place, is it Russian? No that isn't it.

The one called Ryzlar laughs.

It's a cruel laugh that sends shivers up my spine, chilling me to the core.

"Quite pathetic."

He leers at me, looking me up and down like a piece of meat. I involuntarily step back, from the corner of my eye I notice a thick branch lying next to a grave, perfect.

I rush to grab it, but they spot my move. I have barely bent to grab my weapon when Ryzlar is in front of me, there's no time to register how fast he just moved because all I feel is pain.

I fly back in the air and collide with Dad's grave, screaming. The pain is excruciating and my vision blurs, I can barely breathe from the force of the kick to my stomach!

I wipe my eyes to clear the blurred vision as they approach.

"Careful Ryzlar, he wants her in working condition."

Through the fog of pain I pick up on one thing, if someone wants me then that means they plan on taking me, taking me where? Are they part of a sex-trafficking group, they look like they might be? Fear courses through my body eradicating the pain, but something else sparks within me, I can feel it building, it soothes the bruises, warming me from the centre of my chest. It spreads over my body in gentle waves that make my skin tingle.

Ryzlar takes a step forward, I know he is coming to take me, I can't let that happen, I have seen enough movies to know that I will not get out of this alive.

One true thought penetrates my brain, Fight! Something within me ignites, I see it happening but don't know how, I look at them through an orange-red haze. A pressure builds in my chest and then from within me, a charge shoots up my arms and bright yellow fire bursts from my hands, it strikes Ryzlar in the chest spinning him high and far across the graves. As soon as the surge leaves me I collapse, I feel weak as if I've just done a six hour workout. I have no idea what just happened.

The other man stares at where Ryzlar fell before his focus is back on me, and boy, it is full of rage. I grasp for any form of weapon but I can barely move.

"Wrong move bitch." He snarls as he moves to grab me.

That's it I am dead! I can barely grasp the rock I want to

use to smack him in the head!

As he grabs my hair yanking me up, I scream from the pain, my vision blurring some more but then he releases me and I fall to the floor, in a crumpled mess. I hear scuffling from a fight, I try to turn towards the commotion. Dazed I manage to focus enough to see the tanned skin and ruggedly handsome face of the guy from the cinema. And wow his hotness factor just increased threefold, because he is kicking this guy's ass. Both are moving so fast, faster than I know anyone should be able to move, I'm struggling to keep up with them. I close my eyes to try and gain my senses, I probably have a concussion and so I am not seeing things right. There is a sickening crack and what I can only imagine is a body falling to the floor by the sound of the thud. I open my eyes and I am staring right back into the black soulless pits of Ryzlar's buddy. I scream, again, trying to shuffle back from the dead guy, panic grips me as I try to escape.

"Hey, you're alright, I got you."

The hot guy gently grabs me, pulling me up into his arms, though I am still fighting, I know he's just saved me but he has also just killed someone.

"Calm down, I am not going to hurt you."

I can't help it though, all this weirdness and then what I just did to Ryzlar is too much, I can't breathe, I want out. I keep fighting. I just want to get away.

"Let go of me," I scream.

Before he can reply a large branch whacks him across the head, his eyes glaze slightly and his grip releases me. I pull away, fearful that this is Ryzlar coming to get me again. Another whack of the branch and the hot guy rocks forward hitting the floor. Behind is Sky, trembling with the branch in hand. She looks shocked and surprised that she managed to take him down, she looks at me and nods if I am ok. I nod back, still trying to get my grounding. Sky steps in to hit him again.

"No Sky...don't ...I think he helped me."

"What?"

"The other guys, he took them out... well one of them anyway."

I lean over to look at him. Whoever he is, I know he didn't mean any harm, I hadn't sensed danger off him the night before, but then again what the hell did I know about sensing danger. The fact he just killed someone with his bare hands was a testament to how dangerous he actually is!

"Rae we should go, we need to get back to the house."

Sky is shivering, I can feel the fear rising in me again too. I just feel bad leaving him here with the two guys.......My thought trails off as I look around, the other guy and Ryzlar are nowhere to be seen. Other than a scorched patch on the ground by Dad's grave there is not one body in sight.

"What the hell, where are the bodies?"

"What bodies Rae?"

"The two guys Sky, I hit one and then this guy came along and killed the other."

I push past Sky heading to where I thought I saw Ryzlar's body fall. Again, nothing but a black scorch on the earth.

Sky leans down and feels the ground, she pulls her hand back quickly. "Shit, that is hot."

"Where did they go?"

Did they just spontaneously combust? But isn't that a myth?

"Maybe they are vampires?"

Sky even has a serious face on her. I am dumbfounded

"Really? That's the best you can come up with, vampires?"

"Well I don't see you coming up with any good ideas and this is pretty bloody weird," she says gesturing wildly to the ground.

I look at the scorch mark, I can feel the heat coming off the ground on my legs. The mark itself isn't any particular shape, almost star shaped, with a slight crater like a mini comet mark.

A moan sounds from behind us. Shit he must be waking up.

"Come on," I urge.

We dash off back towards the house, running as fast as we can, ignoring our sore feet. We exit the little path and run full speed nearly colliding with a group of people.

"Sorry," I mumble as I try to push through. But there are people everywhere. In the background I hear sirens and I can see smoke coming from just up the road, right where our house is. Dread forms in the pit of my stomach. I look at Sky, she is thinking the same thing. We start pushing faster through the crowd, not excusing ourselves as we virtually slam into people until we hit the police blockade.

"Hey, girls you can't go any further."

I try pushing past him, both me and Sky shoving him, but another officer jumps in to stop us.

"Girls you can't go any further, this is a crime scene."

"Our house is up there," Sky screams.

The officers stop, looking at each other, then turn to face us.

"What number girls?"

"Thirty-five," I reply

Their faces say it all. I can feel my legs give way as a gasp from the crowd behind us ensues.

"Our Mum, where's our Mum?"

"Come with us."

The officers escort us round the barricade. Our neighbours are with a policeman on each door, some are just watching with horror on their faces, others talking to the officers. All stop and stare, sorrow and sympathy etched on their faces as we pass them. We turn the corner of our street, smoke billows in great clouds and before us stands the remains of our house and to the side on the once pristine front lawn lies a black body bag. I see Rhonda running towards us, but I can't hear anything, just a high-pitched buzzing, everything slows down. I see Sky scream but I can barely hear her, my breathing becomes heavy. I look from the bag to our house, it is completely black, remnants of our home litter the street. Everything gone! I look at the bag.

Mum! I try to step forward blackness clouding my vision but Sky's screams are the last thing I hear.

CHAPTER 5

Skylar

I just sit here numb, it's like a haze around me, the bustling of the hospital seems far away, the voices are partially muted, I feel dead inside. How can this have happened? I may not have always seen eye to eye with my Mum but it didn't mean I didn't love her. And now she is dead, and the last thing she saw of me was me running away. Thinking back to those few hours ago I can now see how panicked she was, no not panicked, she looked fearful. I keep replaying the events of the last two days in my head, the dreams that me and Rae share, the girl murdered down our road and those two men. I have no idea what is going on but I feel like I am being torn apart, it's too much. The guilt. The pain. I'm only vaguely aware that I am rocking in my chair…or maybe I'm on the floor, I really don't know and I don't care. Everything is screwed. What are we supposed to do? I become aware that someone is putting their arm around me, but I don't want the comfort. I shrug off this pathetic attempt of comfort.

"Sky." The voice comes from next to me but it sounds distant

"Sky." It comes again, this time whoever the voice belongs to decides to shake me. "Skylar!" The voice echoes in my head bringing me back to the present, everything suddenly seems really loud. "Skylar." Rhonda shakes me again.

I look at her feeling like I have just woken up, the noise

of the hospital instantly irritates me.

"What!" I half spit at her.

I don't mean to be venomous but I just want to be left alone, to think. I know there will be a lot of questions and I just want some time to think.

She doesn't react to my outburst, she just looks me in the eye, grabs my hand and firmly says to me. "Rae is awake."

She raises an eyebrow at me, almost commanding me to pull my shit together and get up.   All I can do is nod and stand up. I let Rhonda lead me to the room they brought Rae into, she had hit her head when she passed out and had still been unconscious when we got here. In a way I wish I had passed out, to just be out of it and not feel anything. That would be great right now.

As we get to the entrance to Rae's room, detective Wade comes round the corner, the look on his face is one of sympathy and it just annoys me, to the point I just want to slap the look away.

"Miss Morrigan, I am so sor……"

I interrupt before he can continue with this crap "Just stop right there, I don't want your sympathies." I can feel the anger boiling. Because of this idiot they didn't find my Dad's killer, that psycho is still on the loose and it is more than coincidental that only last night a girl was brutally murdered just down the road from us and now my Mum is dead! No one has denied that my Mum died due to foul play, I know in my heart that she was murdered and that girl down the road, well from the photo on the news, she suspiciously looked a lot like Rae. Whoever this psycho is, he is determined to wipe out my whole family! And what about the men who attacked Rae in the graveyard? I bet they had something to do with it. In fact, it could have been them who burnt our home, killing my Mum. Why I don't know! But this prick in front of me could have stopped it all, if he had just done his job. I breathe in deep, pushing the anger down like Dad always taught me, now is not the time for me to lose my shit.

Before he can speak again and annoy me further I put my point across.

"I think rather than standing here and offering your sympathies you should be out there catching this killer, doing your job for once before someone else's life is ripped apart." My hands are shaking with rage. It's dawning on me more and more that the same person or people are responsible for all this, Detective Wade has had three years to find them and he has done nothing.

Detective Wade inches forward clasping his hands together, like he is so used to dealing with people in my situation. His general presence is really annoying me.

"I understand how you must feel and we are doing everything we can to find out what happened to your mother."

I can't help but laugh, it's either that or smack him in his face. "You understand?... you understand nothing. You let my father's killer stay free and then he or they came back and killed a girl, who funnily enough looks just like Rae and then a day later my Mother happens to die by what, a freak bloody explosion. Do not stand there and tell me you are doing everything you can because you should have done everything three years ago."

I can feel the tears welling up, a buzzing starts in my ears and I am shaking all over. I know I am ready to snap.

Detective Wade just looks on edge, I have hit a nerve,

but more importantly his look of failure only convinces me more that I am right, they are all connected.

"Miss Morrigan, I know you feel like we have let you down but there is no conclusive evidence to suggest these deaths are all connected…."

I don't hear any more of what he is saying, an intense buzzing escalates in my ears and then snaps to silence. I snap. It feels like everything is in slow motion, like there is a ball of furious energy in me that just needs to uncoil and release. Even if I wanted to stop it I can't. I am too enraged. I feel it build in my chest, travel down my arm as I clock it back and smack him a full blow in the face. And hell do I clock him one, still in some weird slow motion he flies back crashing into an empty hospital bed and crumples to the floor. The rage is still flowing through me as he tries to get up looking at me with a semblance of fear, I see red. My Mum and Dad are dead, we are orphans. I follow my instincts and go for him again; I can't hear it but I know I am screaming. Before I reach him I am grabbed from behind, I scratch and try to tear away to be free to finish this punk.

Through the haze of rage I briefly hear someone say, "Jesus Christ, how strong is she?"

I am taken to the floor, the impact of the fall stuns me back into reality. Rhonda and the other officer are on top of me pinning me down.

"Sky!! Hey get off her." Rae charges out of her room, skids to the floor and grabs my face.

"Sky, you need to calm down, calm down ok." She strokes the side of my face never taking her eyes off of me. "Shhhhhhhh Sky I am here ok, big sis is here."

As the haze falls away so does all my energy, I feel

weak, I feel dead. And then I just cry. Rae pulls me into a hug and I let it all out. The pain is too intense. Rae just holds me humming a song we used to sing when we were little.

****

<u>Rhonda</u>

I help Rae lead Sky into her hospital room and get her onto the bed. She looks so fragile and broken the complete opposite to the raging animal I had just helped pin to the floor. I stand in the doorway watching Rae sit behind her sister on the bed stroking her hair, like I had seen their mother do for both of them whenever they were upset. A ball rises in my throat. My best friend is dead. She is gone. But I push it down, I can't afford to let that in right now. Sky had very nearly lost control, if I hadn't been there she may well have killed Detective Wade. Crap! Remembering she has just struck a police officer I turn shutting the door behind me.

Detective Wade sits in a chair on the opposite side of the hallway wiping a bloody lip, more officers have arrived and they make a move towards me and the girls in the room. Shit! We don't have time for Sky to be arrested for assault. Before I can wrestle with how best to deal with this situation Dt Wade rises to his feet.

"Stand down officers, leave Miss Morrigan be."

The first officer closest to me stops in shock.

"But sir she assaulted you and to be quite frank I believe she may be on something given the viciousness of the attack."

Detective Wade, wipes the last remnants of his bleeding mouth and chucks the tissue in the bin. "I am very much aware of the assault seeing as I was the one who received the punch to the face."

The other officer looks somewhat sheepish and stands more to attention, definitely a suck ass.

"And as for Miss Morrigan being on something, I think the death of her mother is enough to explain her sudden loss of mental stability. Pain and anger can make you do funny things."

Detective Wade looks pointedly at me, he doesn't believe what he is saying. Whether he does or not, it doesn't look like he will press charges and that is the most important thing.

"But Sir it took myself and Miss Roads to take her down she was that strong…"

Detective Wade raises his hand silencing the officer. "I appreciate what you are saying, but as I said she was reacting off adrenaline. I will personally caution her but I think she has been through enough for today. That will be all, return to your duties."

The officer looks like he wants to say more, instead he curtly nods and follows the other two officers down the hallway.

We watch them leave in silence for a couple of seconds before he turns to me, I cut in before he can say anything.

"Thank you Detective, I know you didn't have to do that. Ever since their Dad died Sky has been different, angry at everything. She doesn't show her emotions well."

I hope he can accept that and to my relief he softens.

"I understand what grief can do to a person, let's just say

it was lucky she lashed out at me and no one else."

Nodding I turn to go back into the girls.

"That said, it may be worth keeping an eye on her, she showed some impressive strength." Rubbing his jaw. "No doubt I will feel it tomorrow. But for her size and weight that's one heck of power she has there."

He stares at me knowingly. Impossible that he could have a clue as to who she is.

I don't have time to dwell on it though as he continues.

"I assume the girls will be staying with you as there is no next of kin?"

"Yes they will," I answer.

"Well they have been through enough for today but I will need to speak to them both tomorrow, ok?!" It's a statement not a request.

I nod. "Of course, what sort of time?"

"I will be round before midday."

"No problem, now if you don't mind I better go check on them."

"Ah right… here is my card in case you need anything. And may I take your contact details in case we discover anything new in the meantime."

Giving him my number I wish him farewell and return to the girls, breathing a small, temporary sigh of relief. The girls won't be there tomorrow, they aren't safe here anymore, their lives are about to be upturned more than they can possibly imagine. Looking at them curled together on the bed, I feel like the worst bitch in the world for what I'm soon to lay at their feet. To me they are still just kids, as much as I ranted to Rosaline about duty I have always seen these girls as my family. And now they are to be thrust into a world of terror and violence with only the tiniest hope of a happy ever after.

But what else am I to do? I need to contact Nix, first thing first is the protection of these girls.

"Rhonda?" Sky asks.

"Yes?"

"Can we get out of here now, I don't want to spend another minute here." Sky rises from the bed and heads out the door, not waiting for a reply.

I eye Rae, not being able to tell how she is doing, she's not an easy one to read. Following behind Sky we walk out of the hospital in silence, I know I should say something, but what?! What on Earth do you say in these situations? I turn to Rae to say something, but the words get lost on my lips when I see her, she is desperately trying to hold it together. Any words I offer would be useless, the only other comfort I can give is to grasp her hand, she clenches on tight until we reach my car.

Getting in and belting up I know I have to think fast, we can't go back to my place, they will be staking it out. I need to get them somewhere safe but without raising suspicion from them, somewhere close but not obvious? I have an idea forming, though I am pretty certain that Nix will kill me but what choice do I have? I get out my phone and send him a quick text to give him the heads up.

Looking in the rear-view mirror, Sky is staring out of the window, whilst Rae is staring right at me.

"We are going to have to go to my mate's house, there was a lot of smoke damage at mine, so it's best if we don't stay there." I hope they buy this. "I grabbed some of my clothes for you to change into when we get there."

Rae continues to stare at me, Sky simply shrugs her shoulders. It is a few seconds before Rae says anything.

"Who is this friend?"

Her tone is hardened, virtually lifeless.

"Just someone I work with, they went away for work so I have been keeping an eye on the place."

It's amazing how easy it is for me to lie; it's so deeply ingrained in me to cover things that I don't even think twice. Once I have to tell them the truth though, that will be the most difficult part. I doubt they will ever forgive me. So many lies, I won't blame them.

"Where is this place?" she asks as I start the car.

Without being too obvious I check our surroundings; they could well have followed us to the hospital. But there is nothing, and that makes me more nervous. I was half expecting an ambush as soon as we walked out.

"It's close to the beach, round the corner from the Rose pub, you know that little shithole on the corner of the Strand."

Something passes in her eyes, I can't tell what it is, anger maybe? Betrayal? But she hides it again. I am starting to get the impression she is keeping something from me, she wants to say but it is causing her a lot of anger. Rage with her is not good. I don't think I could keep her down after having dealt with Sky already. But with that her expression changes, softens a little.

"Ok, that will be better than sleeping next to our……house." Tears fill her eyes "What about Detective Wade? You said we would be there tomorrow?"

"We can always head back there in the morning if you feel up to it, else I can give him my mate's address and he can come to us."

She simply nods and then pulls out her phone. Even though I know her phone has the best protection the agency can offer, I am still not keen on any of us using traceable technology. But to say so now will raise too much suspicion.

I pull out onto the main road that takes us back to our town, all the while constantly keeping an eye for anyone following us.

The rest of the journey is silent, though it only takes fifteen minutes to drive to our town it feels a lot longer. Rae looks at me a couple of times but otherwise just stares out the window like Sky.

The hill we crest leads down to our little beach town and reveals a glorious sight, one I will miss a lot. The town is situated behind two miles of beach and open sea, right now the tide is out so all the sand banks are revealed creating little island pockets from where the estuary runs out to sea. Windsurfers and kite surfers can be seen breezing between the sand banks, the beach is still busy even for gone 7pm, it always is in the summertime, what with all the holiday makers. The sun is starting its slow descent to evening but at the moment it creates diamond sparkles along the whole coast line. A warm breeze flies into the car giving the strong scent of the sea, I love that smell, mixed with the warm air smell you only get in the summers here! The area is a true natural beauty.

But we will be leaving this all behind, we have to, it's our duty and our responsibility. Breathing in the scent and sight for one last time I drift off the main road and take the narrow roads leading to the beach. Let it go now. No point dwelling.

Looking back in the rear-view mirror I notice Rae is on her phone again, she must be talking to Danny. She has never been far from his side and he from hers in all the years they have known one another. I am pretty certain that he is in love with her, but I don't think she sees it though, all she sees is her best friend, a brother. Good job actually that she isn't in love with him too, it's going to be hard enough pulling her away from him. But he cannot come with us, he would only be in danger if he did. I look down at my phone to see if Nix has replied and still nothing! It's unnerving, he is vigilant and always on his phone, I can feel the fear starting to creep in, what if his place isn't safe? What if he has been found, attacked, dead even? I can't think like this, I have to keep a cool head, my training has always taught me that fear will get you killed. You have to suppress it, you have to be fearless, then you don't hesitate, then you survive.

Rounding the corner I hit the tight road that leads to the back of his maisonette, relaxing I tune into my sensors, letting a calm energy wash over me, breathing in deep I still as I pull into the back driveway, sinking deeper into the meditative like state. His parking space is free and so I pull the car into his spot and close my eyes, breathing deeper. I call on the energy within me and around me, sending out feelers to pick up on any danger, if there's a disturbance in the energy around me I will feel it. Everything gives off energy, and I know how to pick up on different energy signatures. I sense nothing, no danger. In fact, I can only sense two people in close proximity from the neighbouring house. Rae's irritated voice breaks through my calm state, great, I've been so immersed I hadn't heard her.

"Rhonda!"

Blinking out of my meditative state I tune back into the car. "Sorry, what did you say?"

"I said, is your Friend," putting great emphasis on the word friend, "going to be ok with us just staying at his…. her place?"

Rae is nothing but super intuitive, even in her grief-stricken state she still wants to know it all, she is wary but of what I can't tell yet. Time to give some honest details. "He," I emphasise, "won't mind, Nix is hardly ever in, always away working."

"Nix? Is that his name?"

It's always been my nickname for him. "Yes, it's short for Phoenix … come on let's head in."

Getting out, I open the door for Sky, she is still in a dazed and numb state. She briefly looks at me, and wipes a tear from her eye.

"I am ok."

She gets out by herself and looks over to Rae who is on her phone again. She looks up from texting, glares a little at me, it lasts for the merest second but I swear that look said 'you're a liar'. But within a second her face is replaced with a hint of a smile. She heads round to Sky's side.

I grab my bag and do one last sweep with my mind to make sure no one is here, satisfied I walk over to the girls, leading them into the small fenced garden that blocks his tiny patio space from the car park. It is a quaint little space, a table and chairs sit just off centre, small pots of green bushes are dotted here and there interspaced with large garden candles. Many a night we had sat out here in just quiet peace, but it feels cold without Nix's presence. I look at my phone again, nothing! I up end one of the chairs and unscrew the soft base, shaking it slightly until the spare key falls out. Sky isn't even paying attention, but Rae raises an eyebrow as if to say 'Paranoid much?'

Opening the door I can tell Nix hasn't been back all day, the place is stifling from the windows being shut, I want to switch on the lights and open all the windows but I daren't.

"Come on, come in."

Both girls seem to pause at the entrance then moving Sky through first, Rae follows shutting the back door behind her. We all stand in the dimming light for a moment.

"Make yourselves comfortable, I will try to air this place out a bit."

Sky jumps up on the kitchen counter and looks around, absorbing all she sees, something catches her and she nods. "Do you think he will mind if I pinch one?"

I follow her gaze, cigarettes! Usually I would be dead against it, her being so young but I just can't, not when she still looks on the verge of tears. I walk over and grab them and one of the many spare lighters on the shelf. Turning to Sky I hand over the box.

"Don't smoke them all ok!" I give her a small smile.

She nods jumping off the counter and going out into the courtyard. I look at Rae who is busy on her phone

"Do you want a drink or something?"

She pauses typing, looking up at me and gives a small smile. "Yes, that would be good thanks."

"Help yourself, fridge is just over there and glasses are above the microwave. I am just going to open up the bedroom windows a little and let them air."

She moves past me into the little kitchenette, I peer outside at Sky again just to check she is ok. I am pretty certain she inhaled that first cigarette in one breath. I quickly move to the back of the maisonette, not wanting to leave them out of my sight for long. I open the smaller windows in both bedrooms and the bathroom. I know they can get into this place by means other than a window but I am not willing to risk it by opening up all the big windows. I do a quick check of Nix's room, bed is made, he may not have come back last night, but then like me he is military trained, being clean and tidy comes naturally, same as leaving no evidence. This place probably doesn't even have a single fingerprint of his.

Finding nothing to hint of where he might be, I message him again: 'Where are you? Need evac asap'.

I pause for a few seconds, waiting for a response, but what comes back is a message saying 'Delivery failed'. Making sure the girls are not in the hallway I call him; the line just goes dead. Shit. A cold foreboding runs over me, either he is keeping a low profile and is off the grid or Nix is dead. Whichever it is, I need to start planning without him.

I am about to call the agency when I hear a commotion coming from the kitchen, I burst out of the bedroom without thinking of keeping to a human speed and come to a forceful stop in the lounge.

Sky is glaring at Rae, no not at Rae but at a card in her hand.

Rae is gripping a carton of fresh orange juice, she turns on me with a look that could kill. "Is this NIX?" she yells, thrusting forward a picture of Nix, Rose, their Dad Leon and me.

But I don't understand why a picture could make her so upset?

"Rae please calm down and explain to me why you are so upset?"

"What are you not telling us?" she screams.

CHAPTER 6

<u>Rae</u>

As soon as Rhonda leaves the room I immediately go snooping, none of this adds up and I know for sure she is keeping something from us, I am starting to not trust her motives, I can't put my finger on it but my instincts are screaming at me. I start rummaging in the drawers, there are no visible photos on the walls, in fact there is little to no personal items anywhere, which is just fuelling my suspicion. Every drawer I open I come up empty, so I head into the kitchenette, Sky walks in from the back, and just stands staring like I am a crazy person as I rummage, I am not even being careful, I simply don't care.

"What are you doing?"

"Keep your voice down, and keep an eye on the door for Rhonda." I turn to the fridge opening it, there is fresh milk, juice and food in there. If this Nix is away with work like Rhonda is saying, why is there so much fresh shit in here? I grab the juice and feel it has already been opened and only half left. I slam the door shut as I do so I hear a rustle on top of the fridge.

"What the fuck are you doing Rae, your acting a little mental?"

I ignore Sky and reach atop the fridge, there is a card, it's a birthday card. Sky is still chattering on at me but her voice is tuned out from the ringing in my ears, it's one of those put-your-own-picture-on-it cards. In the middle is an attractive dark-haired, tanned, dark-eyed Nix, the exact same guy who I saw at the cinema and who came to my rescue in the graveyard. On either side of him smiling at the camera is my Mum, Dad and Rhonda. What the fuck is going on?

Sky's voice comes through. "Rae, do you want to explain this now!"

She says it loud and clearly irritated with being out of the loop, I thrust the card in her face, she looks and some colour drains from her face.

"It can't be a coincidence that this Nix was the one who rescued us, I am pretty sure he has been following me too and he was the one Mum was on the phone to this morning," I say.

Sky's eyes turn steely as she looks from the photo back up at me. "I didn't actually get a look at the guy who rescued you at the graveyard but I have seen him before. This was the guy I saw Mum arguing with the other night. And remember I told you Mum had lied about where they had been the night Dad was murdered? And that they looked like they were on some double date at the Rose pub, the shithole just around the corner from here! Well what is the betting Nix and Rhonda were the other couple?"

All my frustration, anger, pain and loss is welling up. "What are they keeping from us," I almost scream.

Rhonda suddenly shoots into the room, I am enraged, but even through the red I note how quickly she moves.

"Is this NIX?!" I mean to yell, but it is more of a screech, I am shaking with rage, and by the sudden ashen face on

Rhonda she knows she's been busted.

"Rae please calm down and explain to me why you are so upset?"

I ignore her comment.

"What are you not telling us?" I scream

She goes to talk but holds back as if not knowing what to say, or maybe not knowing how much to say. More lies no doubt.

I chuck the card at her in disgust, I throw the orange juice at the wall, exploding pulp goes everywhere.

"Rae, calm down ... now."

Her voice is stern and authoritative which just flips my little bitch switch

I am beyond calming down and who the hell does she think she is to tell me what to do? She goes to step forward as if to grab me and I lose it. That is all I can say, I completely lose it, I can feel myself getting hotter and hotter and can just see red, I know I am smashing stuff up but it is as if it isn't me, like I am watching from the inside but have no control. I can see Sky step in to try and stop me but Rhonda shouts at her to stay clear, behind her in the doorway to the back garden Danny stands in total shock, no not shock, he looks terrified. As I stare at him, I suddenly realise he looks terrified of me, I turn to Sky and she is wearing the same expression, she cradles her arm and I see a burn spot. Shit, did I do that? I turn to Rhonda, but the only thing I see is a fist and then light explodes behind my eyes. I crumple to the floor like a sack of spuds. For the second time today I pass out, cold!

****

Danny

I can't move, I just stand there in utter shock, what the hell just happened. This is just unreal, Rae's eyes had literally been glowing, like on fire glowing, it hadn't even looked like her, and her hands had glowed like embers of charcoal. Sky is yelling at Rhonda, but I don't pay attention, my eyes are glued to Rae who is now a crumpled mess on the floor, looking at her now she doesn't look remotely terrifying at all. And it hits me, this is my friend, my best friend who called me for help, she's just lost her mum and home, and here I am standing like a complete twat while she lies unconscious on the floor.

I go to move over to Rae, but Rhonda stops me with her hand on my arm. I look at her hand and then back up at her, I simply stare at her, I have no idea what is going on but if she doesn't remove her hand in two seconds I am liable to punch a woman for the first time.

"Get your hand off me!"

"She is not safe to be close …"

She doesn't get any further, I wrench my arm from hers and weirdly it takes all my effort, she's got one hell of a grip. I move down to Rae, scooping her into my lap, she's got a little blood trickling from her nose but nothing overly serious. However, I only imagine the ache she will feel judging from Rhonda's hulk grip. I bet she packs quite a punch too. Sky is pacing back and forth glaring at Rhonda, who is staring at Rae, there is definite regret in her eyes for sure, but she also looks massively on edge and even a little wary of Rae. I look squarely at Rhonda.

"What the hell is going on, Rhonda?"

She doesn't answer.

"I get a call from Tom saying Rae's place just exploded and that Rosaline is dead, then I get repeated texts from Rae asking me to come to wherever you were taking them because she thinks she's in danger."

Still nothing. I really am starting to become irritated, but judging from Sky's constant pacing I know I have to stay calm. Sky can be a wild one when she's angered.

"Rhonda, she thinks you have all lied about her Dad's death, about her Mum, about this guy who rescued her."

She snaps up on that. "What guy?"

"Really!! That's the one bit you pick up on ...unreal."

"Danny seriously, what guy and why did she need rescuing?"

Sky stops pacing, she drags out a cigarette, lights it, no care for whoever's house this is.

"Before Mum...." She struggles to not cry for a second, taking a pull on her fag she continues, "Mum had been acting weird for the last few days, constantly asking where we were, who we were with. Then this morning she was going on about us all going away, we had a fight and then she slapped me, so I ran out."

Even though Rae had told me all about it, it's horrible seeing Sky have to tell this, the last time she saw her mum was in anger.

"I ran to Dad's grave and Rae followed me, then these two huge guys turned up..."

Rhonda tenses moving towards Sky just a touch.

"What did they look like?" Rhonda asks.

"They were butt ugly, bold, tattoos everywhere, dressed in black and…and their eyes looked black, like no whites, just black, probably contacts. Anyway, Rae said we should run so I did, only she never ran with me. I got halfway across the field when I heard her scream. She had tried to protect me, so I ran back but by the time I got there, there was another guy. I thought he was attacking her so I hit him over the head with a fallen branch." She looks down a little sheepish. "I am pretty certain it was your mate Nix, Rae recognised him in the photo."

This is all insane, I'd believed Rae when she told me, she has never been one to make something up, especially something so elaborate, but there had been a small part of me I suppose that had hoped she'd imagined this. Listening to Sky now recant the story fills me with dread. Looking down at Rae she starts to open her eyes, once she focuses on me, tears well in her eyes, the last time I had seen her give this look was after her Dad died, I had hoped to never see that look again. I hold her hand and squeeze, letting her know I am here for her. She smiles, closing her eyes and breathing deeply trying to regain control. Rae starts to sit and I move back against the wall whilst helping her to a seated position, her head must be throbbing from Rhonda's punch.

"What happened to the two men Sky?" Rhonda's voice cuts through, she moves over to the back doorway, stepping out and shutting the back gate. She returns, getting out her phone and making a call. Clearly no one answers as she hangs up in frustration and fear reflects in her face.

When Sky doesn't answer, Rhonda moves slightly forward, hands up in a I-won't-harm-you-manner. "Sky please, what happened to those men?"

"I don't know Rhonda, by the time I got back they weren't there, Rae said she had hit one but when we looked where he had fallen there was just this weird small crater with scorched grass, it was even hot to touch."

Rhonda goes quiet leaning against the counter. "And Nix, was he still out by the time you left?"

"Yes.... But he was breathing," Sky explains.

Rae and I just sit in silence, I watch Rhonda, her body moves and stature more than indicate to me that she has some kind of military training, she moves and stands a lot like my Dad who is a general in the marines. I don't know why I never noticed this before. It is like she is a totally different person to the mellow Rhonda I have known for years. It's something Dad has always drilled into me to pick up people's mannerisms, behaviour, how they dress, what things give away their true nature. Some would think he's paranoid and sometimes it does come across that way, but he has seen some of the world's most evil people, he simply wants me and those he loves to be protected.

No one speaks up, Rae wipes the small amount of blood from her nose and leans against the wall next to me. We all watch Rhonda, waiting for her to explain what the hell is going on. With a resigned sigh, she pulls out a chair, gesturing to Sky to join us.

"I will tell you what I can, but after that we have to

move, it is not safe here. Do I have your word that you will come without resisting?"

I can't hold it in anymore, "That entirely depends on what you have to say." I glare at her.

She holds my gaze. "I think by the time I am finished you will understand the urgency...." She takes a deep breath, clearly not knowing where to start.

"I am not who you think I am. Yes, I am your parent's best friend but I am also your guardian, I was entrusted to protect you if anything happened to them."

"What do you mean protect us? And who from?" Rae says angrily.

"I am part of an agency called STAR, Strategic Tracking and Removal, we are a secret global organisation entrusted to hunt down and kill non-human entities."

Silence! None of us speak, none of us can speak. This is insane, Rhonda is insane. I am about to speak this thought but Rae gets in first.

"What do you mean non-human entities?"

Rhonda sighs, sitting back on the stool and pinches her brow. "I mean beings not of this world."

Silence again. I'm really starting to hope that I am stuck in some sort of bad hallucinogenic dream. I pinch my arm but pinch Rae's by accident.

"Ouch ... what the hell!"

"Sorry I meant to pinch my own arm, see if I was dreaming, cos you know...this all sounds..." I look to Rae and Sky for back up.

"Bat-shit crazy," Sky pipes in, she steps forward,

advancing a little on Rhonda. "And you expect us to believe that you are what ...Scully or something?" Laughing, she throws her cigarette out the back door. "Aliens exist do they?"

The last comment said in red hot anger. And who can blame her, their Mum has just died and this is the explanation Rhonda is giving? I personally would sock her one. Rhonda just looks at Sky and waits, as if she doesn't want to anger her more. Well sod that I can't keep quiet anymore.

"If you want us to believe anything you say, I suggest you get talking."

Rhonda doesn't take her eyes off Sky, it's a wary look like the one she had given Rae before, but she continues. "STAR was initiated over 1000 years ago; we consist of a small percentage of the human population who have certain genetic enhancements. We protect the rest of humanity from entities beyond the realms of this world."

Sky laughs again, this time a little hysterically. "Are you believing this shit?" she says directly to us.

I am too confused, scared and worried for Rhonda's sanity to speak, Rae simply nods.

"Go on," Rae says.

Much to Sky's dismay, Rhonda continues, "Several thousand years ago a race of beings called the Asteria found their way to Earth, they posed no threat and helped humanity enter a new era of civilization, helping to build cities, farm the land and so on. The Asteria developed relations with certain humans, essentially creating a new breed who contained the genetic code that all STAR agents now have."

"So," I say trying to formulate the right words, "You're basically, what, some kind of super human?" That's pretty cool! But unfortunately we live in the real world where super powers only exist in comics!

"You could put it like that, yes Danny. We are actually called Hybrids; we have enhancements that the rest of humanity does not possess yet."

"Yet?" I ask.

"As is the way with evolution, all humanity will adapt and evolve over time." More than likely judging from the uber excited look on my face at the prospect of gaining some kind of superpower, Rhonda adds, "But this will naturally occur over many thousand years."

Of course!

"Anyway the world lived in peace with the Asteria for a few thousand years, they would come and go between worlds. Human's celebrated them as deities, from Zeus, Apollo, hell even to a certain level God!"

Mumbling under her breath, Sky remarks, "And I suppose Santa is real too!"

Rae ignores Sky, but Rhonda scowls at her.

"I know this sounds far-fetched, like a mad person talking, but I am telling you the truth. Everything you think you know you don't."

"Ok   so   what   exactly   were   these….
Asteria…people…things?" Rae asks.

"They were pure energy, the light, the source of the universe. They could manipulate the elements, re-design the atomic particles around them, even fold time itself. They are what all beings in all the realms strive to be. But they are not the only powerful beings out there, there must always be a balance, always an opposite, with the light comes the dark. The Shades. Beings that over thousands of years have tired of their shadow world. They seek worlds of light to destroy and concur, spreading their darkness everywhere. And just over 500 years ago they turned their attention to Earth, a great war ensued and many were killed on both sides. The Shades were nearly wiped out as they were unaware of the hybrid presence on Earth. As such they were defeated and driven back from our world. But the Asteria were greatly diminished, and they warned us that another war would come to Earth and that we needed to prepare. They retreated to their own world to replenish their race, but since then no one has seen or heard from them, we don't know why or what has happened to them. What we do know is that more and more Shades have been entering this world, the war is coming, quicker than we thought and without the Asteria we may not survive a direct attack."

"So where are the beings of light?" I ask

"We don't know, there's been no communication and no means of contacting them either. We fear with their diminished forces that the Shades may have eradicated them."

"But that doesn't make sense, if they destroyed the light then why haven't they attacked and wiped us out already?" Rae asks.

"Because of us hybrids, we have increased our numbers and don't forget there are Seven billion humans on this planet, we have developed some pretty destructive weapons.

Unless the Shades have amassed an army equal to the last war, they could face a good possibility of losing again! And they won't take that risk! We know they have been doing a lot of recon and infiltrating, we need the Asteria or to be able to harness a similar power."

Sky had been silently stewing by the back door, smoking cigarette after cigarette. "Not that I even remotely believe you but what has any of this got to do with us and Mum and Dad?"

Rhonda pauses, probably deciding what information to give next, or what far-fetched story will fit the one she has already spun. But the slightest re-arrangement of her face tells me whatever she is about to say next will certainly be a lie. Reading liars is a skill my Dad taught me, he is literally a human lie detector!

"Your Mum and Dad were hybrids as such so are you, but you are untrained and so very much open to attack."

No one speaks, none of us expected that answer, even though she is definitely lying, there is some part of this that is true, which part I can't tell just yet, so I decide to delve a little deeper into this madness. "So why weren't they trained if they would be at such a risk?"

"Because Rose and Leon wanted their girls to have a normal life for as long as possible. Being brought up for the sole purpose to protect your world, to fight and kill is not what any parent wants for their child."

Of all the ludicrousness of this story, this is the only part that makes the slightest sense, I still can't imagine gentle Rose and Leon being all powerful super warriors though! It's literally laughable, having been brought up around Marines my whole life I'm used to what tough men and women look like.

"I know this sounds insane and you have no reason to trust me, but even though I have hid things from you, I have never caused you harm, have I? I need to get you to a safe place right now," she emphasises the words 'right now'. She flashes a pleading glance to Rae and Sky.

"Please I can explain in better detail later, but right now you're in real danger."

Sky scoffs. "We're not seriously going to go anywhere with her?" she says to both Rae and I.

Rae just looks conflicted, she is usually the logical one and Sky the open-minded sister, but I can tell she is believing some of this story and wants to know more. Judging by what she told me happened earlier I'm beginning to think maybe someone is out to get them. An idea forms in my mind, one that can appease both sides.

"No, we won't just go anywhere with you. And yes, that means I am going wherever they go. But from everything that has happened I appreciate we need to get to a safe place."

Rhonda looks like she may lose her shit. "So, what are we going to do?" she says through gritted teeth.

"Easy, you take us to my Dad at the commando HQ. You said we need somewhere safe, where better than a base packed with fully trained marines."

CHAPTER 7

<u>Rhonda</u>

This is not what I had planned, I try to argue that I can have a team extract us but they are having none of it, I need to earn their trust, so I agree that the commando base is the next best place. The Shades won't dare attack us there, but we have two miles to travel to get there. I message the contact I have at the base; I have never met him but apparently he is the best, totally human, but in a position of need to know. If we don't get there in the next Twenty minutes he will send back up, not to mention if we get there in one piece we will need someone to let us in. Just because we are friends with Danny, did not mean his Dad can just let us into a military base. Danny has his head down busy messaging his Dad whilst Rae watches quietly, she hasn't spoken much, just absorbing and thinking, whilst Sky is by the back door, smoking yet another cigarette. I try Nix again, hope had flashed through me when Sky mentioned she'd knocked him out, maybe he's still alive? But if so, why hasn't he come back, why is his phone dead? I try his number again; a dead tone greets me. We can't wait any longer. I have to get these girls out; we've already been here too long.

"Come on, we have to go now," I say heading out the back door, I pause before the back gate, sending out my sensors and falling back into a calm meditative state. I feel for anything disturbing the natural energy around us. Nothing! Thank god.

"What are you doing?" Sky grumbles as she almost walks into me.

I open the back gate, still scanning the area and hurry them out. "I was sensing for danger."

Unlocking my car, I keep sending out my sensors, digging deep into my energy field to create a cloak over the girls, it will help shelter their energy signature a bit, but it won't be enough to hide them. Everyone has an individual energy signature, an aura of differing colours, most people's change colour with their mood from green when jealous, to pink when in love to red when angry. Some evil humans like murderers and rapists have dull and dirty brown auras, they are not pleasant to come into contact with and it usually takes all my willpower to not kill them on the spot. A Shade's aura is far worse, it is black, fully black and absorbs the energy around it. Sky and Rae's auras are unique, they are gold, though Sky's is flecked with purple, and this makes them harder to hide. They stick out like sore thumbs.

Sky pushes forward and jumps in the front seat with me, leaving Danny and Rae to get in the back, not that they complain. Both are silent.

"What the hell is sensing the immediate area?" Sky asks curtly as I start the car.

I open the secret panel next to the steering wheel and press my thumb on the print recognition screen. "It means I am like a radar, I can pick up on disturbances, the differing energy fields everyone puts out."

Sky laughs. "What, like Yoda?"

"Yeah actually a little like that!"

With that she shuts up, shaking her head inevitably thinking I am crazy, it must sound like I am, but the Star Wars reference is actually quite close to what I am doing.

Recognising my print, multiple compartments and screens pop out of the dashboard, state of the art radar screens, satellite tracking, weapons. Pulling the headset on I dial into STAR's base.

"What the hell?" Sky looks amazed, pushing a button, she squeals as a gun is ejected.

"Don't touch anything." Grabbing the gun from her lap, I check and load the gun ready.

I tap the screen for the car's cloaking, with any hope combined with my own cloaking that will be enough to shield them from the Shades.

"Are you like James Bond too?" Danny is revelling in all the gadgets.

"Something like that," I mumble, concern rising in me, the line is not connecting to the agency, I try all the lines, but nothing.

"Shit!" I exclaim.

"What?" asks Rae.

"I can't connect to my base command, it's like all the lines don't exist anymore, it's the same dial tone I had with Nix's number when we got here."

"So what does that mean?" Rae leans forward peeking at the screen.

I look down to my phone and the message I'd sent to my contact at the Marine base has bounced back as unable to send.

"I don't know… Danny, has your message gone through

to your Dad?"

He gets his phone out of his pocket and checks. "No, it says delivery failed...hold on." He dials the number and pulls it away from his ear, looking at his phone and then to me. "Nothing but a dead tone."

I ram the car into reverse and speed out of the narrow road and head to the high street which leads to the beach road, it's the busiest way to go but also less chance of an attack than using the back roads. My heartrate elevates, I have never been so alone, someone has always been on the end of the line or Nix beside me. The fear that I might fail the entire world starts to overpower me, but I have to get it under control, I cannot afford to freak out, they need me to be strong.

"Rhonda what is going on?" Sky asks.

"I don't know, but the communications tower could be down. Danny, do me a favour and try ringing Rae's number, I want to see if all signals are down as a whole."

Danny dials Rae's number, she looks intently at her phone, if her phone doesn't ring that means they are here and have shut down the town from outside help, and that will be bad. If it did ring, that means something very serious has happened to STAR and possibly the commando base, I don't know which is worse.

Nothing happens. How the hell did they shut down a whole town? More importantly where the hell are they?

"What does this mean?" Rae asks.

Danny listens to his phone. "It's like a dead line like my Dad's, no answerphone, no nothing."

"It means they are here, they know you are here and they are coming for us," I say it so cool and calm, pulling on my big girl guardian pants. I will do anything to protect them, anything.

I round the corner by the supermarket, the road then leads right down through the heart of the town all the way to the beach. Pubs and restaurants line this part of the high street, most nights, especially in the summer (like now) the pavements are teeming with people. But tonight even though the sun has barely set and it's a humid Friday night, there is no one to be seen. Lights are on down the street, even some outside tables have empty glasses on them, but the street is barren. I increase the cloaking on me and the girls, sending out my sensors when suddenly I am hit with a force of energy unlike no other, they are everywhere, they've cloaked themselves. The screens in the car suddenly light up like the fourth of July, I screech the car to a stop, the car's radar picking up their presence, up ahead dark figures appear like mist in the road, two at first, then another, and another and then more.

Sky smacks my arm in panic, Danny just repeats Shit-shit-shit, Rae just stares ahead fear making her eyes water. Stepping out of the darkness their pale skin glows in the early moonlight, ink black tattoos stretch over their skin, eyes pitch black, dressed in leather with weapons strapped to their backs, it's like something out of a vampire movie. But this is real, shit just got real.

****

Skylar

I can feel a scream rising in my throat, I see what is up ahead but Rhonda hasn't yet seen what I am seeing right next to me. I smack her arm, again and again until she turns.

"What…."

Her words fail her, eyes wide in horror, I hear Danny and Rae suck in a breath, it's pure mutilation, the bodies of people are piled up on top of one another in each pub and restaurant, blood is everywhere. Now under the street light, I can see the entire carnage, blood and parts of people. I suck in a harsh breath that is more like a sob, I don't want to look but I can't tear my eyes from the bodies. Panic like nothing I have felt before overcomes me, and I scream. The open eyes of the dead stare back at me, some have tongues removed, others arms severed, some are nothing more than a torso. I can hear Rae and Danny panicking behind me. In front, the line of black-clad figures move forward, blood dripping from their hands, they are savages, their dark eyes fixed on us as they rush forward.

Rhonda kicks the car into reverse deftly flying us back and around the corner we just came from with ease, the figures race forward at a speed that is humanly impossible. Rhonda pulls a gun out and starts shooting out the window, all the while reversing back up the high street. Behind us a couple of people are about to cross the street.

Still screaming I reach over and beep the horn simultaneously yelling, "Move… bloody run!"

Rhonda manoeuvres the car to the other side of the road to avoid them, as we pass the two people they freeze in shock midway across the road, two of the dark shadows following us peel off from the group and attack the couple, cutting their heads off where they stand, other bystanders scream in horror as their twitching bodies fall to the floor. I can't scream anymore; tears stream down my face.

"Oh god," I cry.

"Sky," Rhonda yells, "Reload this gun."

Half handing it half throwing it at me, I manage to catch it by the barrel and holy hell it's hot.

"Ah crap…how do I reload this?" I've never held a gun, let alone reload one.

"The left compartment has the mags … get them!"

It's amazing that she can give these instructions at the same time driving a car in reverse up the street, avoiding hitting anyone or anything as well as swerving to avoid these demon alien's hell bent on killing us. Now that is multitasking! I look for the left compartment, but this is a spy car, the compartments are not the most obvious, I just start tapping everywhere, frustrated by my slow speed, Rhonda leans across touching the furthest panel, and out pops a compartment.

"Hold on," Rhonda yells.

Two figures pounce on the car and a sword plunges straight down through the top of the roof, right in between us. I scream as another one lands on the bonnet and eyes me like I am a particularly delicious meal, he pulls an arm back to smash his way through the windscreen, I am dead! But Rhonda spins the car round from reverse, throwing both of them off the car, but the others have gained on us.

"Go-GO-go!" I screech as Rhonda floors it forward, the car barely stopping. Another creature jumps on the roof and rips out the sword that is still embedded, it then trusts it back down through the roof narrowly missing Rhonda's shoulder.

"Gun and mags, now!"

I grab them off my lap and hand them to Rhonda and as calm as anything she removes her hands from the wheel and reloads, never taking her eyes from the road. The sword is wrenched again from the roof of the car, I know it will be driven back down and this time we may not be so lucky.

"Rhonda!" I yell nervously.

In slow motion I see the sword break through the roof, this time right above Rhonda's head, she shifts to the left avoiding the point that would penetrate her skull, she points the gun to the roof and fires, a body tumbles off the roof down the bonnet sword in hand, she swerves the car and the corpse flies off hitting one of the other Shades. They are running at a similar speed to the car, and we must easily be going at Fifty mph.

"Holy hell!" Rae screams.

Two of them are casually running alongside the car.

"Sit back," Rhonda instructs me.

She points the gun over me and fires out the window, the bullet hits the first one square in the face, but the second dodges, she fires again and again but it dodges every one of them.

My ears ring with the sound of the gunfire, it's actually quite painful, and all I can really hear now is constant ringing. She grabs more mags from my lap and like a pro unloads and reloads, raising the gun and not looking as her eyes are on the road, she fires multiple rounds, all with a direct hit, the alien creature falls to the ground.

"Up ahead!" Danny screams.

Three of them block the road.

"Hold on." Rhonda puts her foot down; she can't be seriously considering ploughing into them? Can she? I desperately try to grab my seat belt but it's too late, I look up as one of them smiles, it raises it's hand and makes a swipe motion, just before we are about to hit them, the car flips, high, turning over in the air, the scream is caught in my throat as I am looking up at the concrete, if we land this way we will all die. But the car continues to turn, flipping upright and landing hard on the other side of the road. We spin out of control, Rhonda desperately holding onto the wheel trying to keep us from flipping again. We plough through a fence and into someone's garden, and brake just before we hit the house.

****

Rae

Not a second passes before my door flies open and a huge tattooed hand reaches in and hauls me out, I kick and scream but the creature, or whatever it is, it's too strong and I am flung to the ground. I hear Rhonda firing shots, but she is on the other side of the car and I cannot see her, I can only see the hulky beast above me. This one is similar to a man, in the sense it has a similar shape to a male human, but a lot bigger. Its skin is pale with an almost blue hue, black oily hair is slicked back from its face, scars and tattoos are etched over every bit of visible skin, skin that is insanely cold to the touch that it actually sears my hand. I scream and try a twist I learnt in my MMA class to escape, but he simply flips me back pressing his big foot right on my chest, expelling all the air. I can barely breathe let alone move. He looks down bending closer until he is no more than a few inches from my face, eyes as black as night pierce my soul, and then he chuckles a deep humourless laugh.

"How did you kill Ryzlar, you seem so pathetic?"

The sound of his voice is booming with a slight rasp but he also has the same twang of accent like Ryzlar. He presses harder onto my chest, I wheeze desperately trying to pull air into my lungs, my vision blurs. I am losing what little oxygen I have left and the weight of his foot on my chest feels like a brick wall. If I make it out of this, I will certainly have cracked ribs.

"RAE!!" Skylar screams.

I turn my eyes in the direction of my sister's voice, I can vaguely make out that she is being held by another tattooed figure, this one appears to be a woman, she is slighter built, though still very lean and with hair braided to the middle of her back. She may be smaller than the guy on top of me but she still radiates a huge amount of power. But this does not stop Sky from putting up one hell of a fight, her captor struggles to keep a hold of her, as Sky tears at her face, kicks and thrashes. My vision starts fading fast as my lungs burn to the point I fear they may explode and then it suddenly starts to numb, I lose feeling to my legs and arms, and I know this must be death. Blackness spots my vision as the last vestiges of pain leave, the world around me reduces to darkness and muffled noises. A loud crack brings me momentarily back followed by more pain as the monster above me presses harder, cracking my ribs, laughing as he slowly drains the life from me.

I am only vaguely aware of one of the monsters holding Sky yelling at the one pinning me down to not kill me. But I know it is too late, I feel death coming for me. I seek my sister through the black spots obscuring my vision, I need to see her one last time. Finding her she is crying hysterically watching me as she is pinned back now by two female creatures. I try to smile and say I love her but my face can't move, I can do nothing but stare at her as I feel everything go cold. As I am about to close my eyes and just let go, I feel a sudden release, air floods my lungs, I gulp in the oxygen, a little too quickly, I cough and then the pain erupts over my chest all the way up to my head. Yeah something is seriously broken, but I can't stop coughing, and I can't catch my breath, I can only take in tiny gasps of air which isn't enough.

I try to shift to my side but that causes more pain, I swear I can feel my lungs bubbling, a rib has probably punctured my lung. All around me I can hear gunfire, shouts and small explosions.

"Rae…Rae?!" Skylar is by my side "Rae, talk to me."

But I can't, I can barely shake my head in between coughing or more like choking.

"Rhonda!!!! RHONDA…she can't breathe."

"Out the way." A man's voice sounds through my hazy fog of pain. "Rae, where does it hurt?"

I look up into the deep set brown amber eyes, flecked with gold, I recognise those eyes, it's Nix. But I still can't speak, I motion as best I can to my ribs, the pain is so intense I am close to passing out…again! I feel him place a hand on my sternum, which if I wasn't so out of it with the pain and trying to fight the urge to cough I would certainly bitch slap his hand off. A liquid warmth radiates from his hand, spreading through my chest, I've never felt a heat like it. It continues to spread until it envelopes my entire body cocooning me. The pain gets less and less, I can breathe without it hurting, without coughing, I slowly breathe in the much-needed oxygen as my senses come back to me, my broken ribs barely hurt anymore. What the hell?! My eyes shoot open meeting the intense stare or is it a glare from Nix, the golden hue in his eyes have dimmed, they are now the darkest shade of brown and to be honest not the most welcoming.

"You done lying down?" Without waiting for my response, he flips me to an upright seated position. "Get up, we need to get moving."

He stands behind me, grabbing me under my arms and hauling me up. His tone and manner really flips my bitch switch.

"Excuse me for almost dying, sorry it was so inconvenient for you but I can get up by myself." I shove his hands off me and turn to Sky.

I embrace her so hard, pulling back I check her for damages but she seems ok except for a little cut on her forehead.

"Are you ok?"

"Yeah I am fine, what about you. God Rae I thought you were going to die on me too."

Water swells in her eyes; I grasp her and pull her in for another hug. I thought I was going to die back there too. "I'm ok……" Then it hits me, I should be dead, why am I not dead? I turn forcefully back to Nix. "What the hell did you do to me?"

He rolls his eyes. "That's your thank you?"

Is he always an ass? That itchy feeling to bitch slap him rises back up as it had outside the cinema.

"Thank you! But I will repeat, what the hell did you do to me?"

Before he can answer, which I doubt he would do anyway, Danny and Rhonda run over. Poor Danny looks battered, a brilliant bruise forming over his nose, and fresh blood trickles from his eyebrow and his t-shirt is all kinds of wrecked. He looks like he has just gone a few rounds with Mike Tyson.

Both Sky and I run in to hug him.

A little overwhelmed with all the affection it takes him a second to eventually wrap his arms around us both.

"Ah thank god Nix, I thought you were dead," Rhonda exclaims.

I turn in time to watch them give each other a hug, it's more like a back slap than anything like the hug me, Sky and Danny are giving each other, but each to their own. It's then that I truly notice the carnage around us, bullet casings and bullet holes are everywhere, and where the dead bodies of the monsters should be there are scorch marks, just like the ones from the graveyard. Whoever's garden this is, it is entirely destroyed, the front window and door are also shattered. But more importantly I finally notice uniform clad marines everywhere, two are helping the family out of the house, shielding their eyes. Two tanks are blocking off the road, there must be well over fifty armed marines, one of which I recognise as Danny's Dad. Relief floods his face when he sees Danny, he marches forward, dragging Danny in for a hug.

Danny's Dad; General David Pierce is pretty much the highest rank you can get to in the Royal Marines, he has a very domineering look to him, at well over six feet he is a towering mass of muscle and brute force regardless of his age. He, like Danny, has an all year-round golden tone to his skin, blue eyes, strong jawline and I imagine back in the day his hair would have been the same shade as Danny's but it's now a buzz cut ash grey. The general was usually stern looking, though he is very pleasant I knew him to be quite hard on Danny (rightly so seeing as he knew all about this), but for a few moments his face softens as he embraces his son. Danny's an only child which may have also added to why the general is always so protective of him.

The General sets Danny back.

"Dad you came ...I can't…"

"You ok Danny?" General looks him over, taking in the cuts and bruises.

"Yeah, I am all good, just a few bruises."

The general smiles a little, lightly slapping Danny's arm and then turning his attention to us. "You girls ok?"

"Yes Sir." I always call him that, even though he always insists I call him David, but it just doesn't seem right.

Rhonda and Nix approach, both saluting the general, he salutes back as do the other officers who are currently in the immediate area. Weird, are Rhonda and Nix high ranking in their organisation. For the life of me I can't remember what the hell they called their agency?!

Rhonda speaks first, "All the coms are down, I wasn't sure you got my message?"

"I didn't get a message from you, coms have been down

since 20:00 hours, our operations have been working to fix it but it was Nix who alerted us to the situation."

So all forms of communication had been down not long after we got to Nix's, that makes sense and explains why Rhonda hadn't gotten through to her organisation, why the general had not replied to Danny ...it didn't explain though why Nix hadn't contacted Rhonda? We had last seen him in the morning at the graveyard some twelve hours ago. If communications hadn't gone down until a few hours ago then where the hell had he been?

"So where have you been?" I open my mouth without thinking, the words tumbling out, "My sister didn't hit you that hard over the head."

I cross my arms and pointedly stare at Nix, I don't trust him, I don't trust any of them really, everyone has lied to us and they will probably keep lying.

"Seriously? That is what I get for saving your life …Twice might I add!"

Oh yeah, shit. Forgot about that. But I am past caring if I owe him one.

"For your information from the moment I came to after your idiot sister hit me over the head, I repeat, after saving your life, I have done nothing but fight my way to get back and help you all."

Nope I am not buying it, he just took down one of those monsters by himself in no time at all, did he really think anyone will believe it took him over half a day to fight his way back to Rhonda's side?

"So why didn't you ring Rhonda, why are we only just seeing you now?"

"Rae...." Rhonda steps in front of me, anger brewing on her face at my accusations. God, I don't even know what I am accusing him of, but I just don't like him, not one bit.

"What Rhonda!? Having been lied to all our bloody lives you expect us to just accept his story, or yours for that matter?" I pointedly look at him again, stepping forward slightly. "Over twelve hours you have been off the radar, no communication, no nothing."

Nix laughs. "Is she being serious? Look kid, I wouldn't expect you to understand anything about warfare, but if you haven't noticed shit has just got real. The world you knew you can forget about. I don't have to explain myself to you."

"Why you piece of...."

"Enough" The General cuts in, "Back down," he growls at us both, he is so authoritative even Nix steps back. "We can discuss this further once we are back at base, our first priority is to make sure you are safe." He pointedly looks at me and Sky, which is weird.

What's so special about us, surely we all need to be safe?

He motions to an officer behind us. "Let's get them out of here."

The officer lightly grabs our arms, ushering us towards the two big trucks parked on the side of the road, where the hell had they come from? I'm about to argue the toss at being manhandled, which Sky is audibly doing already, but then notice numerous officers are now working on collecting the array of bullet casings littering the ground, others are busy hosing away the blood, a wall of trucks blocks the view of the garden we had ploughed into. It's just like those conspiracy films, one massive clean-up operation, all evidence removed. Absorbed by the swiftness of the clean, I linger too long watching because the officer behind gently prods me in the back

"Prod me again and my foot will meet your ass!"

The officer smiles apologetically. "Please be quick we need to get you back to camp."

He has a slight twang to his accent, not the best with accents but it's almost Jamaican sounding. His smile is wide, warming and genuine, so I oblige. Nodding he jumps up into the back of the truck first, leaning over with a hand outstretched to grab mine, he pulls me up no problem.

"Thank you." I search his badge for a name. "Lieutenant Anderson."

"Pleasure." He gestures to where I need to sit, he then leans over the truck helping Sky and Danny up.

As Sky moves to sit next to me she mouths, "He's hot."

Yes, even in the face of absolute chaos and death we can both clearly appreciate a fine-looking specimen when we see one. I smile and laugh looking back at Lt Anderson, but I am only met with the steely gaze of Nix who has just entered the truck.

CHAPTER 8

Danny

This is so unreal, I can't believe that my Dad knew about all of this, I get why he didn't tell me, he probably couldn't, sworn to silence and all that but it still stings to know he was hiding something this big from me. We are not exactly close, but that's more because of our massively differing personalities, where I'm laid back, my Dad's hugely uptight and always on edge. Clearly for obvious reasons, no wonder why he hammered me so much about every little thing, he'd been trying to protect me. Screw that, he should have told me, being best friends with Rae ultimately put me in the line of fire and a heads up would have been nice. I look up trying to judge his expression, he briefly looks at me sternly and then returns to training his gun out the back of the truck. My Dad and the pretty boy Anderson are both watching our six as Dad would say. So far nothing's caught their attention, the drive though a little bumpy, is, fingers crossed, going without any surprises, to be honest I don't think I have the energy to take any more. I hurt all over, every bone in my body aches, the cut on my head is giving me a pounding headache and all I can think about is if they managed to kill all of those monsters?

My mind swirls with even more questions. How are they going to cover up all those dead people on the beach road, there must have been hundreds of people? I want to voice my questions but every time I think to talk that Nix guy just scowls at me as if to keep me silent. Who is this dude? Nix leans into Rhonda and whispers something, the truck is so noisy I can't hear a word, I can tell Rae is trying to hear too, she is tense, and scowling deeply back at Nix.

She looks to me, grabbing my hand for a little squeeze, she mouths, "You ok?"

I nod, squeezing her hand back, I hurt but I don't think there is any serious damage. The worried expression stays on her face, she looks me over, clearly not believing me. I bet I look a mess, I feel a mess, not my most awesome look. Rae on the other hand still looks perfect, her hair is browner in this light and though it's somewhat messy given what we have just gone through it somehow looks like she's styled it that way on purpose. With the dirt smeared on her face she kind of reminds me of Lara Croft, a pretty badass look she's rocking right now. She smiles at me before turning to Sky who is leaning on her, Rae envelops her in a hug, she has always been a great big sister, even though they've grown apart a bit since their Dad died, Rae has always made such an effort to be there for her. Sitting back a little, I wince when the uncomfortable metal seat digs into my sore legs, god I need to lie down on something super soft. Thoughts of my super king size bed fill my head, but I shake it off, it will more than likely be a while before I can properly rest.

I note that Rhonda and Nix have stopped talking, they stare at Rae and Sky and then back to each other, a look passes between the two of them and my unease blossoms. I do not trust them, not one bit, saving our lives or not, something a lot bigger is going on.

"We're nearly there," my Dad calls out.

Out the back of the truck I can see we have an escort of

big Humvees; all weapons are trained out the various windows. What will people be thinking if they see all this? Though with the camp being so close to town it is quite normal to see the marines out and about training, at this time of the night people will probably assume it is just another drill. It must be after midnight by now, looking up, the sky is completely clear, every star is visible and the biggest moon I have ever seen lights up the sky. It's one of those nights that even without a light you could quite easily walk around in the dark.

Either side of the road is lined with farm land, corn season's well under way and so the fields are full of towering corn, off to the East side I can just about see the sea, the moon light, even from this distance, reflecting off of the water. Must be some kind of super moon, not that I know shit about lunar cycles.

Movement catches my attention in the middle of the field, it looks like the corn rows are moving, my breath catches as I watch intently, a chill running up my spine, but then a breeze blows over the field rustling all the corn, and then nothing. I keep my eyes trained on that spot until it disappears out of sight. Breathing a sigh, I relax back in my seat, but the chilled feeling doesn't leave me, it's got me on edge and I'm so glad when the bright lights of the camp illuminate the truck, I adjust in my seat so I can see through to the front window. I have been here many times over the years but I've never quite seen it like this, at every tower and along fences are armed marines, the bright beams illuminating a vast area around the camp. The camp's on high alert! Regardless of all the guns, this is the safest I've felt in the last few hours, those monsters won't stand a shot at getting through here.

Our truck is ushered through, barely stopping for the usual checks you have to go through, as we enter my Dad turns to me.

"We're going to get you all to med centre first then we will reconvene in thirty minutes."

The truck pulls up outside the medical centre, it is a simple low-rise concrete building, none of the buildings in the camp are pretty. They aren't meant to be but this one is by far the worst, dark grey in colour, hardly any windows, doesn't exactly invite recovery if you ended up that badly injured that you had to stay in there for a while. But Dad had once said it was made of the toughest material, the lack of windows was so if the camp was attacked those in the hospital would be safer, most enemies always direct their first round of attack at the injured, also cutting off any medical help.

Dad and Anderson jump out the truck first helping us all down, and I gladly take the help because I am hurting something bad, I'm obviously not hiding it that well when I catch the look of concern on my Dad's face.

"You alright son?"

"Yeah just feel like I've been hit by a train."

He nods and escorts me inside, I turn to check Rae and Sky are following, they're right behind me and they too look a little more at ease with the armed presence all around us. As we enter the reception of the medical centre a couple of doctor's approach, two men roughly in their late thirties' early forties, both are well built, clearly done a few tours but their faces are kind, they smile at us as they approach and then salute Dad.

"Have you been prepped as to the situation?"

Both doctors still in salute position, answer, "Yes sir."

"Officer Brown, will you examine the two ladies and Officer Dudley, this is my son, he seems to be the worse for wear. I want a thorough check over. As fast as you can."

"Yes Sir."

Officer Brown motions for Rae and Sky to follow him, Rae turns looking at me, grasping my hand again.

"I will see you in a bit." She smiles weakly.

"Sure thing." I wink back at her and wince, dam even winking hurts.

Officer Dudley notices the wince. "Where does it hurt?"

"Everywhere to be honest."

"Ok follow me, first things first to the x-ray department, make sure nothing is broken."

Great, bet my life something is, based on how many bones I have broken in my body.

Officer Dudley escorts me down the same corridor as Rae and Sky are heading, looking back I notice Rhonda and Nix remain at the reception area. I turn to Dad, who I'm a little surprised is following me, I thought he'd have far more pressing matters to attend to. But I'm grateful nonetheless, this is the most amount of time I have spent with him in a few weeks. At the corridor junction Dad steers me in the opposite direction to Rae and Sky, we all look back at each other at the same time, even though I know we are safe I am still a little panicked at being separated. I momentarily stop walking; Dad gently taps me on the shoulder.

"They are being taken to a more private room, this is a marine corps so there are no proper facilities for women."

"Oh, yeah, sure ok."

The unease from before is back, probably caused from all the crap that has happened today. I remind myself that we are in a marine camp, surrounded by heavy fire power, we are safe! Regardless though, the pesky feeling will not go away. I try to shake it off as I follow the officer into the X-ray room.

"I will just be out here, ok son?"

"Ok Dad."

I smile at him, trying to hide the pain of having to get up on the stupidly high bed, who the hell made these things so high, don't they realise that most people who have to get on them will be in a lot of pain! Idiots. Officer Dudley clearly notices that I am struggling and comes round to my side to aid in getting my legs up onto the bed. As he bends his shirt gapes a little at the back of his neck and I notice he's got a tattoo, some kind of symbol that looks like a glyph of some description, but I can't make it out properly, it looks cool. I'm about to ask what it means when pain flares up my side as Dudley moves my legs up onto the bed. I cry out, a little taken by surprise, yeah something has to be broken, then again what if it's internal bleeding, though I am pretty certain I would be dead by now if it were that.

"Sorry, as soon as the X-ray is done I will get you some pain killers. Now stay as still as you can, do you have any metal on you?"

I nod through the pain removing my watch and phone,

handing them to him. The pain is slowly subsiding now that I am lying down and a wave of exhaustion comes over me. This bed is actually quite comfortable, I can already feel my eyes getting heavier and I twitch back to the present. Now is not the time to fall asleep.

"Try and stay still this shouldn't take a few minutes, I will just be in the other room."

Officer Dudley exits through the other door, I assume to where the controls for the x-ray are, I can still see my Dad on the other side of the door through the small window, he is watching me and I give a small reassuring smile. The lights in the room dim and a low humming starts above me as a number of high-tech panels lower. They are concave and attached by arms that are fixed to a big machine on the ceiling, each panel has small glass type squares that seem to flicker with light, there are six panels in total and they move alternately from left to right in a semi-circle over my body, going from one side up and over to the other side. Christ, how much funding did the bloody military have, I have had numerous X-ray's before and they were nothing like this, I imagine this is a lot more like an MRI or CT scan, just without being shoved in a tunnel.

The humming from the machine is quite soothing and I can feel it helping reduce the uneasy feeling I still have. I'm just about to start counting the grooves in the ceiling when the panels all aligned and drift back up to the machine attached to the ceiling, folding in on themselves until they create a shell over the black box underneath. The humming ceases and the lights come back up and Officer Dudley re-enters the room, he is holding a computer pad and turns to the blank wall opposite where I lay. A screen comes to life with my x-rays on it, he flicks through them, studying each one for a few seconds.

"Well you don't appear to have broken anything, there are also no visible fractures, no internal bleeding, I would say your pain is caused from severe bruising. I will X-ray you again in a couple of days just to make sure there are no micro-fractures as these often don't show up in the first X-ray."

He turns towards my dad and motions for him to enter and relays what he has found.

"Good." My dad's face softens a little.

"Let's get you patched up and some pain killers in you." Officer Dudley presses a button and the bed I am on moves so I am in more of an upright position.

Another officer enters with a tray, placing it on a wheelie table and moves it next to me.

Dudley comes over, flashing his torch in my eyes asking if my head hurts. "Well you are going to need some stitches to your eyebrow and we will need to keep an eye on you for concussion too." He prepares a needle, injecting some localised anaesthetic to numb the area.

"Dad how are Rae and Sky?"

"They are fine son, as soon as you're done, we will liaise with them, just focus on staying still."

Even though the officer numbed the area it's still gross to feel the needle threading through my skin, not to mention my head is starting to pound along with every other bone in my body. God, I want those painkillers, they better be the good shit too!

Within half an hour I'm all patched up, doped up with some pretty hefty pain killers too, literally the best shit I've ever had, my headache is already easing and I'm feeling somewhat light… airy.

"Normally I would advise you to lay down after taking these but given the circumstances, I do insist you are aided to the meeting room."

The door opens and the officer from before enters with a wheelchair.

I scoff. "I don't need to be wheeled."

"This is an order, or you can lay down and rest whilst the meeting goes ahead," Dad demands.

And as much as I want to fight him on this I know better.

I nod as Dudley helps me off the bed and into the chair, god this is so embarrassing, I don't need a bloody chair, but I also want to be in this meeting. I just have to suck it up.

"I will take him." Dad motions to the others to stand back.

He wheels me out the door and turns right down the brightly lit corridor, we pass various personnel before entering an elevator at the end of the corridor. Once in the elevator, silence falls upon us. Dad holds his hand against a keypad and then enters a code, we head down, far down. We go beyond the minus one level that is available on the main elevator buttons.

"What the…?"

"I never wanted you to be part of this son."

The elevator finally stops at minus

fifteen.

"This is top secret, restricted personnel only."

Dad enters another code on the pad and the doors open to an expansive hall, it is huge, like a small underground city!

****

Skylar

My stomach rumbles as we wait in the meeting room, in the underground fortress for Danny and David, should I call him General now? Who the hell knew, I'm still in shock, I just cannot fathom what the hell is happening to my life…? Our lives. Only Yesterday Rae and I were two normal sisters who had lost their Dad, now we are parentless, homeless, freaks of nature with Monsters from another world hunting us! How oh how does any of this make sense? People keep asking me if I'm ok, and all I can do is nod, I just can't speak right now, I keep swinging from pure rage at the lies we've been told to overwhelming grief at all we have lost. I know that if I open my mouth to speak, I will lose it and throw a massive rage fit which will inevitably get me kicked out of this meeting, and I need to hear what they have to say. Rae knows, she just keeps my hand in hers and speaks for me. Rhonda keeps glancing over, she looks worried, like she had after the hospital, not that I am surprised she probably doesn't want me to go psycho on people again. Neither do I. Right now, though my mood is getting worse because I am so damn hungry, we haven't eaten since… god …since last night, no wonder why I am so Hangry.

I whisper to Rae, "I am so hungry I may have to start eating my own frigging hand."

"Yeah same here, hold on."

Rae gets up and moves over to Lt Anderson who assisted us down here after our initial once over by the Doctor. Rae leans in and says something, he smiles, as she leans back he laughs and she laughs too but it is a little squeaky. Dear god she is trying to flirt? Rae is rubbish at flirting. Though this time she seems to have it more together than usual, in fact he seems pretty darn receptive to her flirting. I roll my eyes a little and laugh to myself. Lt Anderson is very cute, but nothing compared to the hotness that is Nix, dear god now that is a fine piece of a man, bet there isn't a single inch of him that isn't ripped. I look Nix up and down, he had to be around six foot three and definitely got that brooding look down to a tee. I watch him as he talks to Rhonda but every so often when she turns her attention to the other officer they are in conversation with, Nix's gaze falls on Rae, he does it numerous times and I can't work out why he is scowling at her? What, because she is flirting? I stare too long because he senses my eyes on him and his gaze falls on me. And wow, I feel fried right to the spot, warmth floods my cheeks and I tear my gaze away to some other officers working on a dashboard at the other end of the room. I can tell he is still staring at me and it takes all my willpower to not look back. That had been a very loaded stare, full of hate and disgust! Why though, what the hell have I ever done to …. Oh yeah…I had smashed a branch over his head …twice!

This shit is so weird, my life has just gone down the crapper and I don't even know who to trust, well other than Rae and Danny.

Speak of the devil, behind Rae the door opens and Danny is wheeled in by his Dad, holy shit he must have been worse than we thought.

Rae and I move towards Danny but the General holds up his hands.

"He is fine, this is mandatory so he can attend the meeting, Danny suffered quite a bump to the head and with the medication prescribed I would rather he didn't fall from dizziness and hurt himself again."

Rae just ignores the General and marches in to hug him, I follow behind.

"You sure you're ok?" Rae asks.

"Yeah just feel like I've been hit by a train, but I'll survive."

"You better?" I say as I lightly punch him on the arm, he winks back at me and I stick my tongue out doing my silly cross-eyed face. That makes them both laugh, as I look up and my gaze collides with Nix, he is stern, his eyes shut down from all emotions. Jesus what happened to the smiling man I had seen next to my Mum and Dad in that photo, the look he keeps giving me is like I have just murdered someone, and it's getting on my last nerve. "What's your problem?" I throw at him.

He blinks like he hadn't expected me to call him out on it. I cross my arms; he looks around as everyone goes silent looking at me.

"You have been looking at me like I am the devil incarnate since we got here and I want to know why?"

"Skylar!" Rhonda says sternly.

"It's ok." Nix holds up his hand. "Not that this is the time to be talking about this but I am keeping an eye on you, if you remember it was only a few hours ago that you knocked me out and then according to Rhonda you attacked a Detective at the hospital, you clearly have some anger issues, so I am making sure you don't act on them."

What the actual f.... "Excuse me, who the hell do you think you are?" Says Rae stepping in front of me before I can respond. Jesus I can handle this myself.

"We have just lost our mother, watched our home burn to the ground, found out everyone has been lying to us and oh yeah that's right nearly died by monster attack tonight...So excuse us if we seem a little enraged."

With every word Rae says she takes a step closer to him, squaring up. Nix does not seem bothered, nope not one bit, in fact he looks somewhere between amused and slightly impressed, especially since now the ass is smirking back at her. I definitely think Rae is going to punch him!

"We have urgent business to attend girls and if you cannot act in the appropriate manor you will be excused from this room," The General barks.

What the hell did we do? Well I had brought this up in front of the room, but still! I go to open my mouth but Danny pinches me, shaking his head a little, looking round the room, there are a lot of military personnel in here, probably not the best time. And I want answers as to what is going on. I nod to the General, looking over at Nix I give him my best bitch look possible and grab Rae's hand, she is as tense as me but I manage to move her away from him.

"You kids can sit here." The General motions to the other side of the long oval-shaped table.

I despise being called a kid, especially in front of so many people.

As we take our seats there is a gentle knock at the door, Lt Anderson goes over to answer and takes a tray of sandwiches and drinks from a younger officer. The General looks on, unimpressed.

"Sir, they haven't eaten in a while and I know this will be a long meeting."

I don't wait for the General's response, as soon as we sit down, I dive into the sandwiches, handing some to Rae and Danny too. They are just cheese and ham sandwiches but right now they taste like little squares of heaven. I am so absorbed in eating that I don't realise the General has started the meeting.

The General stands at the end of the table, a screen flashes up behind him, showing a map of the town and local area, various points are marked with a light.

"As of 20.00 hours today all coms have been down, I have sent out various units to each of these communication towers, all have been destroyed, not only that but somehow the satellite feed is down and all landlines. No one within the town can communicate outside and we have contained the attack as best we can, for now we are on our own. However, I was hoping that with the clear lack of communication, STAR would have sent a unit to investigate?"

The General does not hide the fact he is clearly not a fan of the STAR agency.

Nix addresses the room as a whole, "The last communication I had with STAR was to advise them that I was going to locate Rhonda and the kids and that we would be needing an evac from the town as soon as I confirmed I had them. It is protocol for STAR to give at least Twelve hours before the lack of communication would warrant them to send out a rescue unit."

I can't help but roll my eyes, this STAR agency sounds like a load of crap to me, twelve hours before sending out reinforcements? Christ those monsters will kill most of the town in that time.

"It is imperative that we get in contact with them, we don't know how many Shades are out there, we need some backup to protect this town, too many have died already," The General says pointedly at Nix. "I suggest Morse code to try and contact your agency."

He points to the officers sat lining a bunch of screens and computers that look like part of a spaceship.

"Here send this." Rhonda scribbles something down on a piece of paper and hands it to the officer stationed behind her.

He then takes it over to the others manning the screens.

"Whilst we are attempting communication, I want to know why the hell this attack happened, we were informed there had been no activity?" the General barks to Nix and Rhonda.

"There has always been some activity, low level though, most resulted in attacks on specific individuals," Rhonda says.

"Like the attack on our Dad?" Rae asks.

"Yes."

The General speaks my mind before I can. "But why? Why specifically their family, it is obviously no coincidence that Leon was killed and now Rosaline?"

Nix and Rhonda look at each other in silence, Jesus

they're still not going to reveal everything even now?

"I understand that some information is restricted, but right now you need to give me more to go on." The General straightens, addressing the whole room, "Anyone who is below level eight clearance needs to leave the room ...Now!"

A number of officer's rise, no questions asked and exit the room, leaving a mere handful behind.

"Danny you too." He motions to an officer who comes to escort Danny.

"No way, after all I have been through, I deserve the right to some answers." Danny stands up from the chair.

The General does not look impressed with him. "This is a case of national security... and to be honest the more you know the greater the danger you could be in."

His Dad's face relaxes almost pleading with him to leave.

I shake my head; we are already in danger and keeping stuff from any of us will end up with us in more danger or dead.

I stand and speak, "Whether you tell him now or we tell him later he is going to find out."

"Yes, we all deserve to hear the truth, especially as it seems it is us they are hell bent on getting too," Rae adds.

The General looks questioningly at Rhonda, he then motions to the officer to back away from Danny and sits. "I suggest you two start talking."

Nix stands taking the lead, of course, he is probably the better liar, our only hope of getting any of the truth is that they probably can't bullshit a General.

"As you all know we have been building a defence against the Shades, not only amassing an army but also hiding the one weapon that can end this war, it is this weapon that they are now after. I believe they have been tracking those that may know its location, your parents, Rhonda, myself and a few others know the location."

"What is this weapon?" Rae asks.

"That's classified!" Nix answers sternly. "The agency believes the Shades have been operating undercover for some time now, we believe they have evolved to adapt to certain environments."

The General nods, as do the remaining other officers, I look at Rae and Danny who look as confused as I do.

"What the hell does that mean?" I question.

Huffing a little before he answers, God the guy is the biggest ass hat ever.

"It means that they are able to blend in, to look like us."

I'm so confused. "But those … things that attacked us looked nothing like humans?!"

"No that is what SOME of them look like, as with any race they don't all look the same, or did you not pay attention in school?"

Before I can throw a sarcastic remark back, he continues.

"There are different races within this species, the ones who tore up the town are the most vicious, though they are more brawn than brains. The ones who we believe have infiltrated varying levels of our society are the most dangerous, highly intelligent, powers that are unknown, and god knows how long they have been here."

"So how exactly are we supposed to know who they are or where they have infiltrated?"

The General looks unnerved, not surprising as this may mean one of those beings could be here on the base! Shit, someone in this room might be one of them. I look around at each of the officers, but I am at a loss, how the hell could you tell! I just hope I would get some kind of raised hairs on the arm vibe if there was one in here. Right now, everyone here just looks very human!

"The weapon will be able to track them. Not only this, it also has the potential to dispose of them collectively."

I note Rhonda is very quiet, she isn't bothered that Nix is doing all the talking, but she doesn't seem to like something about what Nix has said, she pinches her brows in disapproval but quickly schools her face again. Maybe he has said more than he should have? This is one crazy situation, I don't understand any of this and no one is really explaining anything, it's like no one cares how much we have just lost today, I don't know how much more of this I can take. I'm about to get up and say something when a creeping feeling spreads up the back of my neck, it isn't that cold 'someone-just-walked-over-my-grave' feeling but it's similar and warming. As the strange feeling spreads the sound of everyone in the room fades becoming a muffle and then suddenly everyone freezes as a haze spreads across the room, like a light fog. What the Hell!

"You need to get out of here Skylar."

I literally jump out of my chair as I hear the voice behind me, I collide into the table and trip over the chair next to me.

"Woah, woah, slow down."

I turn to face the voice from behind me and see the guy from my dream. Arms raised as a sign that he is no threat he slowly approaches.

"It's me, Theo."

Oh boy does he look just as hot as I remember he did.

Leather trousers with a tight dark purple t-shirt over a lot of ripped muscles, his arms I notice are tattooed, something I had missed before and this time his frigging eyes are illuminated, like neon bloody purple.

He moves closer to me and I stand back behind a chair, not that a chair can protect me from someone who can clearly freeze a room full of people. Funny that the one thing that is stuck in my mind, other than his general hotness, is how much this would piss off Nix, I look over at the frozen Nix, laugh and raise my middle finger.

"Skylar."

My attention flies back to Theo, and I am immediately captivated by his eyes.

"I don't have much time so listen carefully, you and your sister are not safe here, they are coming, they know you are here…." He shuts his eyes and when he re-opens them panic radiates across his face.

"Shit, they are here already, you all need to get out."

He is suddenly in front of me, my chair I had held as a defence weapon is gone, I don't know how, but I am very aware that he is a mere inch from my face.

"There is so much you don't know and I promise when we get the chance I will tell you, but you cannot let them take you, you have to hide."

He pauses again closing his eyes, when he opens them he grasps my face.

"Go……Now!"

In a blink of an eye Theo disappears. I'm sitting back in the chair and Nix is still talking, Rhonda is staring at me like I am mad, I probably look mad as I start patting myself all over, what the hell just happened? I breathe in deeply and as

I do I feel a breath on my neck and a whisper.

"Skylar go, now."

I stand up and scream, swatting the air like a crazed loon. "We need to go now."

"Sky, what the hell is wrong with you?" Rae jumps up and holds onto my shoulders

"I don't know but we need to go, they are here."

There is a low rumble, and everything around us shakes ever so gently.

"Shit, they are here," Rhonda says.

CHAPTER 9

<u>Rae</u>

One minute we'd finally been getting some answers and the next all hell breaks loose. I don't know how Sky knew they were here but alarms sound everywhere, the room shakes some more and dust falls down from cracks forming in the ceiling. I am suddenly extremely aware that we are underground, the scary thought that we could be buried alive is very real, and I do not want to die that way. Rhonda grabs my arm and I grab Sky's, who in turn grabs Danny, smoke slowly starts to billow down the hallway outside, as screams and gunfire can be heard, but I can't see too far in front as Nix's hulking frame is taking up most of the room, behind us the General and Lt Anderson bring up the rear. We move quickly down the hallway. The General then whistles to grab Nix's attention, we all stop as the General makes his way to the front.

"Take this exit here, there is a secondary elevator, if that is down, take the third exit on the right, the tunnel will eventually take you out onto the common, but it's long and there won't be any escape if they are aware of the escape route."

Nix salutes the General and moves to the entrance of another hallway, Rhonda follows suit. I'm confused, surely he isn't going to stay if those things are here in this underground trap, what hope do they stand?

"You're not staying?" Danny asks, gripping his Dad's arm.

"I am the commander of this camp; I have to make sure everyone gets out. You need to go with them, get to STAR and some form of safety." Danny tries to interrupt but the General grasps either side of his shoulders. "I will be fine Danny, but I need you to get out. This is my duty to these men."

He leans in and hugs him but I'm certain he is whispering something to Danny. Danny stiffens and pulls back with a nod, then turns back to me as the General shouts an order to Lt Anderson who salutes him and then continues to follow us.

"Come on, we have to go," Danny says, but he winces with pain.

"God Danny, we should have brought the bloody chair." I move to help Danny but Lt Anderson throws Danny's arm over his shoulder.

"It's ok I got him, come on we need to hurry."

Damn right we do, the gunfire is getting closer and the smoke is getting thicker making it difficult to breathe without coughing. The alarms are deafening as we make our way down the hallway, at the end is an elevator, but even from here I can see something is wrong. As we get closer, the door is clearly bulging, the elevator must have fallen from goodness knows how many stories up.

"This way," yells Lt Anderson as he diverts right, at the third door he presses his palm to the scanner and the door opens to a dull light room with another door on the other side. He presses his palm again on a small screen and moves Danny behind him as he raises his gun to the door.

The door opens, cool air hits me and a long tunnel leads ahead, gradually grading up, it isn't very big and is pretty much all rock except for the interspersed lighting. Lt Anderson steps in, gun still at the ready and pauses, no sound comes from up ahead, but there is plenty coming from behind us. We file into the tunnel and I hear the door shut and lock behind us, I have never been claustrophobic but I feel it right now, the tunnel can only be a mere five foot wide and no more than seven feet high, we can all easily touch the ceiling, with Nix being so tall he keeps having to duck out of the way of the lights hanging from the ceiling. Still moving, I look behind me to see Lt Anderson continuing to help Danny, his poor face screwed up in pain and the narrow width of the tunnel means that Anderson can't support him as well.

I stop. "Danny are you going to be ok?"

He gives me one nod, the pain obviously too much for him to speak.

"This tunnel was due to be expanded in the coming weeks, sorry man I can't get a good grip," Anderson says.

"It's ok." Danny pauses taking a breath.

Suddenly Nix is right behind me, the heat from his body infuses me, his breath catching on the back of my neck is warming in this cold, rocky tunnel. "We can't stop for a break, there are things in there who want us, we …."

There goes the warm feeling, god he is such a personable prick.

"Yes, we got it OK." I just grab Danny's hand and squeeze it offering a little extra support, he weakly smiles and we start forward, I turn round to Nix who is still stationary. "Come on then."

He looks like he wants to strangle me, but I don't care, I

just want out of this damp tunnel.

We continue up the dimly lit corridor for what feels like an age, in fact it's probably only been ten minutes. Though we are not running, we fast walk and I can tell it is really starting to wear on Danny especially as the tunnel is on a constant incline. I am about to demand a quick minute breather for him when a loud bang suddenly reverberates up the corridor from behind us, gunshots echo followed by a scream.

"Run!" Nix orders.

We all take off, Danny biting down on his lip in pain and hobble running as best he can. We keep running for a solid couple of minutes and then all the lights shut off, we all come to a stop colliding into one another in the pitch black. I scream, but a hand wraps round my mouth stifling me to a whimper, the hand smells of cigarettes, Nix.

"Shhhh, everyone hold hands, Rhonda, take the lead."

Nix's big hand grabs mine to guide me, I grasp it tightly, regardless of what a prick he is I know he can get us out of here. I pull Danny along as Nix moves forward, I can see nothing. God, I hate the dark, I really hate the dark, this is more than just dark it is nothingness, so black I can't work out anything in front of me. My breathing quickens, I hate this, it reminds me of the dream, and I feel the panic rising and not knowing if something is going to jump on us from behind just makes it worse.

It is a paralysing fear and it makes me stop dead, I'm usually really good at fighting down fear and just going for it, throw yourself in I always say, but right now I am stuck. I can't move. Oh dear god I am that stupid bitch in the horror movies everyone always yells at to move her ass.

"Rae? You Ok?" Danny asks feeling my back.

Someone gently grabs my chin, I can feel their face is a mere inch from mine, the smell of his cologne lets me know it is Nix.

"Rae, the exit is not far, in less than two minutes you will be out of here, you just need to hold onto my hand, I won't let go and I will get you out ok. Take a deep breath for me."

I nod, closing my eyes, stupid thing to do when in the dark, I take in a deep breath and try to steady myself, but Nix's cologne clings to me and is rather intoxicating, and not in a bad way! It is really nice actually, quite sweet smelling. I like it. But now is not the time to be thinking of how good Nix smells. Rae! There is something coming behind us and I am frozen here like a complete idiot absorbed by how good a guy smells?!

"Come on, you can do this." I say to myself.

Nix tugs my hand again and I grab Danny's, we move off just as another bang echoes up the corridor, this time something else can be heard, it sounds animal like. Nix rushes forward and pulls us with him, I trip and scuff my arm against the rock, warmth trickles down my arm. There is no way in hell we could make it out of here without Nix's help. We suddenly come to a stop; I crash into the back of Nix banging my nose on his shoulder.

"Owww," I start.

"Shhhhhhh…" Rhonda harshly whispers, "Anderson?"

"Excuse me." Lt Anderson pushes his way through. There must be a door ahead with a security panel as I hear a click sound and the door opens. It must be past midnight, the moon is so bright it lights up everything around, I have no idea where we are, but I am flooded with relief that we can get out of this tunnel. I step to the side to help Danny out. Sky is already standing outside face to the stars. The air is so much warmer out here than it is in the tunnel, almost like stepping out of the airport into a warm country. I'm just about to step over the threshold when a low growl comes from directly behind me. Rhonda's eyes are wide, I clench Danny's hand and he turns to see what is wrong, the look on his face says it all. And then suddenly with such force I am dragged backwards, back into the dark corridor at such speed it slams the door shut plunging me again into darkness.

I scream, like I have never screamed before, I try to grab hold of whatever I can, but end up ripping my hands as I'm dragged. I kick out at whatever has a hold of me, making contact. A grunt and growl comes from whatever the hell this thing is, and it releases its hold on me. I scramble away, not being able to see anything, I just focus on moving up the incline of the tunnel. If I thought I had been terrified before it was nothing compared to this, this is a hundred times worse. I turn to get up and run but the thing launches itself at me just as I make it to my feet, I slam into the wall, crumbling to the floor, and it hurts like hell but I know I have no time to catch my breath. Forcing my legs to work I twist to get up but it drags me again. I scream, dear god I'm going to die in this bloody tunnel. I fight back, kicking and swinging my arms, with everything I have but whatever this creature is I feel it tear or bite into my leg, I scream again and again as the pain spreads consuming my mind.

Suddenly it lets go of me and I hear a crunch, a gurgled growl and a high pitched keen, like a dog, and then nothing.

"Rae! Are you ok?"

It's Nix, thank god. I am crying, it is all I can do, I can't form words, let alone think how the hell did he find me so quickly. Who cares, I just need to get out of here. Another animal sound comes from way down the tunnel, there is another one.

"I got you!" He scoops me up. "Hold on ok."

And then we move way faster than I know any normal human can move, the next thing I know we were out in the open.

"Shut it...quick Lieutenant," Rhonda orders Anderson.

I look up at the stars, they are so bright, so beautiful, my tear-soaked face absorbing the moonlight. Nix doesn't stop moving, we are in a little copse up on the common, looking around it is just an old bunker with a few new modern structures around it.

There's a security fence surrounding the tiny compound with cameras at each corner.

"Come on we got to keep moving, there's another in the tunnel," Nix instructs.

"Over here, there's some transport." Anderson indicates to the other side of the bunker where a large Humvee truck is waiting.

Nix places me in the front whilst the others pile in the back with Rhonda and Anderson who assume position in the open back, weapons at the ready. Nix pulls at some wires, igniting the Humvee like a total pro.

There is a loud bang. Looking over to the door of the tunnel, it bulges outwards, something with a lot of force is about to break out of there. Without hesitation Nix floors the truck, smashing through the fence, avoiding the trees with ease in the dark. Gunfire explodes behind us,

Skylar screams. "Oh my god, what the hell is that thing?"

Turning as best I can in my pained state, I see Danny holding Sky, both are looking out the back, but I can't see past them. Winding down my window I stick my head out to look and my heart literally leaps into my throat. The thing is similar to a human but is covered in black hair, well more like fur, sharp claws glisten in the moonlight from its hands, long fangs protrude from its mouth and its red slit eyes narrow in on me. It pretty much sums up what a mythical werewolf or something must look like! More disturbing though is the incredible speed it's running at, dodging bullets easily and every second it gains proximity to our truck. In one bound it launches itself at Rhonda and Anderson! I hear Nix swear as he swerves the Humvee around a tree, the creature misses its aim, crashing straight into the tree, with a deafening crack, its dark body falls to the woodland floor, unmoving. I keep watching until it's completely out of sight, heart rate still racing, I turn to Nix.

"Is that what grabbed me?"

He gives the briefest nod, still concentrating on the land ahead, we are tearing across common land, I can't get my bearings even with the moon light everything is still very dark up here.

"Jesus, what about my Dad, those things were in the compound?"

Lt Anderson kneels by the back window. "Don't worry about your old man, he is one of the best, nothing can bring him down."

I know that won't ease Danny's mind, it doesn't ease

mine either, that thing had dragged and threw me like I weighed nothing. But the General has decades of training and the whole frigging Marine Corps to back him up. He will be fine. He will be fine! We continue driving over pretty rough terrain with no lights, how Nix is doing it I do not know, but the bumpy ride is doing nothing to help the pain radiating from my leg where that thing had caught me, I don't want to look. So I just keep on biting my lip to stop me from whimpering. With a final bump we burst out onto a thankfully dead road. Nix puts his foot down and we zoom along the road. Lights still off! I am not sure how I feel about it. I mean nothing can see us coming, but given the situation what choice do we have?

Everyone stays quiet, there are still so many questions, so much fear. I have no idea where we're heading, I feel too exhausted to ask, trusting Nix will get us somewhere safe. Taking some narrow back roads, we come to an opening that runs alongside the mouth of the estuary. Right by the water's edge is a small boathouse with a lean-to on the side. Nix parks the Humvee under the lean-to, jumps out and then pulls at something in the ceiling, a tarpaulin ripples down, covering the entrance.

The place looks like it hasn't been used in a while, the wood is rotten and old leaves are piled around where they've been blown in.

Lt Anderson exits the Humvee, still on edge. "What is this place?"

"It's a safe house Nix and I found, other than their parents no one else knows about it," Rhonda answers ushering Danny and Sky out. "We should be safe here for a couple of hours to figure out a plan of action."

I open my door but before I can move Nix is there, he picks me up, closing the door behind and waits for Rhonda to open the door to the house. Surprisingly the door isn't locked! Great they've brought us somewhere that anyone can walk into.

Clearly seeing my expression Rhonda adds, "There are other forms of security other than locking a door." Winking she walks in.

"What, is the place booby-trapped?" Sky chuckles sarcastically.

"Something like that," Nix omits. "But don't worry the traps aren't for us!"

I feel like a complete invalid with Nix carrying me, I am pretty certain I can walk and to be honest even though I appreciate him saving my ass I do not want to be this close to him. Acutely aware of every muscle in his body, and his smell, god it is so good, he literally is the hottest man I have ever seen, like superhero hot! Get a grip Rae snapping myself back to the room!

Nix gently places me on the rather old and very unkempt kitchen counter, clearly this place has barely been used, a thick dust layer is everywhere, even the windows are grimy. Looking out I can see nothing but pitch black and a reflection of the moon on the river, with the lights on in the house, anyone will be able to see that someone's home.

"There is screen camouflage over all the windows and doors, from the outside it looks dark in here," Nix says looking at me intently.

What the hell, can he read minds too? I redden hoping that's not the case, because I've had some very hot thoughts about him.

Thankfully he is no longer watching me to see just how red I am sure I have gone; he pulls the hem of my trouser up to view my wound, the state of my leg is pretty horrific, three deep gashes stretch from the back of my knee to midway down my calf.

"Holy shit balls, Rae!" Sky is by my side in a flash.

"I will get the kit." Rhonda dashes out the room.

Nix grabs some scissors from a drawer gently cutting the trouser leg to mid-thigh and then places a stool under my foot. "You hurt anywhere else." Looking me over.

I look at my arms, they are scraped and bruised but otherwise ok, I shake my head, the pain starts to kick in.

"Why can't you do your voodoo thing like before?" Sky asks, wafting her arms around like something out of Harry Potter.

Nix raises a brow. "By voodoo thing you mean healing," he says pointedly, shaking his head he goes and washes his hands. "Healing requires using energy, a lot of energy, this is not a life or death situation like it was before."

"But she's in pain!" Sky insists.

Oh yeah, I am in definite pain, the sudden air on my wound has totally sensitized it, and god it hurts.

Sky interrupts Nix before he can speak, thoroughly pissing him off again judging by the dark look on his face. "Plus, if those things come back for us she is going to need to run!"

"Hey what about me, I am in pain too!" Danny chirps in, he has been very quiet sitting on the other stool watching us. "Don't see anyone rushing to heal me?!"

Nix rolls his eyes. "That's because they are not after you, you just got caught in the crossfire, you will heal just

128

fine by yourself. They have zero interest in you."

"Wow your people skills are epic." Danny slides off the seat and walks over to a nearby sofa. "On that note I am going to get some shuteye whilst I can!"

Something is up with him; he is a little off! Of course he's off, he's worried about his Dad, combined with his own pain I am surprised he hasn't run away from us. Rhonda returns with a small case. Sky just crosses her arms standing firm, gearing up for an almighty go at Nix.

"Look...Sky If I healed everyone's injuries I would need to sleep for a week and that would make me pretty useless to you if they find us and we need to fight!"

"I thought you said they wouldn't find us." Sky jabs her finger at him.

I definitely think Nix is going to strangle her. "Sky." I grab her hand; she's only trying to help. "Go check on Danny," I say in a low voice. I squeeze her hand to assure her I'm ok, she looks from me to Nix.

"Fine," she huffs and barges past Nix without looking back.

Rhonda opens the kit which is full of small bottles I assume contain medicine, creams, sprays, basically a miniature pharmacy.

I glance back at Nix. "You know you don't have to be so damn rude all the time."

Rhonda laughs a little. "He has always been this way, only nice to the people he knows!"

"Well given the situation he might want to think about changing his attitude."

"I am right here!" Nix says in an irritated manner.

We both look at him, I smile. "No shit Sherlock."

Rhonda hides another smirk.

"You know what...." Nix moves towards me, but Rhonda steps in blocking his way as she examines my leg.

"Go clean up, Nix, we only have a couple of hours here tops, I got this." She eyes him until he relents moving away and out the door across from where I sit. The look I get as he turns before leaving, well if looks could kill I'd be fried to the spot.

"Seriously, what is his problem with us?"

"Nothing, this is a stressful situation, everyone is on edge. Now I am going to clean this but it could really hurt, so I will give you this shot to help numb the area." She snatches one of the small bottles and a needle, and it suddenly hits me she could be giving me anything, something that could knock me out or even kill me! But then she's had ample opportunity to kill me before, in fact she's done nothing but save my ass since the hospital.

She pauses with the needle in hand reading my look. "I would never hurt you, Rae or Skylar. I know you don't trust me, but if there is one thing you can count it is this … I will keep you safe!"

I nod, this woman I've known since I was a baby, she has always been like family, god she is the only family we have left.

She injects me just below the first deep gash, it stings for a moment but the effect is almost immediate, the whole area turns numb and before I know it, there is no pain. Bliss.

"Wow I have had my teeth out before and nothing happened that quickly!"

"The advantage of working for an agency like

STAR is that we get all the latest medical advancements. This solution ..." She raises the large bottle with what appears to be clear liquid. "This stuff contains special cells that help speed up your own body's healing on a particular area and this...." Pulling out a thin sheet that resembles a giant see-through plaster. "Is like a second skin, I don't fully understand the science to it but it basically closes open wounds, minimising infections and scarring."

"That is handy, so no need for stitches?"

"Nope none, these are designed for people out in the field. Ready?"

Even though my leg is numb I brace myself, the wound is pretty horrific, good job I'm not blood shy because there's a fair bit. I watch as the clear liquid pours over my wound, I feel nothing but a slight tingle, but I see in amazement how the raw red wounds are pinking a little and closing, this is so cool and way more effective than being stitched up.

"Why is this not readily available in hospitals for everyone?" A little repulsed that this treatment isn't out there for everyone.

"I imagine the science behind this is pretty costly, a lot of the treatments that are in this case are yet to go through the FDA, at the moment I imagine only those in private health care can afford this."

"Of course, make sure the rich are all ok!"

"I know, it's a load of bollocks, stuff like this could save lives and quickly." She lowers the thin sheet to my leg, gently placing it on the gashes, as soon as it makes contact with my skin it moulds to my leg completely sealing it off.

"This will now mix with the fabric of your own skin rapidly creating new skin. Once complete what is left will shed away just like when you get sunburnt. How does it feel?"

"It feels ok, surprisingly I thought there would be some throbbing… maybe that will come later?"

"Maybe, here take this, it's just a normal pain killer a bit like Codeine but without the unwanted drowsy effects."

She hands me a glass of water and I take the pill without question, last thing I want is to be in pain later, I really can't take Nix carrying me round again.

I notice Sky and Danny have been very quiet, I gently lower myself down off the counter testing my leg, it feels tight but otherwise still no pain. I head over to the sofa, Sky is curled in a ball on one side of the sofa and on the other side Danny is spread out with his feet on the table, watching them sleep reminds me just how long ago it's been since I last slept.

"There is a spare bed just through here, you can prop your leg up." Rhonda approaches with two blankets that she drapes over Sky and Danny. "We can only stay a couple of hours so get what sleep you can ok."

I lean over and place a blanket over Sky, sleeping in a bed with my leg will certainly beat trying to sleep in one of these chairs. I nod and move off to the hallway.

"First door on your right," she calls after me.

Just as I get into the hallway Nix appears, I jump, he is like a frigging Ninja. "God don't do that, some warning next time you are going to appear out of the dark."

"So sorry, didn't realise

you would be so jumpy."

"You know what after the day I've just had I am surprised I haven't had a heart attack, so excuse me if my nerves are all shot to shit!" I open the bedroom door without waiting for a reply and slam it in his face. I wait on the other side until I hear him leave, he really is a jerk!

Turning I look at the small single bed, it could have been a mattress on the floor and it would still be heaven. I am so exhausted I pretty much collapse onto the bed, barely pulling the covers over me before I am falling asleep, my last thought is of Mum and the tired, sad look I had seen on her face the last time I saw her. Miss you mum..........

CHAPTER 10

<u>**Skylar**</u>

I'm absolutely shattered but my mind just won't shut down. I lie for a while listening to Rae and Rhonda trying to force my mind to quiet, so many emotions swirl through me, the guilt at my last few moments with Mum had been one of anger and it's chewing away at me. I love…. loved my Mum and I would give anything to have her hold me again, like she did when I was younger and I woke up from a nightmare. She would sing gently in my ear some lullaby, she would rock back and forth whilst hugging me, I felt so safe, so peaceful. I feel tears brimming in my eyes, god I miss her. But I am also so angry at her and Dad for all the lies, especially Dad, he had always looked me in the eye and promised no secrets between us! He had lied multiple times to my face, I don't care if he wasn't supposed to tell me because of STAR or whatever the bollocks they're called, I was…. we were his children he should have told us.

I curl further into a ball on the sofa to quell the anger and pain. I look at Danny, like a typical man he had gone out cold the moment he sat down, now softly snoring! Great!

I hear Rae and Rhonda finish up and I shut my eyes, I don't want to deal with talking to anyone right now and my body is so exhausted I just want to lie here, stewing in my own grief. A few moments later I feel someone place a blanket over me, they hover watching me for a minute and then I hear them move off to the kitchen area.

"They asleep?" Nix's low voice.

"Yes, out like a light."

Someone else enters the room.

"You want a drink Lieutenant?" Rhonda asks.

"Yes please."

I hear the kettle filling and they all appear to shuffle into seated positions.

"Have you heard back from base?" Nix asks.

"No not yet, still radio silence. So, what is the plan?"

Their voices become muffled out by the kettle; they are talking so low I can't hear them. Once the kettle stops which seems to take an eternity, bloody thing, I have missed the crucial part of the conversation.

"We will need to move out in two hours, I suggest we take it in shifts to get some sleep," Rhonda advises.

"I will go first, you two get some kip," Nix offers.

"Ok make sure you do wake us, come on Anderson this way."

Two sets of feet retreat from the room and I hear footsteps going up the stairs. I concentrate on listening to where Nix is, he coughs occasionally, slurps his drink rather loudly and paces around. Once or twice I swear he moves over to where we are lying and just stares? But I can't tell for sure. Even though my mind is clearly awake the rest of me completely shuts down, my eyes refuse to open, god damn mind, shut up! Then it suddenly hits me, Theo! I need to sleep now; I must speak to him. With a decision made it literally takes me all of two seconds to fall asleep. Everything is dark for a minute and maybe I have just fallen into a dreamless sleep, but then am I not totally aware of this right now?

I feel a hand on my arm, I open my eyes, there is fog all around us and I am lying in the same ball as I was curled in on the sofa, but now on hard rock, the same type I had climbed when I first met Theo in my dream. I look to the hand on my arm, strong with long fingers, my gaze drifts up the lean-muscled arm covered in tattoos, to the breath-taking face of Theo. His dark black hair is immaculate, with a curl perfectly styled falling by his eyes, oh and those eyes are a brilliant violet, they actually seem to be glowing a bit. I wonder if his eyes look like that in real life or if it's just part of this dream world?

"Thought you would never come."

He smiles and helps me up, I look down and wince, I'm still wearing the same dirty, blood-covered clothes I had on before going to sleep. Oh crap I bet I look a complete mess. Great!

As soon as I stand, I turn looking around us and try to subtly flatten my hair a little, why oh why hadn't I thought to have a shower first before coming here?

"You could be covered in sewerage and you would still be beautiful."

Oh balls, I forget he can read minds. Dammit! He probably heard that too, in fact I should stop ranting in my head altogether.

"How about you ask me some questions, save the ranting in your head."

I stand slack-jawed, amazed and in disbelief, and also horrified, but he just keeps smiling, like he finds me ...cute?...shut up Sky!!

"Uh yeah, sure," is all I can muster.

He holds out his hand. "Come let's walk and talk."

I look at his hand, why do we need to hold hands?

"You have only done this once, in this realm it is easy to get lost and you very much need to get back to the Earth plane."

I don't hesitate and grab his hand which feels oddly very normal with him. Even though he pops up out of nowhere, is clearly other worldly and the fact I know diddly squat about him, I trust him.

"I am glad, I mean you and your sister no harm."

I smile, still not used to him being able to hear my thoughts.

"So, you must have a lot of questions?"

Right! Questions. There are so many, where to start? "What is this place? Where is this place? How did I get here? Who are you?"

He chuckles, moving through the fog with purpose. "Well this is what we refer to as the between realm, it is a place of nothingness really but if you know the way it can lead to other realms and planes of existence. For most on your world, those that die will end up here before moving on to the spirit realm."

My thoughts instantly go to my Mum and Dad, they have been here? "Where is the spirit realm, can we go there?" I see the look of sympathy in his eyes.

"I wish I could say yes, but the spirit realm is for spirits, not for the living. But know this, it is the most beautiful of all the realms. Your parents will be at peace."

I look down, taking a breath to stem the tears building in my eyes, I will not cry, now is not the time, someone is finally answering some of my questions.

"As for how did you get here, well you have astral projected."

I vaguely recall reading something on that when Rae and I had found the information on the ascended masters.

"That is right, an ascended Master however can move their whole form through the planes, right now though your body is back at the boat house but your spirit is here, you have projected your spirit."

Something about the last time I was here springs to mind. "The last time I saw you though, when I woke up back home, I had dirt over my hands and feet?"

"That is because the last time your whole form passed through to this realm, you had ascended, I was surprised that you had the power to do that, you are developing much quicker than I expected."

"What does that mean?"

He lets out a small laugh and I feel I am missing something important. Around us the fog thins lifting a little, the ground feels softer almost like we're walking on grass but I can see the same rock as what I woke up on.

"What you did on your first time took me years to master."

Wow, ok now I feel a little awesome.

"Yes, wow indeed. Come, we will be out of this in a moment, you will love this."

He gently pulls me along a little faster, the fog lifts more and a light warm breeze ruffles my hair, it smells like a warm summer evening on the beach. Suddenly the fog is completely gone and the view is amazing.

We are in a small cove; towering cliffs rise up virtually closing off what must be some kind of ocean on the other side. In front a small jetty protrudes out from the beach several yards into the bay. It reminds me of those secret beaches you see in Thailand or somewhere equally exotic. The sand is white and untouched, and the sky is so clear I can see more stars than I have ever before. The moonlight glistens on the water's surface, creating the perfect mirror of the stars. The water is so clear I can even make out the coral a few meters down. This place is breath-taking, I move forward letting go of Theo's hand, flicking off my shoes as I make my way to the water, dipping my toes in the water is warm and inviting, nothing like the cold sting you get at our home beach. I step in some more 'til I am calf deep, tiny fish the size of my fingernail swim around and glow like they have their own light, small shoals of them dance around in front of me in a graceful pattern. This is like heaven.

"It is, isn't it?"

I turn and look at him and in this light he is even more awe inspiring, seriously how can any man be that damn good looking.

He smiles. Oh shit. Thoughts Sky, he can hear your thoughts!! I turn my back to him, desperately trying to hide my embarrassment, I really need to get a handle on my thoughts. Then suddenly he's behind me, I hadn't even heard him enter the water.

"You should take a good look at yourself and try to see what I see."

He's so close behind me I'm acutely aware of every inch of him, he turns my head gently to look at the water, my reflection and his stare back at me. It's like standing next to a god, there he is all perfect and then there's me, big doll eyes, pale as a ghost and what resembles Edward Scissorhands hair.

"All I see is a mess." My clothes are all ripped with dirt and blood over them, gross!

"All I see is beauty."

I turn to him and scowl. "Well you should have gone to Specsavers!"

He laughs, a real hearty laugh and oh my god if it is not the sexiest laugh I have ever heard. I just need to stop thinking, mind reader here.

"So you didn't answer all my questions ...where are you from?"

He takes a hold of my hand again and leads me back to the shore, and up onto the jetty, we walk to the end and sit with our legs hanging off the edge. The water must still be shallow, I can see the bottom but this time there are some bigger fish swimming around down there. I wonder if there are any sharks.

"Yes, but they won't bother us." Theo smiles brightly.

I smile back.

"But yes, back to your question, where am I from? Well I am sure you can tell I am not from Earth, I'm originally from a distant realm called Erebus, but that land of my birth no longer exists."

"Oh wow, I am sorry, what happened to your home...planet?"

He pauses, looking out over the water, a sadness creeps over his gorgeous face. "It was drained of all life, nothing now can grow or survive there. I can barely remember what it looked like before. I am told it was once the most beautiful place, more beautiful than this." He gestures around us. "But a darkness grew there and swallowed it whole, now I roam the worlds without a true home."

That is so sad, my little town of Doversham has always been home and no matter what, I always know it will be there, I can't imagine not having…I catch myself as the realisation that I now no longer have a home either. Our house is gone, monsters are tracking us, we can probably never go back, we would only endanger everyone we know. It hits me like a ton of bricks, knocking the air out of me, I'm homeless, parentless and on the run, I can't stop my tears, they just come, unrelenting, having held them back for too long. A wracking sob escapes my lips and Theo just pulls me into a bear hug, stroking my back as I cry and cry and cry some more. My life as I know it is over, and for what? I don't understand why my family is so damn important?

"I will help you uncover the truth."

He leans back gently cupping my cheeks making me look at him through my blurry vision.

"I promise I will help you and keep you safe."

"I don't understand any of this, why us?" I gulp in some air and wipe my face, annoyed at myself for breaking down. Standing, I pace the jetty, Theo just sits there watching me, no doubt waiting for me to explode.

"All I know is my parents worked for some kind of world …government…agency thing, now they are both dead, everything we thought we knew is a lie and now for some reason these monsters are dead set on killing me and my sister." Placing my hands on my hips I turn. "You knew they were coming back at the camp, how?"

He must know something, more than he is letting on. He seems undeterred by the accusation. "I knew because I have been keeping an eye on you."

"Why?" Because that's just creepy.

"I had been tracking a Fae…."

"Sorry, what is a Fae?"

"They are like a sniffer dog, can track anything across any realm. Anyway, it was tracking you. The night that girl was killed, it had led them virtually to your door."

"But why are they tracking us?"

"You must have something they want."

"Like what?"

"I don't……." Breaking off Theo remains completely still, his gaze sliding to the water.

"Theo?" I come closer behind him looking where he is, the glittering glint from the moon and stars has suddenly gone, I look up, clouds are forming and fast, like a storm is coming. Theo jumps up grabbing my hand.

"We have to go."

He moves away from the edge of the jetty as the water starts to churn and bubble, lightning strikes overhead and a bolt shoots into the water followed by an almighty clap of thunder that shakes all around.

"Run!"

There is no time to process what's happening, Theo propels me along the jetty, behind us I hear the splintering sound of wood smashing, it draws my attention and I look back, the jetty is being torn apart by something unseen underneath it. I scream and increase my speed, Theo keeps holding my hand as we fly across the sand, I barely feel it, sand should usually slow a runner down but not us, we dash back into the fog, not stopping or looking behind us. The sound of the thunderous storm can still be heard, though now it seems to echo all around us, but I can see nothing but fog. Theo does not slow the pace and I daren't ask why, I just keep running. After a few more minutes of straight out sprinting my lungs are starting to burn, and I can feel myself slowing, how much longer? Thankfully Theo must have picked up my distress and slows, bringing me to a gentle jog and then stops, he is barely out of breath where as I am gulping the air down.

"What…was…that?" I ask whilst catching my breath.

"That was the work of a very powerful being, I don't know how they found us there, they shouldn't have been able to track you in that realm?"

"Why not?" I thought he had said something about their sniffer dogs could track me anywhere.

"Because that is my realm, I created it."

I don't think I heard him right, he created a realm? Thunder echoes again, Theo takes my face in his hands.

"I need to send you back fast, I will be in touch soon, don't try to find me, I will find you ok! Now this may hurt a little."

I have no time to ask why it will hurt or even say goodbye, he literally hurls me, one moment I am looking into his beautiful eyes and then next I fall off the sofa as my sleeping body crashes into the coffee table.

"Ouch …bloody hell!" I roll off the table onto the floor, thus hitting my elbow, I curse loudly again. I hear pounding footsteps from behind me.

"Skylar, what the hell, are you ok?" Danny says helping me sit upright on the floor.

"Sky?!" Rae's voice is panicked.

I know everyone must be in the room, god I bet I look like a crazy person.

"I am ok." Theo hadn't been lying when he said it would hurt, he'd totally winded me. I bend my head in between my knees to get my breath, but more so I can come up with an idea as to why this just happened, they're going to want some kind of explanation and I only trust Rae with the actual truth.

Rae rubs my back soothingly. "Sky, what happened?"

"I don't know I must have had a bad dream and jerked awake in my sleep, I felt confused as to where I was so must've tripped over the table or something."

Rae, Rhonda and Danny all look on sympathetically, huh maybe my drama teacher had been wrong about me being a terrible actress.

"Actually, you kind of convulsed and then flipped onto the table," Nix says with his usual flat I-don't-give-a-crap tone. He walks around the sofa looking around as if he is expecting someone else to be here.

Does he know what I can do? Does he know about Theo? I school my look to one of confusion when he stands in front of us. "What do you mean convulsed? What like a heart attack?" I say in my best dumb ass sounding way.

"Sky you're too young to have a heart attack," Rae says soothingly whilst shooting a dirty look at Nix.

He just stares back at me for a few seconds, his look is really unnerving, I'm not a fan of him and I can tell the feeling is mutual.

"When I said convulsed I did not mean a heart attack, I meant one moment you were sound asleep and then next you were shaking and then throwing yourself on the table."

Lt Anderson approaches with a cup of hot tea, handing it to me. "After the day you have had I am not surprised you had a nightmare, I pretty much threw myself out of my bunk in my sleep after Afghanistan, the mind has a strange way of expressing itself."

I take the tea from him, smiling, he just helped back me up.

Nix heads towards the hallway. "We have got an hour before we should leave, I suggest if you want more sleep or shower do it now."

Relieved I look down at myself, a shower is definitely needed, plus I want a few minutes alone time to process everything I have just learnt from Theo, for starters what the hell had come after me in that realm? And if Theo created that realm just how frigging powerful is he?

****

Rhonda

The moment Sky is in the shower and the others become occupied in the lounge drinking tea and eating what few tinned goods we have stored here; I head up to the loft to Nix. Climbing the narrow staircase to the top level, I spot him at the far end by the window where the old rickety balcony is. He is supposed to be keeping watch but his gaze is distant, hearing me he looks over, smiles slightly, his smile never reaches his eyes anymore, I miss that about him. The last ten years have hardened him, changing his usually light hearted, slightly obnoxious, playful persona to someone who now rarely jokes and prefers solitude than the company of others. I stand by him, crossing my arms as I lean on the window edge and watch the sun start to rise creating a light pink colour across the sky. A chill creeps up my spine and the hairs on my arms bristle, the foreboding feeling reminding me of the phrase 'Red sky in the morning, shepherd's warning'.

"We can't trust her."

I sigh, shaking off the chill, I knew this was coming, but before I can talk he continues.

"This isn't just about the darkness in her, I am almost certain she is projecting."

But it isn't possible, projecting takes years to master and requires a highly skilled guide.

"Nix, there is no way Sky is projecting, why would you think that?"

"You didn't see it, the way she flipped off the sofa, I have seen it before when you are suddenly thrust back into your body from the ether."

I haven't seen it before but I'd read about it, Nix is the one with intimate knowledge of Astral projection, he'd studied with the guides themselves back at STAR.

"Not just that but I am certain she is not alone when she projects."

"What, you think Rae is too?"

"No... I think she knows someone there, I thought I sensed him back at the camp when Sky suddenly started saying we needed to get out."

Of course, in all the rush and Rae being injured I had forgotten to go back over just how Sky had known we needed to get out.

"Then I caught the tail end of his scent again in the lounge." He pauses taking a breath.

A sneaking suspicion I know where he is going with this, but it can't be him? However paranoid Nix has become, he has never been wrong about this guy, he would know his scent from anywhere.

"It's Theo, he's back."

CHAPTER 11

<u>Danny</u>

The hot shower water on my sore aching body feels amazing as well as being clean! I feel even better after taking the painkillers that Rhonda gave me, they had acted fast and don't appear to leave the drowsy feeling like the last one I had, bonus, as I have a feeling, we're going to be on our feet a lot today. Very reluctantly I turn the shower off and get dry. I check my phone again, nothing. Still nothing from Dad and my calls won't connect, I'd even tried connecting with Mum who is away for business in the states (thank god) but that line won't connect either. I am really starting to worry that something awful has happened to my Dad. Lt Anderson keeps assuring me that he will be fine and that he has been through much worse, I am not sure what is worse than monsters attacking but he seems very confident that Dad will be ok. It does nothing to ease the dread that is building, the feeling that something really bad is going to happen soon.

The words my Dad had whispered to me before we escaped the camp whirl through my head.

"When you get the opportunity, get away from them, STAR can't be trusted, the girls, they are dangerous."

I have no idea what he meant, the bit about STAR I can understand, this secret agency who no one has heard from in the last twenty-four hours is supposed to help us? Yeah right,

I barely trust Rhonda let alone some supreme spy agency. No, what is really throwing me was his warning that the girls are dangerous, how are Rae and Sky dangerous? It just makes no sense, Dad's known them since we were all in primary school together. The only thing I can think of is that he meant being around them is dangerous because of the people…things that are after them for this weapon. Clearly they think their parents had known the location and so must have passed it onto their children. Yeah that makes sense, but as logical as I want to make this, it does not match the tone my Dad had used to warn me. He genuinely saw them as being dangerous in some way.

Maybe I am just overthinking all of this, I'm still so tired, hurting and worried, I can't think straight just yet, I need to just wait and hear from Dad. A knock at the door jars me out of my thoughts.

"Danny, you ok?" Rhonda asks from the other side.

"Yeah sorry I will be out in a moment."

Quickly I dress in some spare clothes Nix found for me, my favourite T-shirt is an absolute wreck, torn, bloody and ripped, I throw it and my shorts into the bin and open the door. Rhonda stands just in the bedroom door waiting for me.

"Sorry, the shower was so nice I didn't notice the time, has anyone heard from my Dad?"

"No nothing yet, come on we are heading out in twenty minutes and need to go over the plan with you."

I nod and we head downstairs where everyone sits in the lounge area, all waiting for me. Shit. Feeling a little bad now for having made them wait, even Rae had had a quicker shower than me. I take a seat next to Rae; she looks at me and absently rubs my arm.

"Feels so much better to at least be clean." She smiles at me.

"God yeah, and fresh clothes." I smirk looking down at my attire, it is nothing like what I usually wear, dark green baggy combat trousers and a grey long sleeved top, a far cry from my usual boardie's and bright coloured T-shirts.

"So, what's the plan?" Sky asks.

Nix takes the lead. "We still haven't heard from your Dad and we can't stay here to see if he calls as the coms are still down so we need to get past the affected area, we have already stayed here too long."

But what about my Dad, what if he is wounded or needs help?

"Shouldn't we at least try to go back to the camp to scope out the situation?" I plead.

For once Nix's face actually softens a little, big surprise maybe he has a heart. "I understand you want to go back, but right now it is just too dangerous, we need to get in contact with STAR to call in reinforcements."

Lt Anderson, looks like he is itching to get back to camp but my Dad had given him orders to stay with us.

"Your Dad will be ok and he would want you to be safe," Rhonda adds.

I look to Lt Anderson, his jaw working and lips pressed thin, he doesn't like the thought of essentially abandoning my Dad and the rest of the camp either. But what could the two of us do? If the camp is overrun with these beasts we will need back up and a lot of it. "Ok, ok, so where exactly do we need to head?"

Nix spreads out a map while motioning to our position.

"We are here, now the easiest solution would be to take a boat and just head out along the coast, but we don't want to be caught out on the water. We need to be able to run if they catch up to us. We can't risk the truck, so we need to make our way on foot hugging the river edge for at least five miles, once we reach Littledown village we can secure another car. I estimate a ten-mile radius for coms blackout. We must keep on going until we can get through to someone."

Five miles, that's not so bad but Rae with her leg could be a problem. "Rae, will you be alright going that far on foot?" I ask.

"Yeah, I will be fine, may just have to take a few breaks."

"Alright, let's get a move on," Nix orders.

We bustle around quickly grabbing any essentials, water, food and a few items of clothing. We find three backpacks which we ram all the stuff in, I lift one to put it on but Rhonda takes it off me.

"It's ok Danny I will take that, you're still injured and this walk will feel longer than it sounds."

I go to argue that there is no way I'm going to be the only guy not carrying something.

"Plus you can help Rae if her leg gets too sore." Without waiting for my reply, she turns shouldering the pack. "Everyone ready?"

We all nod.

Following her down the hallway we exit out the back door and down the very slippery wooden stairs to the bank of the river. The sun's barely risen, the early morning fog clings to the river casting an eerie glow everywhere.

There's a chill to the air this morning, but I am grateful for it, it's waking me up and I need to be alert. We follow the path Rhonda takes, avoiding the muddy bank of the river keeping to the grassy knoll. Nix is up front with Rhonda looking around for any trouble and Lt Anderson brings up the rear, gun still in hand. Without his military uniform there's a strong possibility that if we run into anyone they may panic at the sight of his weapon. At this time there is bound to be a few dog walkers. We walk in silence for what must be a good half hour, the sun is lighting up the fog around us but is not powerful enough to burn it off. Not paying attention to the more difficult terrain I stumble and nearly take Sky down with me, but I grab hold of a crooked tree before completely face planting.

"Shit, sorry Sky."

She chuckles as we both help each other stand up properly. "Don't worry, it's...."

"Shhhhh!"

Nix is ahead on top of a boulder, eyes closed and dead still.

Rhonda motions for us all to stay quiet. The fog of the river is thicker here as a number of small brooks flow into the main estuary, I can barely see six feet ahead, a little unnerving, there could be anything watching us! Rhonda tenses looking back to Nix.

Opening his eyes, he presses a finger to his lips to keep us quiet, then he motions us to follow. As quietly as we can we follow him right down to the river, there is a mini cliff that hangs over the river, it goes on for about a quarter of a mile and is a great fishing spot, you can walk over it easy enough but Nix leads us down into the water. I turn back to

Lt Anderson with a questioning glance but he just pushes me gently forward, his gun at the ready. Nix slowly walks into the water, careful not to make much noise! Easier said than done, I clench my teeth at every slosh of water we make. We get to about waist height, what are we going to do now....swim? He makes his way to the cliff, then stops looking up to where we have just come from. I can't see anything but Nix motions us to move faster and I trust him enough that something bad must be up there.

We tuck under the overhang of the cliff, if anyone looked out now, they wouldn't see us and with all the mist I doubt we'd be seen from further up the river. The river itself does not look very appealing this morning, well these nice clean clothes lasted long.... shit, my bloody phone, I'm waist deep in the goddamn water. I twist away from the river bank to get my phone out, hands try to grab me, but all I can think of is that Dad won't be able to get a hold of me. Yanking it from my pocket, the screen flickers and then abruptly dies.

"Shit!"

I look up, Nix has an arm wrapped round Rae, the other hand covering her mouth, Rhonda is pretty much doing the same to Sky and Lt Anderson calmly motions me to stay still, I am right out in the open, in plain sight. A growl emanates from atop the river bank, I freeze, phone still in hand, as a large dark shadow creeps towards the edge of the overhang, it stays just within the mist, all I can make out are two dots of red, which I assume must be eyes. Oh crap! It retreats back into the mist and two hulking figures appear; they are dressed in black with tattoos over their arms. They stop at the edge of the bank right on top of where the others remain hidden. I look up at them, heart hammering, dear god they could kill me in an instant they are twice the size of the guys you see at the gym all jumped up on steroids. The slightly shorter one sniffs the air, out of the corner of my eye I can see Nix and Rhonda pulling Rae and Sky further under the water until only their heads are above, they slowly start to move up the river keeping under the overhang.

Lt Anderson, on the other hand, hasn't moved, is he not going to escape too?

"Whatcha doing in there?" The big guy asks with a slight accent.

It sounds a little Russian. My mind freezes, what the hell do I say, because of my stupidity we could all die. I look down at my phone.

"My...my phone....it um fell in the water." Yep I need to be way more convincing than this if I want to live. I cough. "My stupid ass dog did a runner, I was trying to chase after him and my bloody phone flew out of my pocket in here. It's totally broken."

They look at each other, their expressions unreadable, the bigger one lowers to a crouch, never taking his eyes from me, the other lifts his head to the air a little and sniffs again. Thank god I'm half submerged because my legs are shaking something bad.

The big one cocks his head to the side, smirking. "Well that is unfortunate for you," he booms.

"Haha yeah you could say that, my Dad is going to kill me." They both stare at me so I continue, "You two haven't seen a dog running about have you? If I lose Lucky as well my life won't be worth living." I laugh nervously.

Looking briefly off to the side I see Nix and the others are much further away. Lt Anderson has positioned his gun aiming right under the big guy, right between his legs.

The big guy pauses for a second as if listening to something and then laughs while turning his gaze back to me. "No, we haven't seen a dog all morning, which is funny because we have our own dog and he usually always picks up on others' scents."

We've been made, I know it, behind them the huge black shape emerges, it's a giant wolf, teeth bared, red eyes and at least five feet tall. As much as my mind is screaming to get away, I am frozen with fear to the spot.

"But we do smell your friends." He leans to look under the bank edge and right into the barrel of Lt Anderson's gun.

Lt Anderson fires, no hesitation, the guy's brain matter spattering all over me, but there is no time to think, the wolf beast growls and launches itself off the cliff right for me, I dive to the side and push hard and fast under the water. I feel the impact of the beast hit the water, its claws just missing scraping my back. I kick deeper out into the river. I can't see far ahead of me, the water is too silty, but I can just make out a hulking shadow ahead, that looks like a fallen tree. I grab hold looking above me as the beast swims around trying to find me. I don't feel stretched for air yet, I know I can easily hold this for two minutes. Living by the sea and surfing as much as I do meant Dad had hammered into me to learn, but I have never been able to hold it over three minutes. Maybe if I swim out deeper I can peek up briefly to breathe without them seeing me.

I'm just about to move when something grabs me from behind, I turn and in a lame underwater effort try to fight it off, but through the murky water I see its Lt Anderson. I motion to him about swimming further out, he gives a thumbs up and we push away from the branch. I count in my head every stroke roughly gauging how far we are travelling; the tide is not turning so thankfully we are not battling a current. After counting to thirty I look up, we're definitely a lot deeper, I thumb motion to Anderson to go up, we slowly kick to the surface so only our faces breach the water, taking a big breath we duck under again, staying down and focusing on the surface for the big wolf.

After a minute of nothing we slowly make our way back up, this time lifting our heads to look around. It's still very misty but now it has lifted enough that I can just make out the shoreline and the giant shape of the wolf shaking its coat by the water's edge. The other guy is nowhere to be seen, I push up further in the water trying to see if I can make out Rae and Sky but mist clouds my view.

"Don't do that, they will be fine, we need to move. Keep to a breaststroke so not to make any noise."

I nod following Lt Anderson's lead, as we move off following the shoreline up stream. The lurking figure of the wolf fades out of sight. "Where are the others?"

"I don't know but we will find them."

A large splash in the water not far behind us disturbs what had been complete calm, we both stop looking at each other.

"What was that?"

Lt Anderson focuses behind me whilst I look in front, the mist clearing a little more and I spot a moored boat a few yards ahead. "Boat, let's move now."

Lt Anderson nods but as we move off there is another splash, this time it is a lot closer behind. I have never been afraid of the water, that whole not knowing what is under you has never bothered me, even surfing in South Africa I'd never felt that panic, but hell I am feeling it now and it powers me on. I kick off, no more breaststroke, I just flat out swim for it. I reach the boat in a matter of seconds and pull myself up by the anchor chain, it's only a small boat so easy enough. Once on board I look over for Lt Anderson, he's still a couple of feet from the boat, I lean over ready to help him but my attention is caught by the large shadow that passes right under him. My gaze follows it, but the combination of the water and the mist makes it impossible for me to follow further than a few feet.

"Dude come on, there's something under you."

Lt Anderson paddles quickly up to the boat looking around panicked, then thrashes reaching his arm up to me, but it is still a little too far.

"Pull yourself up on the chain," I yell.

A few metres behind Lt Anderson appears a huge fin gliding up in the water, as more of the body crests out of the water, I realise it's a massive shark.

"Holy shit."

Grabbing the edge of the boat I lean over clasping onto Lt Anderson's outstretched hand, I heave trying to pull him free of the water whilst he pulls himself up by the chain. The shark smashes against the boat, jaw wide open with hundreds of razor-sharp teeth. Lt Anderson tucks his legs up some more, yelling for me to pull him up more. I twist my body away from the edge of the boat pulling him up and over with me then the boat jars as the shark slams against its side.

"What the hell, is that a shark?" Lt Anderson calls out.

We peer over the edge of the boat, the water churning as the dark shadow lurks below, it is circling the boat, in fact the bloody thing is as big as the boat. I hope it doesn't figure that out else we're screwed.

"We need to get out of here, now!" Anderson commands.

It's a sailing boat, but thank the lord it also has motor power.

"Pull the anchor up," I yell to Anderson. I quickly release a rope attaching us to the mooring. "Let's hope there is some fuel left in here."

I dash to the wheel, the boat key is hanging by its cord, no one down here would think twice that someone would steal their boat from a mooring. Igniting the engine, the boat roars to life just as the shark collides to the port side. We're both thrown to the edge, I barely stop myself from falling back into the water. Lt Anderson smashes headfirst into the boom knocking himself out, blood trickles from his head but there is no time to think about that, the shark is circling back ready to crash into us again.

I run to the wheel, pushing the throttle, the boat lurches forward, the shark hitting the very end of the stern. Holding on to the wheel for dear life I push the boat forward and turn up stream. This part of the river is dotted with other moored boats I will have to wind this one in between them. From what little I know about sharks they are pretty fast and this boat is not. As we come up to the first boat I aim around, the shark splits off in the other direction and then disappears. Looking around I can't see it anywhere, where the hell has it gone? I pass in between two other boats, slowing down so we don't get tangled in the mooring rope or anchor chains.

Lt Anderson groans as he sits up holding his head. "Where is it?"

"I don't know, I can't see it, can you?"

Lt Anderson keeping low to the deck looks over either side. "No nothing"

The mist has virtually lifted, the heat of the summer sun burning the last remnants away, now that we are further upstream the water is a lot clearer, but there is nothing, no trace of the shark anywhere.

"Maybe it is getting too shallow for it?" he suggests.

"Nah the tide is still in, it will still be pretty deep here."

"Maybe it picked up the scent of something else...."

We both look at each other wide-eyed, the others could still be in the water, they may have been against the bank but it's still deep enough for a shark to get to. I start to turn the boat but Lt Anderson grabs my arm pulling out a small device that is beeping and flashing red. "Shit I forgot about this."

"What is it?"

"This is a mini Morse code machine, Nix and myself thought it would be handy to have in case we got separated."

He starts to tap back on the machine, I slow the boat right down. Looking back towards where we have come from, there is still a lot of mist back there, obviously heavier due to the sea. The machine flashes back again.

"They are ok, and out of the water. They can see us... apparently..."

We both look around towards the shore. Desperate to find them I scan the area, I look up towards the hill at the top is a copse of trees, I spot someone waving. "I think I see them." I wave back. Four of them wave frantically back at us. "It's them dude."

Lt Anderson laughs whilst waving and then looking back down at the machine, his face drops, going white, I stop grinning and my wave frozen.

"What?"

"They said there is a massive shape following us, right under the boat."

With an almighty explosion the middle of the boat bows, wood splintering, as the head of the shark bursts through, I only have a second to register that there is something very different about this shark, it has red eyes, the same as that wolf that had jumped in the water after me. The impact sends me and Lt Anderson flying right back into the water.

CHAPTER 12

Rae

I try to shout to warn Danny that he's out in the open but Nix stops me, engulfing me with his broad arms and keeping a hand over my mouth. Out of the corner of my eye I see Rhonda has done the same to Sky. Lt Anderson raises his weapon up towards the roof of the river overhang. The look on Danny's face tells me whatever is up there is not friendly, he just stands there staring, then his eyes briefly find mine and he starts talking to whatever or whoever is up there. Lt Anderson looks at Nix and mouthing the word 'Go'.

Slowly Nix makes me and him sink until only our heads are above the water, hugging the bank he starts to take us upstream, I squirm, no way am I leaving Danny, but Nix's hold is like a vice, I can't get out, so I start kicking.

"Stop it," Nix growls. "Anderson will cover Danny, if they know you're here they will definitely kill him."

My heart hammers in my ears, I can't just leave my best friend, tears stream down my face the further we move away. Danny is still standing there, what the hell is he saying to them to keep them from attacking? We make it a few more yards upstream, still covered by the overhang of the bank, I can just about make out Danny through the mist. He starts backing away deeper into the water, then suddenly a shot is fired, I go to scream but Nix pulls me underwater, holding me tighter, clamping a hand over my mouth and nose, the panic of not being able to breathe takes over. I can usually hold my breath pretty well but being caught off guard is totally different, I need air, I need to see if Danny is ok. I struggle in Nix's arms, somehow through all of this he is still moving me upstream and away from whatever is surely killing my best friend.

We hit a deeper section of the river that runs along the river edge, I am able to really kick out my legs. Nix pinches my arm as if to tell me to chill out but I don't, because why the hell would I? I need some frigging air! He loosens his grip on me, turning me to face him, he pushes me against the riverbank wall. I motion that I need to come up for air, my lungs feel like they're going to burst, he shakes his head, pinches my nose and then next thing I know his mouth is over mine. Shock pulses through me, and I won't lie, a little of something else that I really shouldn't be feeling in a moment like this. The need for some kind of air trumps all else, I open my mouth and inhale relieving the tight burn in my chest, as much as I want more air it is too dangerous to take much more than a couple breaths like this. He places his hands on either side of my face, and nods to me, I nod back, raising a thumb up to indicate I am ok. He indicates to Rhonda and Sky who are also underwater with us to rise, we do it slowly trying not to gulp in air too loudly.

We've rounded a bend in the river, Danny or Lt Anderson are nowhere to be seen, the mist is lifting but I still can't see much more than twenty feet, there is no sound either, just an eerie silence. Nix raises his finger to his lips urging me to stay quiet, I agree as he closes his eyes, he must be doing that thing that Rhonda did back at his flat, checking the area for danger or whatever it was she called it. Suddenly

Nix tenses, eyes flying open, searching directly in front of us, Oh God, what is it?

"Don't move," he whispers.

I glance over to Sky, she looks terrified, I follow her gaze and realise why, a huge fin glides no more than twenty feet from us, a sodding shark! In Doversham estuary?! I can't even begin to process this fact, I have banged on about how with global warming we would soon see sharks in our waters, but I never thought I would actually come face to face with one! Nix's arm slowly wraps back around me, his eyes never leaving the shark, he pulls me gently against him until there is nothing but wet clothes separating us.

And being so aware of just how ripped he is, has my pulse pounding!

The shark fin turns carving its way towards us, any second now it will be game over. Will it hurt or will I just bleed out in seconds? I turn my head away, not wanting to actually look into the jaws of my death. I notice Nix's hand hovering just over the water and a light shimmer and glow emanates from his hand, it spreads in front of us creating a slightly glittered barrier between us and the shark. What the hell is it that? Another STAR secret no doubt! Sky whimpers as the shark glides past us by a mere few feet. I hold my breath; whatever Nix is doing the shark has not seen or smelt us. Suddenly it turns violently, tail flicking nearly hitting us and powers off through the water, out to the middle of the river. Only one thing could have got its attention….

"Oh my god, Danny!"

"We need to get out of the water," Rhonda says as she grabs the lip of the bank and hauls herself up, once up she kneels over leaning to grab Sky who is already waiting with outstretched hands. Nix helps her up by pushing her legs and I follow suit, clambering up onto the bank, a small moment of relief that we are out of the water, but then I hear shouts out on the water from Danny.

"We have to help him." I make a move to get back in the water.

"No, you don't." Rhonda grabs me.

I slap her arm away. "WE can't just leave him!"

"Rae, listen to me, Danny is a strong swimmer and you will be of no use to him by jumping straight back in there, it is looking for us!"

I know how good a swimmer Danny is, he's surfed every day no matter the weather, but this is a god damn shark, I feel utterly helpless, we have to do something.

"Come on the fog is lifting, you see that clump of trees up there, maybe we can get a good visual on where Danny is." Nix suggests. He gently pulls me by the arm and we all follow him dashing across parts of open ground, who knew if those creatures were still back there looking for us, we had heard a couple of gunshots, maybe Anderson had got them. Oh god, Anderson, I'd totally forgotten about him. Within minutes we reach the trees, the morning sun really blasting through to break up the fog making the whole river visible, though there is still some mist I can see moored boats, maybe just maybe they made it to a boat.

"Look there!" Sky points excitedly, I follow where she's pointing, a boat manoeuvring through the other moored boats and two people on board, it's them. Relief floods me, they made it.

We jog along to the end of the copse waving our arms to try and get their attention silently.

"I can contact Anderson on this." Nix pulls out a small device, it looks somewhere between a pager and a phone.

"It's a little Morse code device that…" he trails off staring in confusion at the boat.

"What?" I ask.

"Oh my god do you see that?" Sky says, pointing.

I look at the boat, but I can't work out what they are all looking at, Danny and Lt Anderson turn to look our way and I start waving.

"They see us." I wave frantically.

"You need to tell them to get to shore now!" Rhonda demands, signalling urgently for them to come to shore.

"What is so wrong?"

"Rae, look in the water beneath the boat." Sky points, then joins Rhonda waving.

My breath hitching in my throat as I look, I'd been so focused on the guys that I hadn't noticed the giant shadow of the shark right under the boat. It backs off suddenly, but only for a run up as it smacks up through the boat. I don't think I just run, barely noticing the others trying to grab me. Everything happens in slow motion, the shark bursting through the middle of the boat throwing Danny and Lt Anderson high into the air, they are going to land back in the water, to that thing, they will die. Propelled by sheer desperation to not lose another person I love, I run as fast as I can. Something in me tingles, a slow burn running from my heart area and down my arms. Remembering what I had done to Ryzlar in the graveyard I instinctively shoot my arms out in front of me, everything turns a hazy bright orange as a ball of fire explodes from my palms and hurtles towards the shark. I stop running and watch my fireball fly at the shark. Everything is frozen, the shark frozen in mid-air still half out of the boat, Danny and Anderson with panicked faces midway from hitting the water, it's like time has suddenly stopped, everything except for my ball of fire. It strikes the shark directly in the head, severing it clean off. Then as if someone pressed the play button, everything continues moving. The body of the shark collapses, crushing the rest of the boat under it and the guys hit the water.

I race out into the river. "Danny! Danny! Anderson!" I scream, heading further out into the river. What if there's another shark? I hear splashing behind me as Sky and the others come dashing in to help. "DANNY!" I yell again.

"Over here," a voice yells back.

I search for the voice and spot Danny; he's swimming towards us and just behind him is Anderson. My eyes never leave him as I wade out a little deeper to him, I'm only partially aware of someone trying to pull me back but I dig into the river bed, not a chance. Whatever I did to that shark I will do it again if another turns up. I don't know how, but I feel oddly energised and exhausted at the same time.

As soon as Danny splashes into range I jump on him, virtually drowning the two of us in the process, wrapping myself around him like a small child I bury my head in his hairline. He just hugs me and walks back towards the shoreline with me attached to him.

"I am ok, Rae."

I lean back to look at him, and I beam, behind me Sky races in to give him a hug too.

"I'm alright too," Anderson says sarcastically, doubled over getting his breath back.

"Ah what, you want a hug?" Nix leans in mockingly to hug him. Anderson whacks Nix on the arm laughing. Nix is actually smiling and laughing.

I think hell just froze over. He looks good when he smiles. But that soon vanishes when his gaze lands on me, smile instantly gone and replaced with his usual brooding glare. I really have such a glowing effect on him!

"What the hell happened? One minute we were shark bait and then next thing the shark explodes?" Anderson asks pointedly at me, but before I can answer Rhonda interrupts.

"We should get to cover quickly before more Shades turn up."

Ushering us to the bank I move as per instructed but if she thinks she isn't going to answer my questions, she is mistaken. "How did I do that Rhonda?"

Her lips thin into a tight line, muscles work along her jaw. "We don't have time to go into it now, we have to get you to safety."

Her voice and face pleading with me, but it is all too much, people don't just shoot fire out of their hands at a giant shark in a small English River.

"No, no, no, no, no, this is too much, why are they after us, why are we so damn important and why the hell can I suddenly explode sharks?" I yell still walking, I'm not stupid enough to stop moving away from where ever those Shades maybe.

"Now is not the time." Nix echoes Rhonda.

Well he can go get stuffed. "No, I will tell you what, now is the perfect time, because if I can protect my sister and friends I will, if I hadn't done that these two may well be dead." I stop momentarily to face them. "If I know what it is

167

I am doing, surely that is better for everyone, you can teach me how to control it, so I can do stuff like you did back there ... though why was mine all fire and yours was like ...shimmering glitter?" I direct at Nix.

Rhonda and Nix look confused, both glance at each other and then back at me.

"My what was shimmering?" Nix asks.

"Your hand," I state but he still looks at me with bland confusion. "You know when we were in the water and the shark was getting closer?" He doesn't respond, just stares at me like I've gone mad.

"It looked like it was coming out of your hand creating a barrier, it looked like glitter......" There was no better way I can think to describe it.

"Glitter?" Amusement apparent to his tone. "You think that glitter was magically coming out of my hand?"

"No, I don't mean actual glitter, just that it shimmered ...I saw it, didn't you guys?"

Sky shakes her head and Rhonda just gives me a bland look that I am wasting their time. Maybe I hadn't seen what I thought, there had been a giant shark about to eat us so it is very possible I hallucinated the whole thing, but that doesn't explain how I just blew said shark up.

"It doesn't matter, what I want to know now is how I can do the things that I have done? First that Ryzlar dude and now a shark....and don't tell me I am imagining things cos that is bullshit!" I point at Nix.

Shaking his head, he huffs, actually bloody huffs at me!

"Fine ...but can we keep moving, stopping is not the best

idea." He marches on not waiting for anyone to respond.

"The truth is we don't exactly know why or how you have manifested different abilities, all we do know is that you express similar power to that of the Asteria and that is another reason why the Shades are so intent on finding and killing you. You pose a threat. No one has heard from the Asteria in nearly five hundred years … for all we know the Shades have managed to wipe them out."

"So I have the power of a god?"

Nix scoffs at me, which really grates because how am I to know if I'm saying something stupid, I have been kept in the dark my whole life.

"No, you simply exhibit some elemental powers…."

Clearly not catching on to what he means he gets visibly annoyed.

"Back there you used fire, harnessed from the Sun's energy," Rhonda interjects. "Do you ever feel more energised when you're in the sun, compared to say at night?"

"Isn't that a given for everyone though, the sun gives you vitamin D, it gives energy to everything?" That's just standard knowledge.

"Yes, but to you it will feel different," Nix says, still walking in front as we head away from the river bank and up to the cycle track that runs from our town to the small city of East View ten miles upriver.

"What do you mean it will feel different to her?" Sky asks, she looks worried.

Christ I'm worried, what the hell am I?

"It is like a sort of tingling, like warmth flowing through your skin, everything feels light and all the aches and pains subside," he continues.

I often feel that, any time I'm directly in the sun, it's like a soothing agent that spreads over my skin, just a minute ago that feeling had increased, rather than a tingling spreading over all my skin it had balled in the centre of my chest and then shot up through my arms. When I had done that to Ryzlar I felt worn out, like it had sapped me of energy, this time I felt more empowered than exhausted. Looking up at the sun beating down on us now, I'm not feeling hot from what must be plus twenty-degree heat, in fact I feel relatively cool and my skin slightly tingles all over, something I've not noticed before.

Nix watches me intently. "You can feel it now can't you?" he asks, falling back so he is more in line with me.

"What am I?" I need to know.

He walks in silence for a few beats. "We are not entirely sure, all we know is that at birth you displayed some abilities, these powers if you wish to call them that then subsided, we didn't know when they would resurface again. By the time you were eleven we assumed it would be once you reached womanhood, around sixteen but then nothing happened until a few days ago."

"What do you mean a few days ago?" Sky says coming up on his other side.

The likelihood that if I have powers so does she would explain why we've been having the same dream?! But why have these powers only just started now? Maybe it has something to do with the dream!

"It was raised to STAR's attention that your powers were unlocked. They called your Mother to summon you in for your own protection, but the Shades were somehow aware of this too…..."

"I'm sorry, but I am really confused as to how anyone would know? Because until yesterday Rae had never shot fire from her hands…I think I would know if she had!" Sky like myself is getting irritated. I get the distinct impression he's purposely feeding us small crumbs to keep us satisfied, but none of it is making any sense.

"The way STAR knew was by a satellite, it picks up infrared signals, it looks for high energy signatures, for a few days it had picked up minor surges coming from your house. But then the other night it happened to pick up a big surge, the agency knew it must have come from you."

He still directs this at me but the way he shifts his attention between myself and Sky I get the distinct impression he's referring to her too.

"Ok that is so creepy, a satellite was spying on our house! Lovely." Sky scoffs.

Something still doesn't make sense. "What energy signature though, like Sky said until yesterday nothing like this has happened?"

He pauses mulling it over. "Maybe you weren't aware you were doing it, the energy emitted didn't need to be like back there fire coming from your hand it could have been steadily emitting while you were sleeping."

OK so the weird dreams we've been having would explain that, but the dreams started months ago so why was nothing picked up before? Though the last few days the dreams had been more intense! Unless it had been Sky's last dream experience? She'd had mud and dirt on her, like she had actually been there.

"So that is how STAR knew, but what about the

Shades?" I demand. I can sense he knows something or at the very least he can hazard a guess.

"Been having any dreams lately?" he asks.

I go cold, goose-bumps rise on my arms, he knows, I can tell he does, it's more of a statement than a question. I should tell him, maybe it would help explain all this, but the look on Sky's face warns me not to, and I can't deny my instincts are screaming at me to keep this a secret. For now anyway. I still don't trust Nix or Rhonda, there are so many lies, they're keeping secrets, so why not us?!

"Dreams? What do you mean?" I say nonchalantly, but I swear I catch a glimmer of a smirk from him.

"Perhaps nothing, but sometimes dreams can spark a reaction, your unconscious mind takes over."

Yeah right, keeping information from us again, guess Sky and I will have to figure out this part of the puzzle ourselves. "Well I don't recall any dreams that would cause this to happen, besides this doesn't explain how the Shades knew or how they managed to find our house?" Memories of our house and Mum flood back, I swear I can still smell the smoke of our house burning, all the emotions that I have been suppressing since the hospital rush back. Did she suffer? Was she burnt alive? Why did they kill her? I quicken my pace until I am slightly ahead not wanting anyone to see the tears welling in my eyes. I need to pull myself together, I can't lose it, not right now, there will be time for grieving later. Taking a few deep breathes the tears vanish, but Sky is at my side, sliding her arm through mine, giving me what comfort she can, sometimes a sister just knows.

Danny joins us slinging an arm over my shoulder. "Well whatever it is that you are, I for one think it is pretty awesome. You're a real badass, like Wonder Woman!" He winks at me.

"I have to agree, whatever this is, you saved our lives back there," Anderson adds from behind.

I turn to look at him with a small smile and regardless of almost no sleep, practically eaten by a shark and soaking wet he still looks all kinds of hot. Something in his eye's twinkles, like he knows exactly what's going through my mind. Check your hormones Rae! I feel the warmth spread across my cheeks and turn around quickly, throwing my full concentration into walking, I hope no one noticed that. Unfortunately, I'm pretty sure Nix had caught that, as he scowls at me, I ignore him and look back to Danny.

"Well don't expect me to wear the outfit." I laugh.

Danny mocks a sad face. "That's the most fun part of Wonder Woman, she's pretty much in a swimsuit." He wiggles his eyebrows at me, which earns him a minor punch in the arm

"Perve." I laugh.

He smiles back at me, it even has Sky smiling for a second, but then our eyes lock and the sadness creeps back in. It's just us two and we are in a whole world we don't know anymore, I have to protect her, she is all I have left. I wrap a protective arm around her as we walk and we lean into one another, we need to talk in private about all we have found out. So far no one seems to suspect that Sky has any of these powers and that's the way I want to keep it.

CHAPTER 13

<u>Rhonda</u>

With the sun soon to peak at noon the temperature soars, it must be at least thirty degrees if not hotter, though it doesn't seem to bother Rae or Nix, the rest of us are dripping with sweat and burning, especially Sky. We had stopped a little while ago to fashion scarves to go over our heads made out of the spare t-shirts I'd packed, but our pace is too slow, we need to get out of the heat before sunstroke kicks in. Thankfully Littledown village is under half a mile away, all being well the other safe house should provide us some shelter before we have to head off again, we won't be able to hang around too long. Even though Shades are creatures of the night the sun will not stop them pursuing the girls, for now we seem to have evaded them but they have other means of finding us.

Always on the guard I stretch out my senses, it's more of an exertion than it should be, with little sleep and lack of food, my energy levels feel stretched to the max but there is little chance of a rest anytime soon. I spread my senses out further, like tiny cobwebs, if any energy force brushes against one of the minute strands it will vibrate all the way back to my mind. I can't stretch it as far as I would like, I need to conserve my energy for emergencies.

Trees line the path we are on, with the river flowing to our left, I check the small wood, weaving the webs of my mind in and out of the trees and bushes. Satisfied there is no immediate threat, I pull my sensors back in, but as I do something ever so slight brushes against it, I pause and immediately send the tendrils back to the spot I felt the disturbance a mere few trees into the wood. Nothing! Closing my eyes as I walk I concentrate harder, but whatever it had been has vanished, if it'd been anything at all. Maybe my exhaustion is warping my senses, I pull my mind back and open my eyes and walk straight into the back of Nix who has suddenly stopped.

His eyes are closed, maybe it had not been exhaustion?

"Nix, you sense it too?" I ask, keeping my eyes on the woods.

He raises his hand to quiet me, the others come to a stop, suddenly very wary. Nix opens his eyes and scours the woods, searching for any tell-tale sign we are being followed.

But I see nothing, I feel nothing.

He stares at a spot, the same spot that I am pretty sure I had felt the brush of energy, but then he looks to me and the others. "Let's keep moving but pick up the pace."

"Why what's wrong?" Sky asks.

"I just thought I sensed something…I take it you did too?" he directs to me.

I nod as I slowly scan the wood again, but nothing, though I know better than to assume it's nothing. "Come on, let's go, we have under half a mile to go."

I gently put my arm around Sky and usher them forward, passing Nix who is still staring out at the wood. I tap his hand bringing him back to awareness, he looks at me, anger clouding his vision. With a stiffness to his body he nods and continues to walk with me without looking back! There is only one person that evokes such a reaction from Nix. Theo is near. What the hell is he doing here? Has he been following us this whole time and why? Is it Sky? I instinctively wrap my arm a little tighter around her.

Nix is convinced she's astral projecting and that she has met him, but that is impossible, she is barely coming into her power, let alone mastering something that usually takes someone a lifetime. Even if, and that's a big IF, she has somehow managed to astral project, why hasn't he caused her harm? In fact, why hasn't he led the rest of the Shades to us? Nix can't think objectively when it comes to Theo, I don't blame him but I need to view this logically.

I know enough about Theo to know he is pure evil, growing up in the agency there were always stories told of certain Shades to instil fear and remind us what we are fighting against. One such story is of Theo, The Prince of Darkness, his powers equal to none but the King himself, it's Theo who had originally brought the darkness of the Shades to our world and all the death caused by the war. It is said he could get into your mind, turn friend on friend, create savage beasts from air and cause all light to drain from the sky. I always thought the stories of him were a little over the top, even knowing what I do I fail to see how one man could literally drain all the light from the sky.

That all changed nearly ten years ago, we had been alerted to a massive surge in energy just off the southern USA coast, the radar had gone through the charts, STAR had known only one thing could cause that, a portal opening from another dimension. A number of us were already in the area and so were sent to the location, Nix, his twin brother Gabriel, Myself and Rosaline along with some twenty other agents were the first to arrive. I remember it as clear as day, the opening of the portal swirled in an almost spherical shape, the edges charged with purple lightning, so much energy was surging at that point it affected the atmospheric pressure above it causing one of the biggest storms in USA history, Hurricane Katrina.

Shades could be seen starting to enter from the other side, a dark land with jagged rock and a night sky that was almost purple, we were heavily outnumbered, there was no way we could stop this army of Shades from entering, we were too few, we needed to close the portal. Gabriel told us that to open a portal that size a few of them would be close to the entrance and would appear to be in a trance like state, they would be using their energy to keep the portal open, if we could kill them then the portal would collapse.

Gabriel had been wrong, the Shades who we managed to get to and kill who looked like they were in a trance had been a ruse for it had been Theo and him alone opening the portal. How he had amassed that kind of power I don't know but when Gabriel tried to stop him Theo had killed him, shooting a lightning bolt square in his chest blasting a hole the size of my fist through him. Time had stood still, the utter shock that had passed over Gabe's face as he fell to his knees, the last essence of life leaving his eyes, still haunts my dreams. Nix bellowed from behind as he rugby-tackled Theo to the floor, but he was easily outmatched, Theo spun him off. But seeing his brother lying dead on the floor fuelled Nix with rage like no other, he attacked again and again until he plunged his dagger deep into Theo's shoulder. With his concentration broken the portal had shuddered and started to fold in on itself, the thunderous sound of the portal collapsing had distracted our attention momentarily, those few seconds had been enough for Theo to escape, simply there one minute and gone the next.

The months following Gabriel's death had been torturous for Nix, STAR had refused to allow him to seek out Theo, instead throwing him into missions to increase security of this planet. The agency may not have given him permission to hunt down Theo but that didn't stop Nix, we helped in any way we could but Theo had all but vanished. I have often wondered if the wound Nix had caused had in fact been fatal. But Nix knew better. And maybe he was right.

Looking at Nix now, no amount of time will ever heal the wounds of losing a loved one, ten years on and the lines of pain are still etched in his face, I have no idea how Sky and Rae will deal with theirs or me. Rosaline had been my best friend since childhood, we'd grown up together, trained together, we were sisters but for blood. The pain and anguish could easily consume me but I force it back down, I am a soldier with a duty, as Rosaline had been, I know my purpose.

"We are coming up to the bridge," Danny says softly, breaking me out of my thoughts.

Looking up I see we have moved slightly inland from the river, over the small hill ahead the path will then lead us down to the old bridge over a small brook and into the village.

Pausing by the last tree I rearrange myself, removing the head scarf and trying to make myself look less like I've been in a fight for my life.

"We need to try not to draw attention to ourselves, we want to leave anyone's memory as soon as they see us." I say

Following what I do, they all smooth their tops, work their hair so it's less of a mess. Nix removes the weapons he has strapped to his leg and hip and places them in the bag, not the most ideal but we can't risk people raising questions.

"Right, just try to act normal, we need to simply look like we have been out on a morning hike. …. just follow our lead." I move to the front. "Let's move."

We start up the small slope. At the top of the hill the old bridge can be seen below, willow trees hanging on either side dangling all the way into the small brook. On the other side of the green is the back of a pub, the Round Tree, it's grassy expanse of a beer garden littered with benches and at this time of the day there are a lot of people enjoying a beer in the sun, most will be too preoccupied to notice us but there are always a few who just like to people watch. As we walk down the slope towards the bridge, I notice a couple of these people watchers, two older gentlemen positioned on a bench closest to the creek but under the shade of a willow tree stare at us intently. I note none of us are talking and we're all stiff as a board, leaning in to Nix I grab his hand, looking up at him.

"We need to relax, smile, laugh, whatever but we need to blend in." I turn over my shoulder, Sky has her arm around Danny's waist and his arm is over her shoulder, he whispers something in her ear which makes her giggle. Rae and Anderson are a little stiffer but have at least moved closer together to chat.

We pass a couple of people walking their dogs just half

way over the bridge, two Springer spaniels and what must be a Chihuahua but looks closer to an overgrown rat. The dogs come bounding over to us, tails wagging wanting any attention we can give.

"AWWWWW so cute!" Rae leans down stroking the springers but her eyes are clearly on the rat…. small dog.

It approaches her and licks her hand making her laugh.

"So tiny," she says, taking on the baby voice that people always adopt when talking to dogs.

Anderson strokes the larger of the dogs. "I would not have taken you for a handbag dog," he says mockingly

Rae just glares, taking no notice as she continues to coo at the little dog, who after initial shyness is now lapping up the attention.

Danny moves forward to stroke one of the springers. "I am with you bro, I like a dog, dog."

The owners who had carried on walking over the bridge pause a little before the end, a man in his mid-thirties and a woman who looks a little younger with immaculately styled wavy blonde hair, a full face of makeup and rather tight looking hot pants. The Chihuahua has to be hers.

"You could be there all day, they love the attention," the man yells back at us.

"Come on Bitzy," the blonde lady calls.

Bitzy! Yeah, the rat is definitely hers. Even Rae raises an eyebrow at the name. The man whistles to get the dogs attention, one of the springers runs back immediately, the other still enjoying the attention.

"Go on then you got a walk to go on." As Rae stands, she gently shoos the dog.

We all turn to walk away when the dog starts growling,

followed by another, I turn to see the rat and the remaining springer have their eyes glued on Sky, and they are really snarling at her. Sky backs off and the little dog moves forward now barking and snarling, the owners come running over yelling.

"Bitzy what are you playing at." She scoops up the now foaming beast and it literally tries to leap for Sky.

I move forward about to swat the stupid thing out of existence but the woman grasps a better hold.

"What the hell Bitzy." She moves back looking at Sky with narrowed eyes.

"Jesus, Barney what's gotten into you." The man also struggles to get the springer onto the lead, the other springer remaining a few feet back not coming closer but growling and whining like it is scared.

Once Barney is firmly on the lead all eyes land on Sky, shit, we now also have the attention of half the beer garden. We need to get out of here, blending in is clearly not working.

"I am so sorry, I have no idea what has gotten into them, they usually just want cuddles," the man says.

The woman busy stroking her Bitzy gives one last glare to Sky before turning on her heels.

"I am really sorry again." Super apologetically, from behind him the lady yells, "Tom come on!"

With that he turns dragging the still irate dog with him.

"What the hell was that?" Anderson says under his breath.

"I don't know but we need to move." Nix nods to the fact that half the beer garden is still watching us.

We walk with more speed, coming off the bridge onto

the walkway which leads to the main street of the village. There is quite a crowd outside the front entrance to the pub, mainly men in rugby shirts smoking, from the noise inside I assume it must be some kind of important match. As we pass the pub I sense someone watching, like a tickle on the back of my neck, a sensation that is oddly familiar, turning I note the two old gentlemen who had been watching us from the beer garden. They make no effort to move but just watch beer in hand until we round the corner. After a couple of yards the tickling feeling disappears, I check behind me but no one is following us.

We are now on the main street, which consists of a post office, a café and a small convenience shop. The street is pretty quiet except for those sitting outside the café, I imagine most of this small village's population are in the pub we passed. We turn another corner to a small green encircled with old cottages, in the middle of the green is a beautiful blossom tree, in the spring it is covered in thousands of small white and pink buds, at the moment it is just a brilliant leafy green with branches that curl and twist creating a huge canopy. We cross directly over the green heading under the tree, as I always do whenever I pass this tree I reach a hand out and touch a branch. I have no idea why I do it, but it is the same as when I am on a beach I always feel the need to kick off my shoes and walk in the sea. With everything that I have seen and know about I never bother to deny myself these small things, maybe it's my body's way of wanting to be close to nature. Who knows? I see Nix look at me as I pass under the tree raising my arm to touch the branch, I expect him to make some kind of remark but instead he reaches out and does the same. We slow down momentarily which causes the kids to look back at us.

"Er what are you doing?" Danny asks, raising his eyebrows. Sky still wrapped around his waist with a look of complete exhaustion which draws me back to the mission.

"Nothing, it's just a stupid good luck thing. The house is just there." Pointing to the cottage ahead.

"Hummm beautiful," Rae chimes looking up at the tree whilst absently touching the branch too.

Anderson notices her doing it and follows suit.

I smile, and stride over to the cottage but before I even place a hand to open the gate the front door bursts open and there stands Bree, hands on hips sturdy as ever even though she is closing in on eighty years old. Bree is an agent, just no longer in active duty, she had been placed here after their Dad died. Her ash grey hair as always is tightly woven back into a bun, the once harsh angles of her face now drooping slightly from age, and her skin has the look of someone who has done a lot of work outside, but her eyes are as fierce as ever, a pale blue. She never dresses like anyone of her age, as she once said 'you have to be ready for anything all the time' and today is no different. She is wearing mottled black/grey cargo pants, black army boots and a thin grey long-sleeved top, but it's the huge knife strapped to her leg that's caught the attention of the kids. Well that along with her piercing stare, she always looks like she is about to tell you off, something Nix is used to as he's always in her bad books.

"Well don't just stand there, get in, why the hell did you come the way everyone can see you." Without waiting for a reply she opens the door wider, hustling us all through.

I'm the last to enter, as I pass her and turn to survey behind us, no one is there, I would have sensed if someone had followed us.

"No one followed us, I made sure to check."

She ignores me, shutting the door and stilling to sense for herself. After a few seconds pass, she taps my hand in the caring way she always does with me. "Always best to double check." She smiles a little at me, looking me up and down, checking for any injuries no doubt.

Bree had been mine and Rosaline's trainer, hard as nails and strict as hell, but outside of training she had been more than that, to me she had been like the mother I never had and I think she had similar feelings towards me as a daughter. My mother had died in birth and my father took off when I was five, to where I do not know. I don't even remember what he looks like, but Bree had known them both, whether it was some silly-founded guilt for my Dad leaving or some ingrained responsibility to someone younger than her, she had taken me under wing and cared for me. She had given me the chance to never feel like an orphan, no matter how harsh she could be I would always be eternally grateful. Plus, I think I am the only one to witness her softer side, something I have previously used to my advantage.

Bree faces the others, her stern glance first falling on Nix, no surprise there, they've always clashed and she never liked how he included me in, his 'obsession' as she called it, looking for Theo, putting me in unnecessary danger she had once yelled at him.

"I suppose you have something to do with this mess?" she barks at him.

Nix glares back, then gives me a look of I knew this would happen. "Why yes Bree, of course, the world is entirely going to shit because of me." He doesn't raise his voice not one bit, keeping it level and matter-of-fact, the last time he had raised his voice at her she had nearly broken his nose. He smiles sarcastically at her and heads into the kitchen, slamming the door behind him.

"Don't make a mess!" Bree yells at him as the door slams. "No good brute!"

I just shake my head, I gave up a long time ago trying to convince her that Nix is a good man and a loyal friend, usually this would be entertainment to me but we don't have time.

"Bree, I don't know if you know…." I am cut off as she holds up her hand. I step back, straightening to attention deserving of her higher rank.

"I know Rhonda." Her eyes never leave Rae and Sky.

How can she know? No one in this village seems aware of what has happened in Doversham? The Shades have obviously covered their tracks or worse they have taken the town hostage to cover that they are here! But some people could easily escape and raise the alarm…. unless they are all dead. The look of pain and confusion must be plastered over my face, she lightly pats my cheek.

"I have my ways, just trust me, I know we need to leave soon."

Before I can ask further her attention returns to the girls. I know better than to press the matter, my questions and worries will have to wait until later. Looking at the girls I see they are wary of Bree. Not that I blame them; she's rather formidable even in her older age. She's a warrior!

"So, these are Rosaline's children." Her voice etched with sadness.

She knows that Rosaline is dead. Again, how if the coms

are down?

Taking a step forward she reaches and grasps each of their hands. "I am so sorry for your loss, your Mum and Dad were two of the best people I had the pleasure of knowing." She smiles warmly which relaxes them both.

"How did you know our parents?" Sky asks.

"I was the one who trained them my dear, as I trained Rhonda." She nods towards the door of the kitchen. "That brute I did not train though."

Sky smirks at the reference to Nix. A loud bang echoes from the kitchen, Nix is clearly listening into the conversation.

"Yeah he is not the most …. friendly," Rae says trying to form the right words knowing that he is listening.

Dropping their hands and standing a little upright, Bree raises her voice a little. "That was a nice way of saying he is an absolute prick!"

I can't help but facepalm, this is going to be a long day. Sky and Rae both try to stifle their laughter, aware of the prying ears in the room next to them. Trying to divert the conversation that could have Bree going on and on for hours, I grab Danny. "This is Danny, Rae's best friend and The General's son. And this is Lt Anderson."

Both offer their hands which she shakes, hard, harder than any woman of her age would, both discreetly rub their hands after whilst watching her with a little awe.

With that Nix opens the kitchen door, coffee in hand. "We really must be getting on," he says impatiently.

The interruption clearly grates on Bree, but she can't argue that urgency is a priority.

"Yes, follow me." She bustles past Nix and grabs his

coffee. "Thanks," she says over her shoulder, drinking it as she goes.

Nix just looks at his now empty hand and then up to me, rage and bafflement tint his features. "I swear to god…" he starts.

"Not now Nix, ok." I rub his arm as I pass him. "Come on we must get going." Everyone follows me into the large, rustic kitchen. To the far side is a door which leads down into the old cellar. Bree waves us over. Why the hell do we need to go down into the cellar? I make my way down the old steep wooden stairs, having to duck under the huge beam that runs along the bottom. The cellar is fairly small, lined with wine racks and the odd box, but to my left a secret door lies open, beyond is a tunnel more modern than the cellar, small spotlights line the ceiling, and the walls are a metallic grey. The end of the small corridor opens into a small underground bunker room, weapons of all variety line one side of the room, guns, bow and arrows, swords, grenades and one big rocket launcher. In the middle is a large metal table with pre-backed bags on it, a satellite phone can be seen protruding from one of the pockets, she has prepared, she knew we would be coming. On the other side is a set of two big screens with an operations panel, the STAR symbol is etched on the corner of the screens, lights flash red where the signal should be coming through, usually it is a constant green.

"You couldn't get through to headquarters either?" I ask, absently tapping away on the keyboard, for what reason I don't know, nothing I do works.

"Nothing since early last night," Bree says, she taps on the panel by the hidden door and it silently closes shut, beeping green once air locked. The air filter kicks in with a slight hiss, the girls jump looking around for the source.

"Erm I thought we needed to leave...quickly?" Lt Anderson says, still eyeing up the array of weapons on the wall.

"We do but not the way you're thinking."

Lt Anderson raises an eyebrow, as do I but Nix speaks the question before I can.

"Then what way do you plan to take us?" he asks haughtily, he hates not being in the know, especially with Bree, ever the control freak.

"The secret way of course." Bree smiles tightly at him, saying it very matter of fact, turning she moves me aside as her hand makes swift strokes over the keyboard on the operations wall. Pressing the enter key, a loud clunk echoes from the far bare wall, the metal lining of the wall splits down the centre, and a whirring can be heard from the other side, light seeps through the space in the centre and then another clunk as the metal wall opens like two doors, the whirring is louder, the light almost blinding, we all hold a hand up to shield our eyes. As the whirring dims to a loud hum I look in front of me, and I can't believe what I am seeing, it is impossible, I have not seen one since Gabriel died. The swirling mass of electric purple light spins like a whirlpool, this is a portal, in Bree's cellar!

CHAPTER 14

<u>Skylar</u>

It's mesmerizing and terrifying all at the same time, I can't stop staring at it, entranced by the now gentle swirling and a rhythmic hum that could threaten to send me to sleep, I am that tired. The shouts from Nix break me out of my trance. Always the dickhead!

"What the hell is that Bree!" Nix's body visibly shakes with rage.

Rhonda just looks in shock, going from Bree to the thing in front of us.

"Oh, don't ask dumb questions Nix, you know full well that is a portal." Bree turns, grabbing the bags on the counter and thrusts one at Lt Anderson who takes it without question but his eyes remain on the portal.

So, this is the form of travel the Shades use to get in and out of our world, can it take you anywhere? My first thought is of Theo! Stupid girl, I barely know him but he is all I can think about. I know he has been following us, I had seen him in the woods, and I'm pretty certain that Nix had sensed him too. Right now though I can't sense him anywhere. The ensuing argument grabs my attention again.

"I BLOODY WELL KNOW IT'S A PORTAL, but why do you have one? Are you crazy? Every Shade in the area will be alerted to this now," he yells as he closes the distance between him and Bree.

She doesn't react, but I see her expression turn ice cold and her muscles tense, she might be old but I won't be surprised if she can put Nix on his arse! "BACK DOWN NOW," she orders Nix. "This is above your security clearance…both of you." She looks to Rhonda before she continues, "I am well aware this will draw the attention of the Shades, which is why we must go, that is an order….and it comes from the top." She spits the last bit out directly at Nix.

Closing his eyes, he clenches and opens his fist, like he is desperately trying to control not hitting her, he wouldn't though would he, she is like what, eighty? But then I barely know Nix, from what I have seen already I wouldn't put anything past him.

Rhonda places a hand on Nix's shoulder and steps forward. "Of course Bree, we apologise, the portal took us by surprise. Where will we be going?"

Bree nods tersely at them both but it is softer towards Rhonda. "Headquarters."

Stepping back, she motions to us all to go through, but I inadvertently step back, something just doesn't seem right, I don't feel safe, whatever waits on the other side will not be good for me. Which is silly because it's the agency who we have been trying to contact for help, now we are being taken directly to them it feels like a trap. There is no reason why, it's just a gut feeling. Bree notes my hesitation as does Rae, who steps back with me, coming forward Bree's face warms and she reaches to place a hand on our shoulders.

"I know you have no reason to trust me, or anyone, but I promise you I am taking you to safety."

The look in her eyes is one of someone telling the truth, or at least believing what she is saying. In truth it is no one on this side of the portal I fear, it is whoever is on the other side, what exactly is STAR? Like any large organisation there is always corruption, people out for their own gain. But what other choice do we have, stay here and keep running hoping the Shades won't catch us or potentially walk into a lion's den? At least this way the attack won't be immediate. I hope.

"What does it feel like?" I ask.

"A bit like the first drop of a roller coaster, in seconds you will be on the other side. Nix why don't you go first?"

It's an order not a request, Nix bristles but sarcastically smiles anyway. "It's nothing, if it helps, close your eyes."

With that he steps into the portal, the purple fingers of lightning caress around his back until it consumes him, the centre mass swirls, crackles and spins a little faster, then slows, the purple lightning calms along the edges.

"Ok you girls next," Bree says.

Rhonda gently shoves us forward. "You will have to go through one at a time, this is only a small portal."

I nervously look to Rae, though I don't want to be seen to be the scared little sister, I am! I had hoped to walk through holding her hand. Rae must sense my fear because she looks at me, smiles and briefly hugs me before stepping towards the portal, she shakes her hand, closes her eyes and without a word steps through, being enveloped by the smoky mass and lightning. For all my tough girl attitude, Rae is the harder one, right now I feel pathetic, weak, like a small child incapable of looking after herself. Dear god I have to man up, I expect I will face far worse soon enough than a bloody portal.

"Sky! Your turn." Rhonda rubs my shoulder, for some reason this really irritates me.

I shrug her off, scowling at her to back off. She is not my mother and I am not a child. Breathing deeply I murmur under my breath, "You can do this."

I step forward towards the portal, unable to close my eyes, it is truly beautiful, like an electric storm but flowing more like water, as I draw near the electrical currents reach out lapping the front of my body. It is warming and pleasant, I take another step and a gentle force tugs me through, swirling mist surrounds me, wind whips all around but it is as if I am in a bubble. Just out of reach through the mist I can see what looks like Rae and Nix, turning behind me I can make out the room I have just left.

"Amazing!" I giggle.

"It is isn't it," says a male voice to my side.

I shriek, I can't help it. But my panic ebbs quickly as I realise it is only Theo. I smack him on the arm, then look around, where the hell had he come from?

"Where the...." I start.

"I don't have time, I can only hold you here for another minute, I won't be able to reach you once you get to headquarters."

"What do you mean?"

Whatever he's doing to keep me here is causing him strain, his brow shines with sweat, I hadn't noticed before but his eyes are the same electric purple of the portal and his hands spark with its energy.

"I mean, there are wards up at the headquarters that will

stop me from contacting you, not all is as it seems. Trust no one but your sister."

"Theo I don't understand…"

"Listen to me, something dark lurks within the agency, I don't know what, but you must be careful, as soon as you can, you need to get out."

"But…"

"No time, you must go."

Before I can say more, he gently pushes me from the small of my back, I take a step because of the force intending to turn around and question him further, but the electric fissures of purple lash onto my arm and pull me forward. Bree was right it is like going on a roller coaster, in the blink of an eye I stumble out on the other side almost face planting if not for Nix catching me.

"Woah."

Nix pushes me back and glares at me, my belly goes cold with the warning Theo just gave me. Trust no one.

"Are you ok?" Rae comes over.

I hug her, I just nod as I am too scared the tremble in my voice will give me away, Nix just remains stoic but lines of rage are visible across his face. Was it Nix, Theo was warning me about?

"What did you see in there?" he asks coolly.

"I don't know what you mean?"

I hear Danny and Anderson behind me, but I never take my eyes off Nix, never turn your back on the enemy, right. Something in Nix's eyes snaps, a steeled glare and I swear his eyes are glowing, that is the only warning I get before he grabs me and flings me up against the wall. The force knocks the air from my lungs and I crack my head on the wall, he pins both my arms to my side, I can't move and my head is already pounding from the force of hitting the wall. I am aware of shouting, Rae is screaming at him and hammering on his back to let me go, but he takes no notice, instead he leans closer, burning me with his stare.

"You've been meeting Theo, haven't you?" he half growls.

I am slightly dazed and so can come back with nothing better than, "What the hell are you talking about?"

"Don't lie to me," he yells into my face as he squeezes my arms.

It should hurt, but all I can feel right now is a rising anger, like it did back at the hospital, why isn't anyone pulling him off me, why is he doing this? More importantly how does he know about Theo? Panic and rage mix in my belly and I feel an overwhelming build of it in the pit of my stomach.

Nix's expression turns from enraged to one of mockery as he sneers, "Don't even think about it."

Think about what? I don't know what's going on but I want him off me, I want him nowhere near me or my sister, he's a danger, he's a threat. And that is my last solid thought, a pressure in my stomach ripples up and out over my skin, everything hums and tingles, a purple haze clouds my vision a little like that from the portal.

I hear Rhonda yelling, "Nix you dumbass get back."

I see a reflection of myself in his eyes, my eyes are illuminated to brilliant deep purple/blue, electricity dances off my hair, my skin glows, I should be terrified but I am not, in fact I feel empowered, invincible and this dickhead has pissed me off for the last time. I don't hold back, I smile and then thrust my arms wide, easily knocking his once death-like grip away, he stumbles back a step, looking more enraged than ever. Everyone is yelling but I don't hear them, my focus is only on Nix. Red hot rage flies up through me and I'm aware I am moving faster than I know is physically possible, I hit him, right in the face, throwing him back some ten feet. He collides with the wall on the opposite side, and I am above him in the blink of an eye hauling him up like he weighs nothing. Blood drips from his nose, I hold him by the throat as the rage whirls around me, electricity shoots up my arm and out into Nix, his eyes widen with pain and his body jerks. I have never been one to cause another pain, but I can feel a glee rising in me as he squirms under my grip.

"SKY let him go," Rae screams from the side of me.

But before I can acknowledge her, someone slams into my side knocking me over, I crash to the floor in a tangle of limbs, hitting my head again. The pain erupts across the back of my skull and whoever ran into me pins me to the floor. I can barely breathe; my eyes fly open and I am looking into the barrel of a gun held by Bree. What the hell?

"Calm down now," she demands, her face is fierce.

Gone is the stern old lady, this is the warrior, capable of ending my life in a second.

"Get off her or I swear to god I will end you," Rae screams at Bree.

"You will do no such thing, now back off and shut up. Rhonda, get control of her now," she barks.

"You Mother f…." Rae starts.

"Rae shut up, she won't hurt Sky, she needs to get her to control herself." Rhonda gently pushes Rae back just a step and that is all Rae will give her.

Bree's attention never leaves me, for an old bag she weighs half a ton.

"Will you get the piss off me; I can barely breathe." Not to mention I'm pretty certain there are stones lodged in my skull.

"Not until I am certain you are back in control," she repeats.

"What are you on about you crazy bitch." I spit back through gritted teeth.

"The power you just demonstrated could have killed Nix, I may not be fond of him but I hardly want him dead. Now are you under control?"

She slowly clicks the gun and ice fear trickles through my veins, I have no doubt she will shoot me in the head without a second thought, Theo's warning comes to me again. Trust No one, something dark lurks in the agency. Is Bree the one we need to fear? Or maybe I am! The look of pain from Nix as I'd pinned him against the wall flashes into my mind, dear god what had I almost done. Would I have killed him? How had I even done that? A tear trickles down the corner of my eye, I have no idea what is going on and I'm terrified not only of those around me but also of myself. What the hell am I? The only place I feel safe is with Theo, and he said he couldn't reach me here, what am I supposed to do? I hate crying, but all the pain, all the loss bubbles to the surface, tears stream down my face. I look to Bree, pleading with her to release me, I don't want anyone to see me break, especially Nix. Her face softens and she uncocks the gun, lowering it but she doesn't get off me.

"All of you wait over there," she says sternly, again still

not taking her eyes from me.

"But…" Rae starts.

But Bree holds up a hand and simply points to the far side, indicating to do as she's told.

I hear Rae's mumbles of anger and their footsteps move further away. Bree slightly turns to see that they have all done as instructed, then she returns her gaze to me. I start crying even harder, is she going to kill me, beat me? I am shaking with fear and my chest is heaving with the effort to not outwardly sob. Instead she shocks me by gently stroking my face, the fierce warrior is gone, now replaced with the softer face of an older lady.

"Breathe in through your nose and close your eyes, it will help calm you." She leans back and climbs off me, kneeling instead at my side.

"What is going on with me? How did I do any of that…oh god I could have killed him." I fight to keep control of my breathing; it is erratic and the tears just stream freely now.

"You need to control your emotions, it is what sets it off, so do as I say, close your eyes and just breathe."

Helping me sit up, I put my head between my legs and do as she says, I don't want to hurt anyone and I also figure if I don't control myself I will end up with a gun at my forehead again.

I rock with my breaths, as I think in my mind, 'in' and 'Out', 'in' and 'out', on repeat until I feel my tears stop. Bree hasn't moved, she also hasn't tried to rub my back like Rhonda did, thank god, maybe she just knows I don't like to be touched. Taking a final deep breath, I open my eyes and look at her, she is calm as if nothing has happened, as if I hadn't just tried to murder someone.

"Better?" she asks.

I nod, I may not be on the verge of a mental break anymore but I am by no means out of the woods yet, I don't trust that my own voice won't break.

"Ok, now you need to stay calm and just explain to me what happened?"

What can I tell her? Theo said to trust no one but Rae, but I don't even truly know if I should trust him? I go with my gut feeling that is telling me to keep Theo a secret. "I, I don't know," I stammer out. "I literally came through the portal, or should I say fell through the portal. Nix caught me and then he just went mental, threw me up against the wall and kept yelling at me that I had been meeting someone called ...Th...Th... I can't remember the name."

I think the lie came across well because Bree's face darkens.

"Every bloody two seconds that idiot thinks Theo is around."

She grumbles, casting a look over to where the others stand. Nix is glaring at us whilst wiping blood from his nose.

"Who is Theo?" I ask as timidly as I can.

"A very evil man," she says slowly, still looking over at Nix. "Theo was once responsible for bringing an army of Shades into this world. Though Nix has a personal vendetta as Theo murdered his twin brother, Gabriel."

I stop breathing, and the hairs on my arms stand up, this can't be true, the same Theo that has done nothing but rescue and help me? My head spins and I am a nanosecond away from breaking again. Should I tell her then? Has Theo been lying to me this whole time? Dear god did he have anything to do with the death of my parents? My thoughts are cut short as Bree turns to face me.

"Did you see anything in the portal?"

Now is the time Sky, but there is so much confusion, I look at her and school my face into a bland expression. "No, I walked in, closed my eyes and the next thing I know I tripped out on the other side." I have no idea why I just lied, but the fact is people are keeping information from me and it feels good to keep something from them. My heart races and I am deathly cold, I need to talk to Rae. The quicker we get to these dam headquarters the quicker I can get some alone time with her. I need help deciphering all I have discovered; we need to form a plan.

"Ok I believe you, but you must learn to control your anger, we cannot have outbursts like that, you have no idea how dangerous that could be."

I scowl at her. "Of course I don't know because no one is telling us anything, you're all lying to our faces and keeping secrets."

My blood boils again and a very slight hum spreads across my skin but I fight it down, I really don't want another gun pressed to my forehead.

"I understand how frustrated you must be, but this is for your own good," Bree says, the softness gone, the soldier in her returning.

"How on Earth would any of you know what is best for us," I spit back at her, I don't even wait for a reply but turn and stomp back over towards Rae. As I approach, Nix straightens, his scowl deepening, fists clench and his eyes darken, I really don't like him one bit, there is something very off about him. I mean a full-grown man attacking a teen girl like that, I inwardly smile though as the memory of me smacking him in the face springs to mind. Not such a little girl it seems. Rae reaches me and hugs me hard; I take the close moment to whisper in her ear. "We need to talk, alone as soon as."

She squeezes me harder and whispers back, "Yes…love you lil sis."

I look up at Nix and glare daggers back at him, he makes a slight motion like he is going to move but Bree bellows from behind me.

"That is enough Nix, leave the girl alone. I don't know what you were thinking but mark my words this will be reported."

"I am telling you; she has had contact with Theo, this was not the first time," he says through gritted teeth.

She strides over to him and stops only a few inches from him. "As your commander I am telling you right now to drop it, your hate for Theo and passion for revenge has overruled your ability to think rationally for too long."

He goes to interrupt.

But she holds a hand up stopping him. "This is not the first time something like this has been brought to our attention, no one else has noticed any appearance of Theo in ten years except you. You really think he is hanging around on Earth just to tease you?"

Nix looks to Rhonda, but she scowls back.

"Don't look at me, I understand your need to exact revenge but attacking Sky?" Rhonda shakes her head and moves off.

Danny and Anderson both move over to us, Danny

wraps an arm around me, bringing me in for a hug, both are looking at Nix like they want to punch him.

"I didn't attack her, I merely pinned her to the wall."

Rae scoffs and pretty much growls back at him. "Ohhhhhh and that makes it ok does it?"

Nix's expression does not change, I truly don't think he cares about anything but getting to Theo, if he had to go through me, he would. "I know she was with him in there!!"

"Enough Nix," Bree yells.

"No, it is not enough, Theo has been following us…more specifically Sky. You sensed him too, Rhonda, just outside the village."

Everyone turns to Rhonda, she looks caught off guard and a little irritated, as if she didn't want to discuss this here and now. She sighs and throws her hands up. "Look I don't know if it was Theo I sensed, but I do believe he or someone is following us."

Nix smugly looks back at Bree. "However, I don't believe for one second that Sky is associating with him." Rhonda adds.

I focus on plastering my most expressive dumb ass face on, sided with a look of exasperation. "I have already told Bree, I don't know any Theo, by what she said he seems like a right psycho and I am not in the habit of hanging out with murderers…." I hope my irritation is masking the fact that just saying Theo's name elevates my heart rate. Why am I covering for a murderer? Yes, he has helped me, but still, it is sounding like he is an actual psycho.

"I know you're lying, at the river house you were projecting, I sensed his aura all over you."

Nix's voice is level, if a tad loud, clearly not wanting Bree to have another go. How the hell does he know where I had been that night? Lie! Lie through your teeth Sky.

"I'm sorry I was what?"

I feel Danny's arm tense round me. "Yeah I think you need to explain just what you are accusing Sky of doing, cos I swear to god if you don't come up with something good in a minute, I will knock you out." Danny spits at him.

Nix just laughs at him; I hate the arsehole more just for that. Danny lets me go and takes a step forward but Anderson grabs him as well as Rae.

"Don't, he is not worth it," Rae says, as she looks back with daggers in her stare.

For a brief second it actually looks like Nix is hurt by what she said, but then it's replaced with his smug smirk.

"I don't care what any of you think, she is projecting and she has been meeting with Theo," he says to Rhonda whilst pointing at me.

Rhonda looks torn, I can tell she wants to believe Nix and I can see some doubt creeping in, I need to throw them off.

"Look I have no idea what this projection thing is you think I can do, so if you can explain, then maybe I can actually prove my innocence."

Bree speaks first before Nix can say more. "Projecting is when the spirit, the essence that is you, leaves the body in what appears to be sleep. It is very difficult to achieve without practice it can be extremely dangerous. Masters of this art are few and it takes them almost a lifetime to achieve. Something I very much doubt you are capable of doing."

"We have no idea what she is capable of," Nix says angrily, pointing a finger at me.

"Enough Phoenix," a voice booms from behind.

We all turn towards the voice, it is only now that I notice we are in some kind of underground cavern, the walls are rocky and the ceiling must only be some ten feet tall, the stone has red hues mixed with black and grey. The Cavern is fairly wide, with no natural lighting, the lights are coming from old skool looking sconces but instead of fire there are weird shaped bulbs. The wall where the portal had been is now just like the other walls and no sign a portal had ever been there, I hadn't even noticed it disappear. I hear the trickle of water now too, in fact looking closely some of the walls are a little wet, that must mean we are possibly below a lake or very close to a river. But where I have no idea, where the hell are we?

But my attention is now on the man in front of me, he is dressed in what I can only describe as a dressing gown, or something you would expect a wizard to wear. The gown, or robe is emerald green with a weird symbol stitched on the sleeves, but from this distance I can't quite make it out. The man is old, maybe not as old as Bree but certainly a senior, and like Bree he looks like he can easily handle himself in a fight. Unlike Bree though his features are softer, more welcoming. He also has long grey hair tied back into a ponytail and a short beard, which just makes him look even more like a wizard, all that he is missing is a staff.

"That is no way to speak to a lady," he barks at Nix and for once Nix says nothing, he just looks to the floor.

Amazing, this dude actually scares him. Behind him are four others of around the same age, again dressed like wizards, though they don't have long hair and their robes are black. The old guy takes a step forward, never taking his eyes off Nix.

Obviously sensing his stare Nix looks up at him. "She has been speaking to The…."

"DON'T YOU DARE SPEAK HIS NAME!" the man bellows.

Everyone is silent, all I can hear is the dripping of water around us, the look on Nix's face though is priceless, whatever power this man has over him I am glad for it, he deserves it! Or does he? I have no idea at this moment if Nix had actually been justified in his attack, I mean I have been meeting with Theo, and more than once, and apparently Theo is a killer. So yeah maybe Nix had been justified. Maybe I should speak up, but I don't want the Wizard yelling at me either, or worse, clearly everyone thinks Nix is a little nuts. No until I know more, I will keep my mouth shut.

The anger on the old man's face softens ever so slightly towards Nix. "You let your heart rule over your head, as such you make brash decisions. We will discuss this at length later." Nix goes to interrupt but the old man holds up his hand. "You are not the only one who has lost someone precious, you will do well to remember that."

He continues to stare coolly at Nix for a few seconds and then his attention flips to us, his features soften again and he smiles ever so slightly. "I do apologize for my son's behaviour; I had brought him up to be a gentleman."

This guy is Nix's Dad?! No wonder why he has such power over Nix, this is hilarious then, he literally just got told off by his Dad in front of everyone! I try really hard not to laugh out loud, instead shaking a little to control myself. I am pretty certain I have been noticed by Nix, his usual scowl deepening even more.

"My name is Tiberius and I am the chief elder of the leaders of ascendance." He bows ever so slightly to us.

I am confused, I thought we were being taken to STAR? I look to Rae and she too looks confused; Danny and Anderson however are tense and look ready to take flight the moment something goes wrong.

Rae turns to Rhonda. "I thought you said we were going to STAR?" she says with a little accusation in her words.

Tiberius chuckles a little, then holds out his hands in a peaceful sign. "I am sorry, we are part of STAR, the agency is quite large, we are from the highest sect of the organisation, essentially we are the ruling government and I suppose in layman's terms I am classed as the prime minister."

Ok that kind of makes sense.

"No doubt you have a lot of questions and there is going to be a lot for you to process, right now though I suggest we settle you in, let you get cleaned up and eat. I imagine it has been a while since you had something sufficient to eat?" It is more of a statement than a question.

Right on cue Danny's belly gives a low rumble. The laughter I have been trying to smother erupts out, I quickly try to stifle it by slapping my hand over my mouth but this makes the sound worse. However, it does bring a smile to Tiberius's face.

"Sorry," Danny says, going slightly red in the face whilst holding his stomach as if that will stop it.

"I will take that as you haven't eaten in a while. Well let's get you that food first, I find new information is always processed easier on a full stomach." His smile widens even more, revealing vibrant white teeth. For an old guy he is in seriously good shape.

He motions to the men behind him and they turn moving off down the hallway still not speaking a word. Taking Tiberius's lead, we follow him down the low-ceilinged hallway.

As we walk Tiberius keeps talking. "This is one of the oldest parts of the compound, you are now walking on ground that was used as a temple well over a thousand years ago. Since then we have built above it and around, I think you will be quite impressed, it's a beautiful piece of natural architecture."

There are so many questions wheeling around in my head, I definitely think I need to write them down or else I will forget.

Anderson though is not willing to wait until after food. "What do you mean compound? And where exactly are we, I will need to contact my commando base, you do realise we were attacked?"

With everything that has happened since we escaped the commando HQ it'd completely slipped my mind that Danny and Anderson must be going out of their minds needing to know what has happened.

"I understand your urgency, we have had contact from General Pierce via morse code, there were some casualties but they were able to drive back the attack pretty quickly. It would appear the purpose of the assault was to acquire both Morrigan sisters but once you escaped, the Shades retreated." Tiberius lets this sink in.

"So, my Dad is alright?" Danny asks.

"Yes, he is fine Danny, we will inform him of your arrival. He will be most relieved!"

Danny nods, looking a bit more relaxed than he had before.

Anderson doesn't, however. "When can I contact the General, I need to know what my orders are." Anderson stops still, causing everyone to stop with him.

I can understand his need to speak to the General, and I too would like to hear from a familiar voice.

"I will personally take you to our command room within the hour, if that is suitable for you?" Tiberius says a little tersely, clearly Anderson's demand has ruffled his feathers a bit.

But why, surely he can understand after all we have been through?

"And me, I want to speak to my Dad myself," Danny adds, standing straight next to Anderson.

The warmth that had been emanating from Tiberius' eyes steels for a second before softening again. "Of course, I will inform the command centre that you will be coming."

Rae glares a little at Tiberius, clearly she hadn't missed that minor change in his manner either, the warning from Theo ringing around in my head 'Trust No one'.

"We would all like to speak to David... I mean General Pierce," Rae chips in. "We do not wish to be separated." Linking her arm with Anderson.

"Not a problem at all, I can understand you would all want to stick together, given what has happened that is only natural. Trust must be earnt!" He smiles warmly, opening his arms a little to gesture that we continue onwards, but the smile is now a little on the creepy side.

"If we get you to your quarters, I must first meet with agent Roads, Barns and Storm so I can have their account on the situation." He directs this more to Anderson than anyone else.

Anderson simply nods back, eyeing him warily.

So, is that Nix's last name? Storm! Fitting actually!

The cave hallway comes to an end, we enter a small domed room with various exits leading off to paths unknown, above each entrance way are ancient symbols carved into the stone work, I don't recognise them at all. Ahead of us is an old staircase that winds out of sight, thankfully this part of the underground cavern is dry, the last thing I want is to slip and break my neck on some old wet stairs, especially after everything we have been through.

The climb is long as we seem to constantly spiral, round and round. I give up counting after the hundredth step, how the hell are the oldies not panting like I am? I seriously need to reconsider smoking, and of course now that I have thought that, all I want is a cigarette. My bet, I won't find any here and to hell if I am asking Nix! Just as I am thinking I need to stop for a breather we come out to a metallic room, a vast contrast to the old rock wall of the stairwell behind us. Tiberius beckons us forward, he seems barely out of breath, as does Bree, Rhonda and Nix. The rest of us are sweating, panting and look generally like hell, so much for the younger being the fittest! Well Anderson is barely sweating, but he's a marine!

"If you can step forward, we just need to scan everyone in the room, this is standard protocol nothing to worry about," Tiberius says.

A quick shooting sound makes me spin, behind us the door closes off to the stairway, the hairs on my arms rise and my breath quickens, I have never been one to feel claustrophobic but I do now. Rae and I move towards each other, Rhonda notices this and smiles.

"Girls there is nothing to worry about this is like a giant x-ray of sorts, it will simply scan us to make sure we are not imposters."

"Imposters?" Danny asks, moving closer to us.

Before Rhonda can answer, the room goes dark momentarily, and I can't help it I screech, but in a second there is a flash of red and then the lights are back on. I am mortified, why did I screech like that? It was only half an hour ago that I was pinning a grown man up against the wall and now I'm screaming like a little girl because the lights go out! Get a grip Sky!

I also realise that I am digging my fingers into Rae's hand, letting go a little I see my nails have made imprints.

"Sorry," I whisper, letting go, but she grabs my hand and pulls me closer, shaking her head as if to say don't worry. That in itself makes me feel even more like a baby, but I am too tense, too tired, too hungry to bother fighting.

A light by the door beeps and goes green.

"Guess we are not imposters then?!" Danny says dryly.

Tiberius smiles. "No, if you had been, the room would go into lock down. We have to be incredibly careful with security at the compound. It will take a little adjusting to but it is for the safety of the world."

The puzzled looks on our faces must have said it all. How long are they intending to keep us here for?

"I am sorry I keep adding to your questions, I promise all

will be answered shortly. Please follow me."

The door opens and we step out into a huge hall, with multiple columns that tower above into arches, it is very similar to a cathedral, the stone floor is polished black and white marble. I tilt my head up noting the carvings similar to those I had seen below etched into the columns and up above on the ceiling is a painting, depicting a battle. From the images I can work out the Shades and some other creatures, but there are also people painted so they look like they are glowing as though the sun is radiating from them. I assume these must be the Asteria, they are blasting beams from their hands into the dark mass that is the Shades and all in between are humans fighting, humans dying, humans fighting humans. I can't even see the whole picture. It literally takes up the entire ceiling, it's amazing the detail, it's reminiscent of the paintings I have seen around the churches in Rome when we went on holiday a few years ago before Dad died. The memory of that last holiday, all of us together stabs at my heart and the tears well a little.

"It is magnificent, isn't it?" Tiberius chimes also looking up at the ceiling.

Taking a deep breath and pushing back the memories, I notice all but Bree, Nix and Rhonda have stopped to look in awe at the painting. "It was painted some four hundred years ago; it is a true work of art."

I can't deny that, it must have taken the painter or painters nearly all their life to do this. Incredible that someone would have that amount of patience. I turn taking in the rest of the hall, there are small trees and flowering plants dotted all over the place, with their own lights, illuminating them in a way that casts beautiful shadows. Close to these are seating areas, a bench here and comfort chair there, I imagine it could be quite a calming experience to simply sit with a book and a cuppa. A small rumbling of my stomach reminds me of just how hungry I am. Looking around I note there are no windows, everything is lit artificially, the walls lining the hall are smooth pale grey stone and most of the walls are covered in paintings or antique looking weapons. Even though there are no windows it does not seem dark at all, and for its size it's relatively warm too, their monthly bill must be monumental!

Tiberius starts off across the giant hall, as we follow him, I am more aware that there is nobody else here in the hall, for a place so big I would have thought it would be teeming with life. It takes a good minute to get to the other side of the hall, as amazing as it is, I am still on edge and cling to Rae's side.

We move through a high-arched doorway and down an empty corridor, again no windows and again no people, I don't know which is more disconcerting. I turn slightly to look at Rhonda, she's obviously been here before, if she thinks it is normal then I will just have to trust her for now.

"Where is everyone?" I whisper to her noting Tiberius is further ahead in conversation with Bree.

Her brow pinches a little, which lets me know that this is not normal. "I don't know, they may have been called in to the great hall."

Rae scoffs "So that back there was not the great hall?"

Rhonda smiles a little. "No that was the common room."

Of course! "Well the great hall must be pretty ...Great!" I say.

"Other than the caverns below, the great hall is the oldest

section of the compound, it has stood for over nine hundred years," Nix says with little emotion to his voice.

I am surprised he even wants to speak to me. He looks at me for a moment and I swear guilt crosses his face, like he is sorry for what he did, but then it is gone.

"Here we are, if Sky, Rae, Danny and Lt Anderson could come in here, you can freshen up, there is some food and drink in there too. As I said I need to have council first with agents Roads, Barns and Storm."

He opens the door to a pretty luxurious room, finely furnished with sofas, rugs and paintings, it is a little on the medieval side, the walls are stone like the hallway and like the hall there are no windows. We still have zero idea where the hell we are.

"Please," Tiberius gestures for us to enter.

I turn to Rhonda who smiles and guides us into the room, she rubs Rae's back as we enter.

Tiberius walks to the middle of the room where there is a table full of food and drink. "This should suffice until we can get you a warm meal later, there is a bathroom over here." Tiberius walks over to the left-hand side and switches on a light, revealing a pretty lavish bathroom. "And there is an assortment of clothes in the wardrobe, please take a little time to relax and we will be as quick as we can." He smiles openly and then turns, marching out the room offering no further conversation.

Bree quickly follows, but both Nix and Rhonda stare at us for a further few seconds, they look unwilling to be parted from us either.

"Agents!" Tiberius demands from the hallway

With a half-smile Rhonda turns and leaves, Nix's eyes

find Rae's for a brief second and then he is also gone. The door shuts quickly behind them, and a soft click is heard.

"Have they just locked us in here?" I ask slightly panicked.

Anderson paces over to the door and tries the handle, it doesn't budge. He thumps on the door a few times, putting his ear to the door to hear if anyone is outside.

"I don't think anyone is there," he says whilst banging on the door some more. "Hello?!"

I try to keep calm but the panic is building and all I can think of is that I wish Theo was here, he had said I wouldn't be able to reach him from here, had he known we would get locked up.

My breath gets a little shorter with every intake, and I'm not the only one panicking, Danny starts pacing too, looking around the room for another way out, but there isn't one.

"Right, everyone needs to calm down," Rae demands.

"Rae, we have been locked up like bloody prisoners," Danny says, still pacing.

Rae laughs a little and then grabs one of the juice boxes on the table, she gestures round the room. "Yeah we are really prisoners."

"Then why lock us in and not say that is what you're going to do?" Crossing my arms, I'm a little annoyed that Rae is so calm.

"I don't know, probably some stupid protocol…. look it is not cool that they did it, but I think now is time for us to re-coup and discuss everything that has happened up to now without prying ears!" We do have so much to talk about, but most of it I can't say in front of the guys, especially the bit about Theo.

Anderson moves away from the door, he is desperate to get back to his command, I expect having to be stuck with us teenagers is not what he signed up for.

"I don't like this, we have no idea where we are, who these people really are or what the hell they want from us?" Anderson leans on the chair.

"I don't think they want anything from us," Danny says motioning to him and Anderson. "But they do want something from Rae and Sky."

"Yeah I kind of figured that a while back," I say sarcastically, I am running out of patience for anyone right now, plus I am super cranky because I am so tired, so hungry and I stink.

"Will you all sit down, eat, drink and rest your feet! We will be able to think far more clearly once we do that." Rae indicates to the table of food and settles into one of the large chairs.

When no one moves she leans forward, grabs one of the many baguettes, flicks her shoes off and tucks her feet under her, curling right into the chair. "Suit yourself," as she takes a huge chunk from the baguette.

"Rae how can you sit there and eat, we need answers, now!" I practically scream with frustration; I am genuinely thinking of beating her with that bloody baguette.

"Sky we are not getting answers any time soon, we have spent twenty-four hours with Nix and Rhonda and all we have gotten is tiny snippets of clues. I expect the agency to be no different. So, we have to think smart. To do that we need our energy and wits. Hence the food! Now sit and eat!" She lifts the baguette in a cheers and then takes another bite.

Danny says nothing but shuffles over to the table to

grab two baguettes, crisps, juice and a giant muffin, he takes a seat on the sofa and then notices we are all staring at him. "What?! I don't know about you but I haven't eaten since…… yesterday afternoon, I've probably lost a stone already."

Anderson laughs. "You're right, we need to collect ourselves and go over the events of the last twenty-four hours." He walks past me and then gently rubs my arm coaxing me towards the food.

"Fine," is all I can muster, I know I am being an unreasonable little shit but I just can't help it.

Anderson and I grab a load of food and then I take a seat next to Danny, the moment my feet are off the floor I realise just how sore they actually are, I kick off my converses and the relief is so sweet.

Soon we are all lost in thought and food, scoffing down through the baguettes with ease and rehydrating with the juice boxes. After five minutes of silent eating I am the first one to break the silence.

"Where do you think we are?" I say scanning the room again, the only thing I can glean is that the brick work looks like sandstone… or maybe it is limestone?

"I have no idea, since a portal can take you just about anywhere … we could be on the other side of the planet," Danny says.

"Let's focus on what we do know, we know the agency is a secret, only those at the top of command, like your Dad know about them. I didn't know anything about the agency until yesterday afternoon and that was only on a need to know. So here is my thinking, that Tiberius guy said part of this compound was very old, some thousand years?"

Anderson asks.

"Yes, that's what he said," Rae says shuffling her chair closer.

"Well it also appears to be pretty big too, it's also close to a lake and it's somewhere fairly warm," Anderson continues.

"How do you know any of that?" I say with half a mouth full.

"Easy. The cavern that we were in, the rock is limestone, the constant drip of water created a lot of the formations that you could see on the ceiling and floor."

I don't remember seeing any of that, clearly I need to pay more attention.

"The water sound was more settled, rather than a rush of a river, which indicates it is probably under a lake of some description. Then the fact that most of this building is made of a similar limestone but still within the European style, I would guess we are somewhere in Europe, more than likely somewhere like Slovenia, there are a couple of big cave systems there. Also, once in the countryside there is a low population so the likelihood of someone to stumble across the compound or to raise too many questions is lower."

Wow, he got all of that from some water and stone?

"That's pretty impressive," Rae says whilst beaming at Anderson.

Like me she probably would never have come close to guessing that. Though I had got the lake bit right.

"He is trained to think like that, a bit of an advantage to three teenagers," Danny grunts out and paces over to the wall, touching the brick he turns.

He is clearly irritated by our situation, probably just

needing to speak to his Dad. And more than likely wishing he had never met us! I don't blame him, we have nearly got him killed, multiple times.

"So how exactly do we get out of Slovenia?" His face reddens a little as he says it.

"I don't know…" Anderson says slowly, possibly gauging that Danny may lose it. "But I will find a way. Like you said, I am trained for stuff like this…well stuff similar to this."

"Really, you're trained to fight monsters and travel portals?" I come out with it before I can stop myself.

Anderson lightly smiles. "No, you're right, I am not trained for that, but we are just going to have to work as a team to figure this all out. Most importantly we need to figure out why everyone seems hell bent on you."

He nods at us, I know he is referring to Rae too, but I feel that since my one to one with Nix this is definitely more directed at me. "We don't even know why; other than apparently we now have magical powers." I emphasise the Now.

"Let's take it back to basics, tell us everything that has happened in the last week, even the smallest details can help."

I get the impression he's fishing for something; I've already decided to keep everything about Theo quiet, I will only speak to Rae about him, I just hope Rae keeps quiet about my whole ascending dream. "Ok, well it really started a few months ago, we both started having this same dream…"

I sit back and listen whilst Rae recants our story, from the dreams, to discovering we were both having the same dream, to Mum acting weird, then to Rae feeling like she was being followed, this one is new to me, but then we haven't had a second to talk about any of this. Thankfully Rae doesn't bring up my ascension dream, maybe it's the fact that Nix has been so adamant that I can and so she doesn't want to risk omitting the truth even to them. I zone out a bit when she moves onto the dead girl, Detective Wade and the brief once over about Dad's death. For only a few days there's a hell of a lot to tell, I'm glad that Rae automatically offered to tell it, I don't have it in me. Now that I have eaten, I feel physically exhausted, I haven't slept in nearly forty-eight hours, at the boat house I had been awake, just in another dimension. I feel my eyes wanting to close and I blink multiple times to try and stay awake, but the warmth of the room, a full belly and the comfort of the cushioned sofa is just too much. Before I know it, I am out cold, falling into a black nothing, no Theo this time to welcome me, just sleep devoid of dreams.

CHAPTER 15

__Danny__

The food has definitely helped give me a clearer head and I had no idea how much my legs were aching until I sat down. I massage my stiff calf whilst listening as Rae recants everything they have been through over the last few days. It is not long before I feel a growing surge of anger towards the agency, towards Rhonda and Nix, and even my Dad! He knew about all of this, screw the top-secret bollocks he should have told me, I could have warned Rae and Sky…All those people in town, dead ... it could have been prevented! And for what? To stop people from panicking, the world had a right to know that our way of life is being threatened!

"Danny…Danny!!"

I look up having been engrossed in my own turbulent mind, I hadn't noticed Rae had been speaking to me. "Sorry what?!"

"I just wondered what your Dad said to you before we left the camp."

Should I tell them, it's not like it is a nice thing to reveal, and Dad had said it in confidence. I shake my head; it's keeping secrets in the first place that has gotten us all into this situation. "He basically told me to get away from you guys as soon as I could." She doesn't look too horrified, maybe she had expected it.

"Well yeah, he didn't look like he trusted Rhonda and Nix, so I doubt he trusts the agency either."

Nope that's not it! Taking a breath, I reiterate what I mean, "No he said to get away from you guys." I gesture to her and the currently sleeping Sky. "His words…. You are dangerous."

I wait as my words and its meaning settle in, at first she looks perplexed, then betrayed and then there it is, anger.

"What the hell!" she squeaks out.

Her raised voice wakes Sky who rubs her eyes adjusting back to her surroundings. "What? What's going on?" she asks through a yawn.

"Oh, only Danny's Dad told him to split from us because we are too dangerous to be around…the man has known us almost all of our lives, if we are so dangerous why has he left it until now to say anything?"

"I don't know Rae, I don't know how much he actually knows, or why he kept any of this a secret, same as I don't know why you can do what you do, there is a lot none of us know."

Sky takes an energy drink as she sits upright, she looks to me gravely. "Do you think your Dad knew what killed our Dad?"

Her eyes brim with tears, wanting it not to be true, god I want it not to be true. But if my Dad has known about the Shades and who Rae and Sky are, it makes sense he would have been briefed about their Dad's death too! My lack of answer speaks more than any words. My Dad had gone to the funeral, he had hugged Rosaline, helped do the gardening through their initial grieving phase. How could he look them in the eye knowing the real reason behind their Dad's murder!

"Trust No one," Sky coughs out, wiping her tear-filled eyes. "We can trust no one." She says it as a statement, but it is only directed at Rae.

"Hey you can trust me; I have never kept anything from you guys." I grab her hand and squeeze. "I am so pissed at my Dad, I just want to hear he is alive and then not speak to him for a long time."

She half smiles but doesn't squeeze my hand back, I feel deflated, I don't want her or Rae to not feel like they can't trust me. I would do anything for her.... them. "Sky I could have left ages ago, as Nix said they are not after me, but I have stayed with you guys cos I will not abandon you!"

"We know that Danny!" Rae pointedly eyes Sky.

"I don't think General Pierce knows much about you or what happened to your Dad, he seemed genuinely surprised that the Shades were coming directly after you." Anderson says, which is a little reassuring.

"Sky?" I ask timidly, her hand still in mine.

She closes her eyes taking a breath and then squeezes my hand back. "I know… I'm sorry I just don't know what to make of any of this, there are so many lies…and what the hell are we?"

She lets go of my hand and it tingles where her touch had been, shifting in her seat she focuses on her energy drink.

"I mean I pretty much almost killed Nix, you blew a shark in half and all we have gotten out of anyone so far is that we have elemental powers…I mean, what the hell is that for a start?"

She looks like she is going to cry and I don't blame her, if it were me, I would be going out of my mind, I am going out of my mind just worrying about them. I move closer and place an arm around her shoulder.

"I have no idea how to really help you, but we will figure this out, you guys are not alone in this. Right Anderson?!"

Anderson had been sitting quietly lost in thought, he looks to all three of us.

"Absolutely, I am not going anywhere and we will get to the bottom of this."

I rub Sky's back and she leans in a little, sniffing back tears, I feel totally helpless, I mean I say I will help, but where the hell do we even start.

"Let's look at this objectively." Anderson leans forward towards Rae. "You guys started dreaming some three months ago right?"

"Yes, it may have been a little before I am not sure," Rae states.

"Ok, was anything going on at that time that could have triggered it? I mean from what Nix said they thought your powers had gone dormant, so why all of a sudden did they start to develop?"

"I don't know......nothing springs to mind." Sky pulls away from me, leaning back onto the sofa, I move away giving her some space but miss the warmth of her body against me. Rae quirks an eyebrow at me but then falls back to concentrate.

"Same, I can't think of anything," Rae says to Anderson.

"Think, it may not have seemed much at the time but something must have triggered this for you both to be experiencing this development at the exact same time, it is just too coincidental."

He is right, for there to have been nothing for over sixteen years something must have caused this, but I come up blank, I highly doubt the stress of end of year exams could cause this kind of a reaction. Though if that were true, balls to going to university, I like my safe human status. Rae gets up and paces desperately trying to think, I can't remember her telling me anything significant, she had been completely absorbed with revision for exams. Sky had been less bothered by them, she did not care for much these days other than having a good time, most of the time she just partied or ……. A vague memory pops to mind.

"Hey didn't you guys say you almost had an accident a few months ago?"

Rae stops pacing and gasps turning to Sky who sits up more.

"What happened?" Anderson asks.

"I'd been at this really shit party and had no money for a cab, so I called Rae to come and get me. We were at the junction along Cliff Road, as we turned to pull out this guy appeared out of nowhere crossing the road, Rae had to swerve into the opposite side to avoid hitting him, but there was a lorry coming on the other side, we were literally going to hit it head on but Rae's rally driving saved us!"

Rae shakes her head. "I don't think it was my driving that saved us, we were heading straight into that lorry, at the time I thought it was just you know the whole life flashing before your eyes kind of thing, but everything slowed, almost like it did before I blew up the shark. I managed to swerve the car in between the lorry and the man. Do you think that is the cause?"

We all look to Anderson who mulls over what they have told him, I would have no idea where to start with this, so I am happy to sit back and let Anderson make the assumptions.

"Well it is possible that as your lives were in danger your power naturally reacted to protect you?"

"Yeah, maybe it was the surge of adrenaline... you remember reading about the mother who lifted a car to save her new born baby trapped inside." I say, recalling the article in a magazine, there had been other examples but that one sticks out the most.

"Did you feel anything else when it happened?" Anderson asks.

"Not that I remember ...Sky?" Sky shakes her head.

"Ok so when after this did the dreams start?" He queries them both.

They both go quiet, locked in thought, Rae sits down again looking to Sky.

"I am pretty certain mine started that night but not the full dream. What about you Sky?"

"Yeah I am pretty certain mine started then too."

"If you don't mind me asking, what exactly happens in these dreams?" Anderson asks.

I had only heard the rushed version of what the dreams were about so it will be interesting to hear it in full. Before Rae has a chance to start, Sky jumps in talking.

"Basically, we are in this really dark place, like you can't see anything, it feels really cold and there is this sense that there is something or someone we need to find in this darkness. Just as it feels like we are getting closer to whatever it is, these bright red eyes appear, like pure evil eyes. Then there is a feeling of something behind us and it breathes onto our necks and then we wake up."

She recants the dream very monotone and quite fast, at the same time as she picks the skin on the side of her thumb. "And it is the same each time?" I ask as something is bugging me about Sky's demeanour.

She looks at Rae, picking some more at her thumb, Rae leans over placing a hand over hers to stop her picking, there is a brief moment of eye contact that seems loaded with questions.

"Yes, that is all that ever happens, the same dream every night for months…. you can see why I have been so tired." Rae laughs sitting back, satisfied that Sky won't peel all the skin off her thumb.

"That is horrible, I am sorry you have had to deal with this for so long." Anderson's sympathetic comment is like background noise.

I am focused on Sky who can't make eye contact with me, she looks down to her hand and at the spot she had been picking, it is bleeding a little. She only ever does that when she is nervous or when she is lying. Why would she be keeping something from us? Maybe it is the fact that Anderson is here?

"What was it that Nix thought you could do again…projecting was it?" I enquire as Sky shifts uncomfortably and resumes picking her thumb.

"I have no idea why he would think Sky can do that, you heard Bree she said it takes years to master, by all accounts Nix seems a little unstable I don't think we should take much of what he says as truth." Anderson jumps in before Sky can answer, she looks relieved.

"I agree, he may have saved our lives, multiple times but after what he did to Sky back there, well that is just unforgivable."

Anger pours off Rae, the last time I saw her get angry she literally looked like her eyes were on fire. Even though I know they are both keeping something back, now is clearly not the time to approach this subject.

"So what are your thoughts?" Rae asks us both.

I honestly don't have a clue, this is all so science fiction, it still doesn't seem real. "Firstly, I think we need to clear out logic, we need to imagine that anything is possible, clearly everything we thought we knew is wrong."

Anderson has a point; god knows what could be possible.

"Ok so following that point, what do we know about elemental powers?" I ask.

"Only stuff that I have read in fiction books," Sky says whilst swigging some more energy drink.

"What sort of stuff have you read?"

"Loads, mostly vampires, werewolves, witches and wizard's kind of thing, I doubt any of it is close to being real though," Sky continues.

"Well we have nothing else to go on so hit us with the basics." I lean and squeeze her hand to encourage her.

"Ok, so from the bits of information Nix and Rhonda have given us, elemental powers are a bit like magic, but more natural. In books they involve earth, air, water and fire, but the people who use them are usually Elves, pixies and nymphs." Rae laughs a little and looks to Sky's ears.

"No pointy ears, guess we are not elves then!"

"No, a lot of this probably won't be relevant to you, but the bit about the natural magic, there might be some truth in that, carry on." Anderson gestures Sky to continue.

"I really don't know, it's been so long since I last read one of my books and there are so many variations by different writers, I just don't know what use any of it will be." She pinches her nose in frustration.

Rae rubs her back but she shrugs it off, jumping up she paces whilst taking long inhales. "Sky...." She cuts me off with her hand, I keep quiet. After a minute of us all silently watching her she opens her eyes, appearing a little calmer.

"Sorry, I could feel it rising." Sky motions to her chest area, an act that causes my eyes to linger there a little too long. "Bree said I have to keep calm, that my emotions trigger the power."

Snapping back to look at her I am pretty sure she catches just where I had been staring, crap, I grab my drink and settle back in my seat pretending to be absorbed with swallowing.

"Then let's talk about something easier," Anderson suggests, he turns to Rae, "How is your leg doing?"

Good conversation change, Anderson, not just a pretty boy. I had forgotten about her leg.

"Surprisingly it feels ok, a bit tight and sore, but for all we have gone through I would be expecting to be in agony by now." She lifts her trouser leg and shows us the back of her calf, there are clear lines of pale pink where that thing had torn her leg, but it looks like it is weeks old scarring.

"Holy shit, that's almost healed." Sky kneels down to

inspect.

"Yeah Rhonda said the stuff she used is like the leading edge in medicine, that it would heal me quickly, though I didn't expect it to be this fast." She looks to her leg, giving it a little poke.

"For what it looked like before, it really doesn't hurt. Do you reckon it has anything to do with my powers?"

"May I?" Anderson asks, she nods and he kneels beside her taking a close look at her leg. "Whatever the cause, the speed at which you have healed I wouldn't be surprised if this is completely normal by tomorrow."

"Yeah I saw what it was like before, anyone else would not have been able to walk on it for weeks, the gashes were like this." Sky holds up her fingers indicating a width of about a half inch.

"I really can't even begin to speculate how or even what you are." Anderson sits back, for the first time looking exhausted and frustrated.

We all remain silent, no matter how much we try to figure this out it is all speculation, there are little to no facts. Anything that we think could be the answer might potentially just lead us off on the wrong path.

"I wonder why this Theo guy gets to Nix so much?" Rae says randomly, she looks to Sky. "Did Bree say anything about him?"

Immediately Sky starts picking her thumb again, she paces before turning to answer, "She said he killed Nix's brother, that he is an evil man."

She says it is almost like she doesn't believe it, or doesn't want to?

"Shit… well I suppose that explains his obsession," Anderson comments.

"And what, you think that it is ok for him to attack me like that?" Sky spits at him.

"Woah, Sky that is not what he is saying." Rae jumps up as Sky has taken some involuntary steps forward towards Anderson.

I swear her eyes have a little glow to them.

"Of course I did not mean it like that Sky, all I meant is that must be why he seems so unstable, grief is preventing him from thinking straight." Anderson remains seated, holding his hands up and just speaks calmly. "It does not justify him attacking you, not one bit. Ok?!"

Sky backs off rubbing her hands through her hair, she looks to Rae, almost on the edge of tears.

I can't help it; I have to ask. "Sky, is there something you want to tell us?" Preparing myself for the inevitable onslaught. Her gaze turns to me and I instantly regret opening my mouth.

"What the hell do you mean by that?" she demands.

I don't even really know what I mean, it is just a gut feeling that she is keeping something from us.

"Don't get mad, it's just, I know you, and I know when you're keeping something to yourself," I say as softly and as un-accusingly as I can.

"Danny!" Rae warns me.

"Look I am not accusing you of anything, I am simply picking up on what I am seeing from you. You're picking your thumb, you only ever do that when nervous or keeping something to yourself." It comes out before I can stop

229

myself. Bloody motor mouth.

"And what exactly do YOU think I am keeping from you?"

The venom in her voice is all too apparent, her eyes are steeled and shut off. But for some bloody reason I can't back down, even though I know I should.

The point she had seemed to shut down, the look she had given Rae all came down to whether there was more to the dreaming, whether she was projecting. Though Nix is clearly insane he was so adamant that she was meeting this Theo guy, it really is making me think, is there any truth to it?

"Have you met Theo?"

****

Rhonda

The door to the girls' room shuts and Tiberius locks it, my unease at the whole situation blooms. Why is he locking them in? And where the hell is everyone? For this time of the day these halls and the common room should be packed with agents, I have not seen one person. I look to Nix, concern furrows his brow as he looks back to the girls' door, he too is not happy about leaving them, but we both know better than to question Tiberius. Instead we follow him in silence through the meandering hallways until we reach his office, myself, Bree and Nix enter but the other elders simply bow and retreat off down the hallway, back towards the girls' room. A twist in my gut spikes, but surely the girls are safe? This is my home, I have brought them to safety, I promised them they would be safe. I turn and catch Nix's steely gaze in the direction the other elders have just gone in, is he too sensing that something isn't right?

"Shut the door Phoenix," Tiberius barks at him.

I step further in allowing Nix to close the door. Tiberius' office is spacious with an oriental feel to it, candles are sporadically glowing everywhere, colourful wall hangings stretch from floor to ceiling covering most of the brick work. There are sofas on either side of the room, but the most dominant part is the monumental fireplace with the huge antique desk in front of it. The desk is made of some kind of marble, black stone etched with blue flecks, some have often said the stone is from another realm, brought here by the Asteria. The same stone is set into the fireplace, giving it a Gothic appearance. Above the fireplace is a large painting of Gabriel, even though he and Nix were twins I could easily tell them apart, Gabriel had a lighter look to him, he was always happy and smiling, joking around and just generally the light-hearted one in the room. The painter captures this completely, even from a distance his eyes light up, as if he has just been caught telling a joke. Nix has always been moodier, even more so since Gabe's death, it is like Gabe brought out the lighter side to Nix. Now I hardly ever see it.

Tiberius moves round the desk, sitting he gestures for us to do the same, there are already three chairs in front of his desk, I nod and take my seat as does Bree. Nix is a little slower.

"Father I need…."

"You need to do nothing, but sit and do as you're commanded!"

I can see it pains Tiberius to talk to his only son like this, it cannot be easy to be both father and boss. Thankfully Nix does not fight him on this one and assumes his seat next to me.

"Agent Roads, let's start with you and just how this mess came to be?" There is a slight accusation to his tone, which really sets me on edge.

"I am sorry I don't think I completely understand your question?" Keeping my voice even, I try not to let him know I don't appreciate his tone.

"Well it is perfectly clear that the sisters have come into their power, but yet they were not handed over to us immediately, as was your duty!"

I am a little stunned at the callous comment to simply hand over the girls, no matter their power they were Rosaline's children.

"I am sorry but until forty-eight hours ago they had not displayed any powers, the only suggestion that something was happening was that Rosaline had overheard them talking about having dreams, that was it. Rosaline and I discussed this and decided to move them the next day, which……"

"Was too little too late, now we have one agent dead, raising questions within the local authority. A town under siege with over a hundred dead and half a marine base now aware of our agency. There should have been no discussion, the moment you both suspected the sisters were developing their power they should have been brought here immediately."

I swallow my rage down before answering, taking a beat of a breath first. "I understand the consequences of our waiting, Rosaline just wanted her children to have a final night of peace, knowing what was to come."

"SHE HAD A DUTY!" Tiberius yells at me.

I am shocked, he is a parent, surely he must understand.

"Her duty was not as a parent, but as guardian. It is why those girls should never have been allowed off the compound in the first place, unfortunately my predecessor thought otherwise."

Is he seriously going to pin this all on me, simply because a mother wanted her children to be kept one more day from harm's way? And if it had been up to him would he have kept the girls locked up?

"Rosaline was a guardian as well as a mother, she did her duty. We both decided the threat was not imminent and that it would be safer to leave in the morning. We all took turns making sure the area was clear."

Nix nods with me, he had stayed in the car just down the street all night making sure nothing appeared.

"But something did happen, didn't it! Our satellites picked up the energy signature from the house that can only suggest one or both of those girls were using their powers."

"But we questioned them on that, until Rae took out a Shade in the graveyard neither one recalls anything else unusual happening."

Tiberius laughs, but it is cold without humour. "And you just readily believed them? Because teenagers never lie do they?"

I have always followed the rules, done my duty, never spoken out of turn but these girls are more than a job to me, they are my family, they are like my own. "I believe that they were not aware of using any power, whether they did in a dream state I do not know. And yes, maybe they are keeping a few things to themselves but they have just lost everything dear to them, they have been thrust into this world in a matter of hours with little to no explanation. Their trust needs to be earned."

Tiberius leans forward never taking his steely gaze from me, internally I want to back away, he emanates such power but I steady myself sitting straighter and not once looking away. Something in my demeanour must meet his approval, he relaxes back in his seat, I release my breath with relief.

"You have been one of our best agents, highly recommended by Commander Barns, no advisories against your record…well none that you were at fault for." His gaze travels to Nix who simply remains stoic. "As such I will give you the benefit of telling me the exact events of the last forty-eight hours and I mean everything."

I nod, taking a deep breath I start to recant everything from the moment Rosaline had messaged me, going over our plans to get the girls out the next day, the death of the young girl down the road to the explosion at their house. Finding Rosaline's burnt body, to the hospital and Sky's first display of her power. I then move on to not being able to get hold of Nix so heading to his house, at this point Tiberius glares at Nix disapprovingly, it was not Nix's fault but I know Tiberius will find a way to blame him for some of this. I explain about Danny and how he came to be part of this before continuing on to everything leading up to this point in time. For forty-eight hours there is a lot to cover and it takes me over half an hour to detail everything, Tiberius only stops me a couple of times for me to reiterate the meaning, one of these times was the fact that Rae had used her power to kill the shark, the other had been Sky falling off the sofa at the boat house. I can already tell he is very interested to hear more about Sky. I conclude with the altercation between Sky and Nix just before he arrived.

Tiberius sits still closing his eyes, I wait patiently not saying a word, it is not unusual for the elders to do this and something I never question them about. After a minute though Nix becomes restless, shifting slightly in his seat, I eye him to sit still, trying to rush his father will be of no use. When I turn my attention back to Tiberius he is watching us both.

"From what you have described agent Roads you have displayed the true essence of what it means to be part of this agency, you have acted within the line of duty and delivered the sisters unharmed with little aid from your fellow agent."

Nix goes to speak but Tiberius silences him with a stare. "You will have your opportunity to speak in a moment."

This does little to appease Nix, who has been more than valuable in helping me keep the girls alive, how can Tiberius not see this?

But before I can voice this, Tiberius continues. "You have done well agent Roads, but your emotional attachment to the girls has clouded your judgement. If you detached yourself, as you should have, then you may have clearly seen what my son spotted, Sky is not just projecting, she is ascending. She lied to you." He pauses, letting it settle in.

But there is no way, it takes years to master projecting and only a handful have ever learnt to ascend.

Even Bree looks dubious, noting all of our expressions he pulls out some satellite footage, he places four images on the table for us to see.

"The radar confirmed it, we re-examined the footage from that evening before Agent Morrigan died, the radar clearly shows Sky in her room, then there is a flare of energy, a few seconds later there is no energy signature at all. Some hours later there was another energy flare and surprise, surprise, her energy signature was back in the room. We confirmed it all came from Sky's room and not Rae's. So now you know the truth, why do you think she has hidden this from you?"

I have nothing to say, the proof is there, how she has managed it I do not know. To be able to ascend at her age is unheard of, the power she must possess must be incredible. But regardless I can still understand why she has not told me. Trust must earnt and she must know I am keeping a lot from her too.

"I knew it." Nix laughs, he isn't even phased by his Father's stern look. "I told you she was projecting and what is the bet she has been meeting Theo too?"

"I agree you were right on the projecting part, but she is a good person, there is no way she would associate with Theo," I state.

"That's because you're too emotionally attached to her, you can't see it, there is a darkness in her, she can't be trusted," Nix yells at me.

I forget where I am for a second, so sick of his inability to see clearly. "I'm emotionally attached? This coming from you, who thinks every bloody thing is something to do with Theo?" Anger quickly rises in me. I just want to punch him one.

"You sensed him too in the woods, but will you back me up on that? No of course not, wouldn't want to tarnish your perfect record."

We are soon on our feet, forgetting where we are. "Back

you up? I have done nothing but back you up every time since Gabe died, every hair-brained, far-fetched mission I have followed you on, I have been the one to believe you. But you are wrong on this." I point a finger at him which he bats away, he is seriously at risk of me beating down on him any second now.

"ENOUGH," Tiberius bellows, using an unseen force to push Nix and I apart, we both topple, ending up sitting on the sofas either side of the room. Tiberius lowers his arms, taking a breath he opens his eyes, they are cold and unwavering now, I think we just pushed our limit with him.

"You. Two. Are. Done. Here," he says punctuating each word. "You have allowed your emotions to rule your actions as such I am left with no choice. You are both demoted and you are to stay well away from the sisters, you will be reassigned back to Doversham to assist your friend the General in protecting the town's inhabitants."

I can't believe what I am hearing, after all I have gone through to get the girls here safely and he is simply going to throw the book at me?

"Father if you would…." Nix starts.

"I DON'T WISH TO HEAR ANYMORE. I have given you an order as your elder, be thankful I am not sending you further afield."

I am shocked, surely he must see we did the best we could, regardless of Nix believing Theo may have been involved, we have fought hard to get everyone here, alive. I look to Bree who has said nothing this whole time, in fact she has barely moved from her chair, I catch her eye, pleading with her, but she is shut down. The dutiful warrior who had trained me in her place.

"May I speak Tiberius?" She looks away from me to Tiberius.

"You may." He nods.

"I agree wholeheartedly with you that both agent Roads and Storm are far too emotionally involved."

I sigh, realising she is never going to back us up against an elder. Duty first.

"However, I do believe they did the best they could under the circumstances. The deaths in the town could not have been prevented even if the girls had been moved sooner, I believe the town was chosen by the Shades as their base. For what reason I do not know, the Shades usually operate undercover, this was a brazen attack that was meant to announce their arrival. Some recon will need to be done to establish why they chose Doversham."

Tiberius absorbs this and nods. Nix thankfully remains silent, this is probably the only time Bree has ever praised him, maybe he is in shock.

"I do think separating Rhonda from the girls would be the wrong thing."

"Why do you think that?" Tiberius asks, he sits appearing to be far calmer.

"Those girls have lost everything they know in a short space of time, they are not trained to deal with their emotions and I feel if you remove the final remaining constant from their life it could ignite their power to an uncontrollable level. They don't fully trust Rhonda or Nix, but they do trust that they will keep them alive."

Tiberius is silent whilst he closes his hands in front of him in a meditative prayer position. "Whilst I understand and take your opinion on board, these girls must learn their place, their lives are not their own, they have one purpose and that is to protect this world. As such they need to be trained and controlled efficiently, Rhonda is not the agent fit for that job."

He is really going to force me to stay away from them? They are my family, tears well in my eyes, but I swallow it back, I can't let my emotions get in the way. I do have a duty and as much as I just want to whisk the girls away to safety, they too have a role in what is to come.

Tiberius shakes his head and sighs, gone is the fierce elder who just demoted us, before us now is a father and friend. "I understand Rhonda, I really do. But there is more at stake than how two girls will feel. Life is often unfair. You will be reassigned to Doversham, you know the town better than anyone else here, you will be a vital asset in uncovering why the Shades have chosen this town especially now the girls are not there. Nix, you will assist Bree in training the sisters, they have some element of trust in you and you are a face they recognise."

This is as good as it is going to get, at least the girls will have someone they know around them, even if they don't like him much. And Tiberius is right, I know the town well.

"Taking into consideration what Agent Barns has said I will not command you to cut all communication with the girls, Rhonda. BUT, do not hinder their training. Do you understand? Any information they receive is to only come through Phoenix or Bree."

I stand to attention and nod; grateful I will still be allowed contact. "I understand."

"For their safety and mental stability, I advise only a spoonful of information to be given to them at a time, enough to satisfy their needs but that is it." He nods to Nix and Bree.

"Rhonda, when you return to Doversham you will also escort Lt Anderson and the General's son, we have no need for them here."

I nod again, but knowing that will be easier said than done to separate Danny from the girls, plus what harm would it do allowing him to stay? The unease from before rises again but I daren't voice my concern. Nix has remained quiet, lost in thought, he looks at me and frowns, is he too feeling the sense that something isn't right?

"Father…."

Tiberius simply holds up his hand. "I will not discuss this further, you have your orders."

He stands and walks to his door, opening it he indicates for us to leave. Bree exits back into the hallway first, I quickly follow but Nix hesitates looking to his father, but Tiberius coldly stares back. Conversation officially over. The hallway yet again is barren of life, it is beginning to feel quite eerie.

"Where is everyone?" I say looking at my watch, it is nearly supper time everyone would usually be on their way to the dining hall.

"As of this morning, everyone has been re-assigned, we have gone into high alert, the compound has been stripped back to the necessary few."

I look to Nix whose frown has deepened.

"But surely that will leave the compound wide open to attack?" Nix says stiffly.

"Yes, the compound may suffer an attack, but bricks can be rebuilt, people can't! As elders we decided it would be better to have our people spread out, if an attack does happen then there should be minimal casualties. Not to mention we need as many eyes out there to see what the Shades are up to."

It does make sense, but there is still something prickling at me, it feels like the answer is hovering in front of me but just out of reach.

"Do you have some concerns about the council's judgment you wish to raise?" Tiberius challenges.

There is no way I am going to voice my concern right now. "Not at all, I was just surprised to see the compound so quiet."

Tiberius' stare softens again and he laughs a little. "Yes, it is actually quite unnerving to have it so quiet, but rest assured the girls are safe here, we have activated every security measure so if anyone not of this agency enters the premises we will know about it before they can take their next step." He places a hand on my shoulder, which should have been comforting but instead gives me chills.

"Now I don't expect you to leave immediately, please eat and rest, yourself, Danny and Lt Anderson can leave first thing."

I nod as he removes his hand, my skin still chilled where his hand had been.

"Let's go collect our guests and allow them to contact the general, I doubt they will be at ease until he has spoken to them," Bree comments, she eyes me steadily and then nudges me forward, her hand leaves nothing but warmth on my arm.

"Yes, well I shall meet you in the command centre,

there is a matter I need to discuss with security first."
Without offering any further explanation, Tiberius turns and
walks quickly off in the opposite direction.

"Come on then you two," Bree says.

We follow, not wanting to say anything in front of Bree.
I look to Nix; he shakes his head just a touch as if to warn
that we will discuss this later. We continue in silence, but I
notice Bree looking at the cameras in the hallway, the
compound has thousands of them, it is like being on big
brother, but they are there for good reason to pick up on any
unwanted visitors. But I now notice what Bree has, each of
the camera lights are off, there should be a little red light to
indicate they are on and working, the whole hallway heading
back to the girl's room are off!

"Shit," Bree curses and bounds off ahead of us.

Running after her we all lock into our powers and within
seconds we are outside their door, it is still shut but a pool of
blood is seeping from under the doorway, my heart leaps into
my throat. No. I have failed them.

Nix pushes past me and Bree, opening the door, the
room smells of smoke and looks like a hurricane has torn
through it. On the floor by the door is one of the elders, half
his face is burnt and a piece of wood from the broken
furniture protrudes from his chest, another body lies slumped
against the wall, completely charred, I only know it is
another elder by the ring still attached to his finger.

"What the hell?" Bree gasps, tears in her eyes for the
dead elders.

But my concern is not for them, where are the other
elders and where are the girls?

The bathroom door is closed, I go over and try to open it,

but it is locked. I knock. "Girls, it's me Rhonda, open up."

I don't hear anything from the other side, I close my eyes and focus on extending my hearing beyond what any human can, I pick up two faint heartbeats and shallow breathing. Nix must've heard it too, I step back as he shoulder slams the door, catching it before it can swing in and damage anyone on the other side. Opening the door my chest tightens, beaten and unconscious are Danny and Lt Anderson. My pulse elevates quickly, where are the girls?

CHAPTER 16

<u>Rae</u>

What the hell is Danny thinking asking her a question like that, of course Sky doesn't know Theo.

"Danny!! Do you really think my sister would associate herself with a murderer?" I yell.

Sky just stands there dumbfounded, glaring at Danny and he keeps staring right back at her, his face getting redder by the second.

"She is hiding something from us, I can tell," he says in a low tone, not taking his eyes off Sky.

Of course, I know she is hiding something and for whatever reason she doesn't want these two to know she is projecting, thinking about it now it may be for good reason! Especially if our closest friend is willing to jump to the conclusion that she has been meeting up with Theo.

Sky's face slowly becomes a mask of serenity, the energy in the room shifts as electricity dances over my skin, I am not the only one who feels it too. Lt Anderson watches her warily as she steps towards Danny leaning down to his level, he swallows hard but doesn't look away.

"You think you know me so well! What am I thinking right now?" Sky spits at him.

"Probably that you wanna junk punch me……. but before you do, we are only trying to help you both and we can't do that if you're……."

Before he can finish, Sky pushes him with such force that the sofa we are both on jolts back tipping Danny and I over and onto the floor. I hear Lt Anderson shouting at Sky, but it is muffled as the energy in me builds, before I know it, I am in front of Sky and pushing her against the wall.

"Calm down sis, Danny is our friend, he is only looking out for us," I say sternly, the energy in me hums across my skin, it is not centred in my chest like it was last time, now it vibrates all over my body.

Sky's eyes are lit up to a brilliant blue-purple, small tendrils of electricity bounce around her iris, it's hypnotic and strangely beautiful. I place my hands on either side of her face, she seems to have calmed.

I whisper, "We can trust them."

She shakes her head, visibly getting more distressed.

"It's Danny, he's like family. He is probably the only person we can trust."

"What about Anderson?" Sky whispers.

"He has put his life on the line for us, he is loyal to the General, he is also on our side."

She sucks in a breath and her eyes dim back to normality, at the same time the warm humming from the energy over my skin disappears. Looks like we are both quickly gaining control of whatever this power is.

"You know your eyes were like a luminous green then, back at Nix's flat they had literally looked like they were on fire." Sky says.

"Well a moment ago yours had little bolts of electricity shooting around them."

She looks disturbed by this; I hold her hand.

"They looked awesome Sky, so cool." I smile to reassure her.

Turning back, I see Danny and Lt Anderson standing close together a little on edge, not surprising seeing as the smallest person in the room just flipped two people to the floor. Sky steps forward a little.

"Danny I am sorry, I didn't mean to take it out on you, I just...."

He smiles brightly and moves towards her to embrace her in a hug.

"It's ok, I just want you guys to know that I am on your side, you can tell me anything."

Sky nods and looks at me as she hugs Danny back.

"So maybe we have been keeping something from you." I start but then stop, what if there are cameras or some kind of voice recorders around here, I don't want Nix to be hearing that Sky can project, it will be all the ammunition he needs for his theory about Theo. "I have been projecting." I say it without thinking.

Sky looks at me with surprise, but thankfully hides it well when Danny looks from me to her.

"You've been projecting?" Lt Anderson asks suspiciously.

"Yes, the first time was back at home the night before ...well you know. Then it happened again at the safe house. I didn't want to say anything until I knew more about what it was that I was doing."

Danny looks between us dubiously, then as if he realises what I am doing he smiles and nods without saying anything further.

Lt Anderson looks confused, clearly not having clicked on to what I am doing. "So, if you're the one projecting, why was Nix making all that fuss about Sky falling off the sofa or when she went through the portal?"

Needing to think fast I just go with my gut instinct. "For some reason I think Nix has it out for Sky, I have seen the way he looks at her, something about her power makes him almost fearful of her."

Sky moves forward and nods in agreement. "He has not liked me since he first met me, although probably bashing him over the head with a branch a couple of times did not help."

Danny smirks, in fact the memory even has me laughing a little.

"And as for at the safe house, I had a bad dream and woke startled."

"OK so you're the one who projects, what is it like?" Lt Anderson asks.

I recall the memory of Sky telling me about her experience. "Well I went to sleep and when I woke up I was surrounded by fog, I walked around for ages until I saw a rock and I started to climb......." I stop suddenly as I remember Sky telling me she had met someone, a man during this projection, she hadn't remembered his name at the time but could this have been Theo?

"You started to climb and?" Danny probes.

I look to Sky, but she is looking to the floor and picking the skin at her thumb again, a prickle trickles up my spine, has she met Theo? Surely she wouldn't keep something as important as that from me? But then when would she have had the chance to tell me, we have been surrounded by people since the hospital!

"I was climbing for what felt like an age……." Now I will have to lie because Sky didn't tell me anymore. "And then I missed my footing, I fell back through the fog, just as I was about to hit what must have been the bottom I woke up in bed, my hands and feet were covered in dirt."

Everyone remains silent, all I can hear is my pulse quickening as I note just how nervous Sky is getting and the fact she won't make eye contact with me.

"I am going for a shower." She jumps up heading to the bathroom.

A click from the door stops her mid stride, we all look to the door as it opens revealing the elders from earlier, minus Tiberius. Without speaking they enter, shutting the door behind them, the hairs on my arms rise as my stomach fills with dread. Something is not right.

The first of the four elder's cold stare settles on me first, his eyes turning from grey to purple, what the hell? There is no warning as a bolt of power is released from his hand throwing me back into the wall with such force it should have knocked me out. But I feel it, the hum of my own energy spreading over my skin, the impact feels more like hitting a bed than a rock wall. One of the elders uses his power to throw Danny from the floor to ceiling and back down again, blood is already dripping from his mouth and he barely looks conscious. Fury builds in every cell, I let it ball into my chest and release down my arms and out of palms like I had with the shark. Its aim connects with the elder sending him back into the opposite wall in a ball of flames, it also hits another on the side of their face releasing his hold on Sky. As he grabs his face screaming from the burning, Lt Anderson uses the distraction to break free from his capture, he army rolls under the elder grabbing some splintered wood and thrusts it into the burning elder's chest. I turn to strike at the remaining two elders but they have Sky pinned between them.

"Take one more move and we will use our power to explode her brain," says the one to the left.

The one to the right with purple eyes raises his hand to her head, her eyes instantly roll back revealing just the whites and she starts to scream.

"NOOO STOP. Ok I promise I won't use my power," I scream.

The elder removes his hand grabbing Sky as she slumps forward, she moans as tears stream down her face.

Anger boils in me, but I dare not use my power, I won't risk her life.

"What do you want?" Lt Anderson says slowly standing from where he has just killed an elder. Both remaining elders look at him with pure disgust and rage, then the one with purple eyes laughs.

"We want nothing from you, pathetic human."

With that he throws a ball of electric energy at Lt Anderson, he has no time to react, it hits him square in the chest and through into the bathroom, he hits the sink with a deafening thud and then falls to the floor unconscious, he doesn't move. My temporary distraction is all the other one needs, next thing I feel is scorching pain in my head, like razors are being dragged through my skull and cutting into my brain, the pressure in my head builds and I feel like my eyes are going to pop out of their sockets. The last thing I hear is Sky's scream begging them to stop. Then there is nothing, no pain, no nothing.

****

Rhonda

Both Danny and Anderson look really bad, blood trickles from the corner of Danny's mouth but he is starting to moan, though his pulse is weak it is steady. Anderson's is weakening with every beat.

"We have to get him to the healers now!" Bree states.

"What about the girls?" I half scream.

"This man will die if we don't get him to the healers now, whoever has the girls can't leave the compound, it has been on lock down since we entered. We will need to get a search party together using only those we trust. Now hurry, Anderson is weakening more." She orders.

Nix scoops up Anderson and runs out the door before we have even got Danny off the ground, he moans in pain but we just ignore it, going for speed. Carrying him between us we race off after Nix to the healer's quarters, upon entering there is already a commotion of healers tending to Anderson. As soon as they see us another two come for Danny, lifting him onto a bed and using their powers to seal any internal bleeding or serious breaks. They move their hands up and down Anderson's body, hovering a couple of inches from actually touching him, I can see the distortion in the space between his body and their hands indicating their power flowing from them into him. There are only a few of us within the agency with this ability, most become healers or go onto to become elders. Nix is the only one in the agency who has this ability who is neither, he chose the life of an agent and with Tiberius in power he was granted this request.

The head healer, Audrea, looks up at me. "How the hell did this happen?" she demands.

"I don't know, they were locked away in one of the secure rooms, we noticed all the security cameras were out, when we got there two of the elders were dead, and these two were locked in the bathroom like this," I explain.

She doesn't once stop assisting with healing Anderson, moving her hands deftly over him. I can sense his heart beat strengthening already.

"Do you think this was the work of the sisters?"

I am stunned and appalled by her insinuation, and she can tell this has not gone down well with me.

Before either of us can speak Danny croaks out, "No it wasn't them….it was your elders…… where are Sky and Rae?"

He starts to sit, but Bree and another healer push him back down.

Audrea coldly looks at Danny. "Are you certain of your accusation?"

Danny pushes Bree's hand off him and sits up, facing Audrea head on he doesn't blink. "I know what I saw, the four of them entered the room and then attacked us, I don't know why, I was knocked unconscious…. now where are Rae and Sky?" He looks at me pleading.

"We don't know where they are Danny."

He starts to move to get off the bed.

Nix gently pushes him back. "Let the healers finish their work on you, we will go search for Rae and Sky."

Danny scowls back at him and then me. "Like I am going to trust any of you to actually help. You promised them they would be safe here, instead you have only brought them to more harm. So, get your hand off me now."

Nix's usual impatience dissipates, we had promised them they would be safe. Danny is perfectly within his right to not trust us. Nix backs off.

"Danny, we had no idea this would happen. We genuinely believed we were bringing you to safety," I plead with him to believe me.

The head of security walks in ushering for us to go to him.

Turning back to Danny "Please let the healers finish their work, as soon as you are healed you can help us look for Rae and Sky, I promise."

I don't wait for an answer but join Nix and Bree in the entrance way with the head of security. I have met Cade a couple of times; he took over the position from his Dad only a few months ago. Cade is a towering mass of muscle, bigger than Nix and always looks like he is about to punch your lights out. From the few encounters I have had with him he has even fewer social skills than Nix and takes his job very seriously.

"I have been informed that there has been an incident, why did you not report this immediately?" His voice is so deep that even trying to keep his volume down it comes out booming.

Before Nix or I can open our mouths, Bree answers with a less than impressed tone.

"It was not reported immediately because there were two individuals on the brink of death. My question to you is, how and why were the security measures down for an entire section of the compound?"

She does not give Cade a moment to answer. "For your knowledge, four of the elders entered the secure room that were holding the sisters and their friends, from an eye witness," she indicates back at Danny, "They openly attacked them, we don't know why, but they have taken the Sisters, it is imperative that we keep the compound on lock down until we retrieve them."

Cade is silent for a second, concern evident on his face. He moves in closer, lowering his voice more. "Are you certain what the eye witness saw was correct?" He says it without accusation, simply a question to confirm.

"Danny is one of the most honest people you will ever meet," I step in.

Cade nods, taking my word. "Then my fears have come to pass, I raised concerns with Elder Tiberius about reassigning our agents, that it would leave the compound open to an attack, he would not listen and reminded me of my place in the agency. I found this to be most unusual for him as he has always been accepting of advice. His orders left everyone with little time to organise themselves before their reassignments. My team has been working around the clock to help ensure the security systems are all in working order, but we have come across numerous glitches, it is as if someone has hacked the system."

A cold sinking feeling of dread swells in my stomach, have we just brought the girls into a trap?

Nix is silent, from what Cade is saying, it looks like Tiberius maybe in on this, but to what end? Surely, he is not working with the Shades.

"My father said he was on his way to see you, just before we discovered the security cameras were down, did you meet him?"

Nix's tone is flat, but I can tell he is barely containing his rage.

"No, Tiberius did not come see me, we were checking the grand hall when one of the nurses alerted us to the incident. I sent the rest of the team to the secure room to keep anyone from entering and disturbing the evidence."

The muscles in Nix's neck start to pulse and his face reddens with anger. "We need to find the girls...NOW!"

He turns back into the healing room; Danny is now sitting up looking better than ever and Anderson is now conscious.

"Are they ok to walk?" Nix demands.

Audrea glares at him before answering. "They were both close to death, of course they shouldn't be walking around!"

Danny shakes his head and jumps off the bed. "I am fine.... thank you." He turns to the young lady who had healed him.

"Me too." Anderson slowly sits up, clearly still in some pain.

"No, you are not, you suffered severe internal bleeding as well as a fractured spine. My healing is good, but I am not a bloody miracle worker, you need to rest."

Anderson shakes his head and sucking in a breath he

stands. "You don't consider all that healing a miracle?" He laughs and holds out his hand to shake hers. She looks dubious but Anderson's warm smile encourages her to accept the handshake. "Thank you for saving my life." He holds her hand not letting go. "You are a miracle worker."

The usually stern Audrea cracks a smile, before sighing and rolling her eyes. She turns and grabs some tablets. "Here take this, it will help with the pain….and you." She thrusts a finger at Nix. "He is forbidden to fight; one small knock and all my work will be undone do you understand me?"

"Got it, just walking for him," Nix says.

They join us over in the doorway, Danny looks up at Cade like he is some kind of god.

"What are you gawking at?" Cade says with a bit of a bellow.

Danny cowers back a bit. "Nothing."

"What is the plan?" I ask.

"We don't know who we can trust, I suggest we head back to my team at the secure room," Cade states and without waiting for a response he starts off back to the room.

I indicate to Danny and Anderson for them to follow, Anderson moves in closer to me whispering in my ear.

"How do we know we can trust him?" Bree hears this too.

"We don't, right now we have to assume we can trust no one." Bree says. Danny sniggers.

"Is that including you?" But Bree is undeterred by his accusation.

"I understand you have no reason to trust any of us, your

experience of the agency has not been a great one, but you will in time learn that you can trust us." She indicates to Nix and I as well as herself.

We round the corner to the secure room, three security officers stand to attention outside, another has a laptop plugged into one of the cameras. They all salute Cade as he approaches.

"Agent Jackson, have you found their location?"

"No, whoever has hacked us is sporadically shutting down various systems at a time throughout the compound. I have found no sign of them on any of the cameras and the infrared has been shut down."

"Is the main security lockdown still operating?" Cade worriedly asks.

"It is for now, but for how long I do not know, whoever it is they are good." He goes back to tapping away on this laptop.

"Where would they take them?" Cade looks to Bree.

"We don't even know why they have even taken them!" She looks back to Anderson. "Did you see or hear anymore?"

Anderson approaches with a slight hobble, he really shouldn't be on his feet right now.

"Yes, I asked them what they wanted, one of them answered back and said we want nothing from you human, then he blasted me with a bolt of electricity, the last thing I remember was his purple eyes."

"WHAT?" I move in front of him using my enhanced speed without thinking, he doesn't even have time to move back in shock.

"He had purple eyes?" I reiterate slowly, I need him to

confirm what I already suspect.

"Yes, why is that so important?"

Cade sighs and smashes his fist into the door. "Only Shades have purple eyes, our council of elders has been infiltrated."

The enormity that the agency has been infiltrated knocks me to the core, we are in so much shit!

"That is impossible, we have wards and other measures in place to ensure that does not happen," Bree barks.

"Bree, I don't want to believe this as much as you don't, if true this possibly implicates my Father as working in line with the Shades." Nix doesn't even look at her, his focus is on the dead bodies in the room.

"Let's have a look for ourselves, shall we?" Cade enters the room; the other security officers move to the side and without being asked exit the room.

We all move into the room, Cade approaches the elder with the broken wood sticking out of his chest first, only half his face is burnt so we will still be able to see his eye.

Cade forces open the lid of his eye, it is a pale blue almost grey colour, looking up he beckons Anderson to come closer to inspect.

"He wasn't the one I saw with purple eyes, it was one of the other two that have Sky and Rae." Anderson looks, pleading with us to believe him, and I do, I don't doubt what he knows he saw.

"Let's examine the rest of the body, see what we can find. Have any of your men touched the bodies?" I direct at Cade.

"Absolutely not, they were on strict orders to guard only."

I kneel down to the body, the four elders have always worn identical black robes, with their haircut the same, from a distance it's difficult to tell them apart, but on closer inspection I see this is council Elder Ethan Rivers. Being able to identify him makes this even harder, though the elders were always distant from the rest of STAR, whenever I had met one, they had always been nice, compassionate and caring. The thought that these men had not only been working against us, but had been in league with the devils that we risked our lives daily to protect the world from, it is just too much.

I sit back and stare, within two days everything I know has crashed down around me and I have no control, no safety net. STAR has always been my safety net, there has always been back up, people to turn to, now who the hell can we trust. I look to Bree; can I even trust the woman I have known my entire life? I shake it off, I can't start doubting the people I am closest to...not yet and not without reason. I inspect the body further, checking for god knows what, a clue, anything to help us find the girls. I pull his arm away to get at his pocket, it takes more effort as rigor mortis is already setting in. His sleeve lifts up a little and I stop when I catch a glimpse of a marking. Pulling the sleeve up further reveals a tattoo, it is a strange symbol that looks a little like the glyphs in the caverns below.

"What have you found?" Nix kneels next to me to take a look.

"I don't know, it's some kind of weird tattoo, I can't make out the meaning though."

He leans in to take a closer look, but shifts back suddenly, a look of confusion on his face.

"Do you know what it means?" Bree asks over my shoulder.

"It is an ancient symbol of the Shades, I have not seen any artefact with this on it. The only reason I remotely recognise it, is because my father once showed me the Asteria records."

Anderson and Danny edge closer, having given up getting any kind of evidence off the burnt corpse against the wall.

"What are the Asteria Records?" Anderson asks.

Every agent in STAR knows about the records, very few of us are actually allowed to see them, let alone read them. Nix had been granted that privilege because his father was a Council Elder, of course he was sworn not to reveal what he had seen, and of course he instantly came back to tell us all about it.

"It is basically the Asteria and Shade history, a dated account that goes back over a hundred-thousand years, before they came to this planet. It tells about the war, the different planets. There was writing just like this when detailing about the shades." Nix holds up Dead Elder River's arm, we all look closer.

"I swear I have seen that before," Danny exclaims.

Now that is impossible, up until two days ago he had no part of this world. He looks puzzled that he can't place where he has seen it.

"I highly doubt you could have seen this before," Cade says so matter of fact.

I can tell it has brushed Danny up the wrong way.

"I can't remember where, but I have seen a tattoo just

like this before."

"Millions of people have tattoos, many with Symbols, I am sure it would look a little similar." Cade is even starting to rub me up the wrong way.

Danny moves closer, glaring at Cade, looking back to the tattoo he looks closer.

"I don't care what you say, I have seen this tattoo before, this exact tattoo."

Cade looks like he is about to jump in with some kind of smart comment but Danny stops him.

"But it doesn't matter whether or not I have seen this tattoo before, my best friends have been kidnapped, for all we know they are being tortured or worse. So quit arguing with me and let's find them!"

Without waiting for anyone he marches off out the door with Anderson quickly following.

Nix jumps up and gestures for us to follow. "Wait Danny, you don't know your way around. I suggest we split up, each taking a section. Anderson and Rhon you take the North quadrant, Danny and I will go down to the caverns, Cade and Bree you take the Southern quadrant, the rest of you keep working on the security system and making sure it doesn't fail. Do you have any radios?"

Cade looks taken aback that Nix is the one giving out the orders, but there is nothing he can do, Nix is higher ranking than him, well he was until Tiberius demoted us, but no one else but Bree knows that. Looking at her now she gives no indication of interrupting him, for once. One of the security officers' hands Cade three ear mics, which he distributes to us.

"Once any of us locate their position, make sure you

radio it through first, the elders are very powerful and we have no idea just how many others are working with them." Nix says.

His comment is to everyone but his stare lingers longer on me, he knows there is no way I will wait for backup. Those girls are more important to me than my own safety. But I nod in return along with the others.

"Right let's get going," Danny says following Nix's lead.

"Anderson, we need to go this way." I point in the opposite direction that Nix and Danny have gone.

"Keep your head Rhonda, fear will cloud your judgement." Bree grips my arm; she knows just how worried I am. With a slight smile she turns on her heel and marches off for the southern quadrant, shouting over her shoulder, "Keep up Cade, we don't have all day."

Cade grimaces a little, clearly mirroring similar feelings that Nix has for Bree. Anderson and I move off up the corridor. I already have an idea where to start searching, the northern quadrant houses most of the agent accommodation, though it would be easy for them to stay lost in one of the many rooms, I hardly doubt it. The Shades and their followers are too egotistical, whatever the plan, it will involve a grander scheme than hiding in the dorms.

"Do you know where to start looking?" Anderson queries.

For someone who almost died and is clearly in pain he is keeping pace with me just fine.

"This section contains the dorm rooms for all our agents, there is also the service rooms and the kitchen, I have a hunch we would be wasting our time searching there."

"Why, with so many rooms it would be perfect to get lost in?"

"That is true, but the Shades would see it as below them to hide like that, I know the elders, their tastes are somewhat grandiose. No, I think there is a better place to start our search."

We pass the healing centre again, this marks the entrance to the north quadrant, but instead of going straight ahead, I take the immediate right down one of the fewer used narrow corridors. I slow my pace, searching for the right wall ornament, this corridor is lined with relics, it always reminds me a little of a museum.

"What are you looking for?"

"It's just down……. ah here it is." I stop as we pass a wooden cabinet that holds an old knight's suit of armour, on the other side is a crossbow mounted to the wall. I look up and down the hallway, no one has followed us. I push Anderson in so the cabinet hides us from the direction we just came from, but it also covers us from the camera on the other side. It is an ideal blind spot.

"What are you doing?" He seems more than a little irritated with me.

"This marks the entrance way to a secret passage. Only a handful know they even exist, they have not been used for over a century. Nix managed to get hold of an old map when we were younger. We used it to explore, well until Tiberius caught us, then threatened to post us to the North Pole if we ever entered again."

Anderson smirks.

"There is actually a station post for STAR agents at the North Pole, it is not a place you want to end up for months on end."

His smile drops realising the truth to my words.

Now looking at the bow I remember it like yesterday, the arrow already locked in the handle, I push down on the feathered tip, it moves easier than it did the last time, which can only mean one thing, it has been used a lot recently. A soft clicking sounds and then silently the door swings open. Ahead is cobbled flooring and dusty stone walls, it is also dark, grabbing my phone, I switch on the light.

"Come on."

Anderson looks apprehensive but follows me nonetheless, as we enter, I push the door shut behind us, enveloping us in darkness but for my meagre phone light. I should have had the foresight to bring a proper torch, Bree's warning rushes through my head 'Fear Clouds Judgement', let's hope a lack of torch is the only downfall to this impromptu planning.

"Where does this lead?" Anderson asks.

"All over from what we could tell from the maps, I think they were originally constructed as escape routes."

Anderson looks panicked.

"Don't worry, the exits have been blocked off for years, those that aren't have the security measures in place, the same as the rest of the compound."

Well so long as the system remains up and running, we could be running out of time. Panic radiates through me, what if we fail? What if the girls are dead? I push back the fear with all my might. I have to think logically, I need to think with my head.

"Give me a second."

Anderson keeps quiet, that's what I like about him he takes all this in his stride, even if he doesn't understand it. I close my eyes and sink into my meditative state, sending the tendrils of my mind out, I sweep the passages for energy signatures, but there is nothing, I can only extend so far and I snap the tendrils back with frustration. "I can't sense anything from here, we will have to keep moving through, I will try again in a bit." I move off not waiting for Anderson to respond.

"But if these passages go all over the compound we could be walking around for hours, what makes you so sure they are down here?"

"I don't know, call it a gut feeling." I look at him, he is dubious about this plan, heck I am a little, but over the years I have learnt to trust my instincts. Right now, it's pulling me in this direction. And so we walk on further into the darkness, I just pray we find them in time.

CHAPTER 17

Skylar

My head is pounding from whatever that jerk off did to me, it literally felt like he was stabbing me in the skull. Though I feel weakened by it, I remain conscious but Rae blacked out and shows no sign of waking up. I feel incredibly alone, god knows if Danny and Anderson are still alive, I can only pray that they are. If there is a god, please, please make sure they are ok.

The elders had taken us through a secret door hidden behind one of the many wall tapestries in the room we had been in, the one with the now purple eyes, which scarily reminds me of Theo, had warned me to stay quiet or he would hurt Rae. I had no doubt he would, so I have stayed quiet, all the way through the dark, musty tunnel, down a lot of stairs, to this place, whatever this place is.

It looks like some kind of worship room; it must be very old because a lot of the statues are worn and some of the carvings I can barely make out. We must be back under the lake again as I can hear water, plus there are loads of formations like the ones Anderson had mentioned.

There are bookcases on either side of the room with what look like ancient scrolls practically stacked to the ceiling. The room itself is kind of circular, with a crater in the centre and stairs leading down in the middle, around it is a bunch of symbols that I can't even begin to figure out. The one thing going through my mind is, are we going to be sacrificed or something. The elder carrying Rae moves down into the crater placing Rae in the centre, the elder behind me nudges me to move but I am frozen with fear.

"Move, or I will forcibly move you." His eyes light up purple again.

They are not the same pure brilliance as Theo's but the similarities I can no longer ignore.

"Who are you and what do you want?" I mean to say it with more force, but it totally comes out as a lame whimper.

"You will find out soon enough, now move."

He pushes me and I lose my balance, half slipping, half falling down the stairs, I twist my ankle as I try to right myself. Crying out from the pain I grab my ankle; I must have landed on it badly because there is already swelling.

"You idiot, he said they were not to be harmed." The other elder who had been carrying Rae turns on the elder who just pushed me. Well at least I know we are not going to be sacrificed, doesn't make me feel any better though, because someone wants us.

"Don't panic Reuben, nothing a little healing won't help." He approaches me with a leer, kneeling, he grabs my ankle, squeezing it hard, I can't stop the scream that erupts from me. It feels like my ankle bone is about to snap.

"Enough Lazar!"

Lazar's eyes pulse with light and he smirks as he squeezes tighter some more to the point, I think I may pass out, then he releases leaving nothing but one heck of a throbbing ankle. I shut my eyes and try to bite back the tears building, I will not let him see me cry.

"Lazar...." Reuben pushes past him, kneeling in front of me he hovers his hand above my ankle, a warming sensation slowly spreads, the throbbing decreasing with each second, it tingles a little and then nothing, my ankle feels completely normal again. I open my eyes and look in amazement at my ankle, the swelling is gone, in fact it feels better than my other foot which is clearly worn out from all the walking we have been doing over the last few days.

Reuben looks to me, his eyes are not purple, just a pale grey colour but they are cold nonetheless.

"Keep your mouth shut and no more harm will come to you."

"What do you want from us?" I could literally smack myself in the face sometimes! What had he just said? I must have a death wish.

Thankfully Lazar the torturer has moved over to one of the bookcases and doesn't appear to have heard me. Reuben leans in slowly, like a cat about to pounce his eyes might not be light up but he is still all kinds of scary.

"I healed you this time, I may not be so helpful next time."

With that he storms off to Lazar. They start talking, looking back at us but I can't hear what they are saying. Looking down at Rae on the floor I move to her, I need her to wake up now, should she have been unconscious this long? I lean in to check she is breathing and so not to piss off our captor I whisper in her ear.

"Rae…...Rae…. please wake up…...Rae."

I shake her, nothing, I shake her again, still nothing. I pinch her quite hard and finally her eyelids flutter.

"Rae ...I need you to wake up ...Rae."

Her eyes suddenly open and she shoots bolt upright, holding her head in pain as she does.

"Where are we? What…."

"Shhhhhhhhhh!"

I clamp my hand over her mouth as both Lazar and Reuben turn around at the disturbance.

"Well, well the little ball of fire is awake." Lazar stalks towards us.

Without thinking I push Rae behind me. My attempt at protecting my sister seems to infuriate him.

"Clearly your last lesson didn't leave enough of an impact."

With no warning to brace myself, the world turns into the most unbearable pain, it literally feels like my flesh is being peeled off, I scream like I have never screamed before. I am only vaguely aware of Rae yelling, I can't see anything, as my vision blurs from all the tears in my eyes. The seconds tick away and still the pain doesn't stop, I pray that I just pass out, every time I think I might, a new bigger jolt of pain rushes over my body. I have no idea if I am standing, lying down, sitting, all I can feel is this pain, my bones feel like they are snapping and my joints like they are coming out of their sockets.

For the first time ever, I pray for death. I am not strong enough for this, I can't do this anymore. My throat is so raw from all the screaming, all I can do is mentally scream over and over kill me, please just kill me. Yet the pain does not stop, he is enjoying this too much, he likes to torture, he won't kill me, he wants me to feel the pain. I mentally scream in pain and rage, a rage I have never felt before one of pure hatred. Suddenly the pain lessens, it is not gone, but compared to before it is absolute bliss. I open my eyes and everything is foggy, I wipe my eyes to clear the tears but there is still nothing but fog. I look to the floor, it is the same black rock with blue flecks that mark I am in the between realm, I look around but see no sign of Theo.

"THEO!" I yell, my voice is like an echo.

"THEO…...THEO…. THEO."

I increase the volume each time until there is a constant echo of his name all around me. I jolt as the pain that had subsided increases, the fog fades a little and I can see Rae above me crying and yelling at Lazar. No - I yell mentally, we need help. NO, I scream in my head. I am back in the fog and the pain subsides again. "THEO, please we need help…. THEO," I screech.

"Sky?" Theo comes racing through the fog, skidding on his knees in front of me. "What is it, how are you here?"

"I don't know but we are in tr……."

The pain increases and his face blurs as Rae's comes back into focus, I don't know if I can hold it much longer.

"Sky...SKY what's happening to you?"

"The Shades, they have us, at the agency………. ahhhhh so much pain." I cry.

As Rae's face becomes clearer and the pain increases again, I see Lazar looming over Rae laughing at the pain I am in, that prick is laughing. I don't know how but I use the rage of his presence to push myself back in front of Theo, the pain fading to a dull throb. I focus on the rage and hold it in my mind, clearly this is what is helping me stay here.

"Sky…."

"Shhh I don't know how much longer I can hold myself

here, the elders are working for the Shades, heck I think two are Shades, one's called Lazar and the other Reuben. I think we are still in the compound, they took us through a secret passageway and we are now in some kind of temple room. They haven't said what they want or what they are going to do, but......."

The pain starts to increase and I am dripping sweat with the exertion to keep myself here. The look of sheer desperate panic on Theo's face instils in me that we are in deep shit right now. He holds my face and a warm sensation pulses into me, the pain ebbs some more.

"Where is Nix and Rhonda?" he asks.

"I don't know, I haven't seen them since they left us in the room."

"Do you have any idea where the compound is?"

I nod the pain increasing again. "Anderson suspected somewhere in Slovenia. Theo will you help us......please."

He draws me into a hug, wrapping his arms around me, the warmth of his embrace is still not enough to stop the increasing pain.

I can see Rae again, I don't have the energy to stop myself from falling back, back to the pain.

"I am coming for you Sky, be strong, I am coming."

With a rush I am torn from his arms and back to the temple room. Then like a switch the pain ends, I shake and twitch.

"Sky.... oh my god Sky." Rae is sobbing, she pulls me into her embrace.

"Unless you wish to experience that same level of pain, I

suggest you sit in silence." With that Lazar moves back over to Reuben, who has not moved, he coldly stares at me, clearly no healing from him this time. Ass hat!

I take a few deep breaths, every intake slowing my heart rate and slowly stopping the shaking. I repeat in my head, Theo is coming, Theo is coming, Theo is coming. But how will he get here, he said he would not be able to reach me once I was in the compound? But then how the hell had I reached him? It doesn't matter, he will come for us, I know it. Heck the guy is a god, if he can create his own realm, then I am positive he can figure out a way to get in this compound.

"You ok?" Rae whispers in my ear.

I dare not speak and just nod back, wiping the remaining tears from my eyes.

"What are we going to do?"

Her whisper is barely audible. I look over to Lazar and Reuben, they have their backs to us, so I quickly lean in for a hug and whisper back, "Help is coming."

I pull back and she frowns at my meaning. I glance back at our captors and Reuben is now eyeing us suspiciously, I have no intention of going through that pain again, so I squeeze Rae's hand to keep her from asking anymore questions. I sit back a little just enough so she can see my hands and start to sign language to her 'Theo'. We only know the alphabet and we have not done it in years, but after repeating it for the third time she finally gets it. Her frown turns into worry tinged with anger, she now knows Nix was right, it is not like I was never going to tell her, I just never got the chance. I stare at her for a long time desperately trying to get her to understand that he is not a threat and he really is coming to help.

"What are you two doing," Reuben demands.

I jump having not heard him approach us, he towers over us, arms folded, studying us like we have just committed some kind of high treason.

Neither of us say a word.

"I said what were you two doing?"

I really don't want to be the first one to speak, but apparently my brain is not attached to my mouth.

"You said to sit in silence."

Rae grips my hand hard urging me to stay quiet, but the thought that Theo could be here any second gives me a boost of confidence, I sit a little straighter and meet his stare. Lazar is still busy looking over some scrolls.

Reuben leans down just a touch and smirks. "I like you; you have character…...but don't for one second think I won't hand out my own punishment if you two try anything."

He straightens, not taking his eyes off me, I feel like he is undressing me in his mind, which is totally gross because he must easily be in his fifties. Yuck. But not wanting to back down, I level his stare with one of my best resting bitch faces. Which only makes him laugh. Double A, ass hat.

"Lazar, are we ready, it won't be long until one of the others find us."

Lazar looks incensed that he has been interrupted, he takes a device out of his pocket and looks. "The system isn't down yet, a couple more minutes and then we can get out of here."

"A couple more minutes and they could be here!" Reuben's voice is stressed.

"You don't think I can take anyone that comes in this

room? The compound is empty, they won't trust anyone else but their little gang, two of whom are humans and probably dead after what I did to them." He smiles, possibly at the memory of what he did to Danny and Anderson. It takes everything in me to keep my mouth shut, I bite my lip drawing blood. He will pay for what he has done, I promise I will make him pay.

"I think you forget just how good Nix is, he is our most elite warrior, he has a perfect kill record. He's certainly gone up against worse than you or I."

Reuben genuinely looks fearful of Nix; I mean I know he is a badass but he's making him out to be some kind of gladiator. I smirk to myself imagining the look on their faces when Theo walks in, then they will really fear for their lives.

Lazar stares at him for some time with a look of disgust. "Your fear of the little hybrid is exactly why you don't deserve a place in our new era of civilization, your fear makes you weak." His eyes brighten with each word.

"Excuse me, but if it were not for me, you would not have been able to infiltrate the agency in the first place. I have more than earnt my place by your king!"

Lazar laughs coldly, and that is more frightening, if I were Reuben, I would definitely keep my trap shut. "If you truly thought of yourself as one of us, then you would refer to Aarion as 'our' king. No, you're just saving your own ass from the inevitable invasion to come. You turned your back on your own people, just to save yourself. How truly pathetic."

Reuben's shocked face turns from one of embarrassment, to guilt to pure rage. "How dare you. You and your kind would still be rotting in the dark lands had it not been for the Alliance."

What the hell is the Alliance? I look to Rae, no one over the last few days has mentioned anything about this, but then no one knew that one of their elders was in fact a Shade.

Lazar pounces forward grabbing Reuben by the throat and holding him up, slowly squeezing. "Your little Alliance has been nothing more than a tool that we have used for our own gain. To think that you have had any significant bearing on what we have achieved is laughable and highly insulting."

Reuben tries to fight back, even using his powers to hurl items at Lazar's back, but nothing phases Lazar, he doesn't even blink. Reuben's face is slowly turning purple and I am sure in less than a minute he will be dead. A beeping distracts Lazar and he drops Reuben like he is rubbish, removing the device from his pocket he smiles, turning his gaze to us. I swallow hard, expecting to be hit with the same brutalizing pain as before.

"Time to leave." He grabs a couple of the scrolls he had been rooting through and moves down into the centre towards us, we both involuntarily move back and he sniggers. Grabbing us by our arms he hauls us upright. "Get up."

As soon as he let's go, I grab Rae keeping her close, I still have no idea how we're supposed to be leaving the compound but I have a sneaky suspicion it may involve a portal.

Reuben is still coughing on the floor at the top of the stairs, Lazar turns to him with pure contempt.

"See, so pathetic, you're weak, your whole species is weak. You really think we would let you into OUR new era!"

Reuben is still trying to get his breath back and can say nothing in reply. I am now wondering if his windpipe is broken, not that I care, just of the two he is marginally the nice one. The hairs on my arms rise and a cool rush sweeps up my spine, Rae squeezes my hand, she must feel it too. Static charges my body and I feel currents ripple under my skin, all around us, thin purple bolts of electricity build, small and few at first but becoming more frequent, a wind swirls around us that is literally coming from nowhere. As the electricity increases so does the wind, I was right, this is a portal, only this time it is opening right on top and around us.

Lazar looks around with a look of surprise and is it a hint of admiration? "Well, well you two really do have some power."

"What the hell are you on about?" Rae says with a little shout to be heard over the wind.

He looks at us intently and then laughs. "You two really don't have a clue what you are, do you?"

Anger rages through me, I am so sick and tired of everyone knowing what we are and leaving us in the dark.

Before I can open my mouth Rae pipes up. "No we don't, so how about you tell us!"

He smirks and I am sure he is not going to tell us anything, why would he, he clearly hates us.

"You both contain the original, pristine power. You are of the light," he says, pointing to Rae. "And you of the dark." Pointing to me. "When your powers combine you can for example create portals in places steeped in energy."

He may as well have spoken a foreign language for all I understood of that, and I can tell from Rae's expression she did not get any of that either.

"We are creating this portal?" Rae asks.

Looking around everything is becoming increasingly foggy, the lightning is stronger and bigger, soon the portal will be complete and then god knows where we will be. Panic surges through me, we can't leave with Lazar, whatever is awaiting us I know will be far worse than anything he could do to us.

"Yes you are, and before you get any ideas you can't stop it, the portal is drawn to your energy, other than dying this portal will open and then you will meet him."

"Him who is him?" I shout over the increasing scream of the wind. Why is this portal so much louder than the last?

Lazar raises his chin in a proud gesture. "King Aarion of course, Lord of Darkness and your new master." He says the last bit with such a predatory stare, I have no doubt this Aarion guy is just like him, or worse.

I grip Rae's hand, tears swell in my eyes, if we thought life was bad before it is just about to get a lot shittier. The fog around us thickens, the wind moves away from us to the outer rim of the crater and the centre where we are stood becomes calm, like we are in a bubble. Just like when Theo had stopped me in the last portal.

"Are you ready?" Lazar asks.

Electrical tendrils shootout and entwine around our arms, I can feel the pull of the portal wanting to push me to the other side, but I fight it, then the tendrils latch on harder and pull. Rae grabs my arm as we both dig our feet in fighting with everything we have.

"I like your spirit, but you can't fight the inevitable."

I can feel both our feet slipping as we are dragged by the portal's force to the other side, I am still so weak from what Lazar did to me I know I can only hold this for another second.

The tendrils thicken around our arms and pulsate, as we are pulled closer, I can make out a man on the other side, he is massive, with tattoos and scars all over him, but it is his piercing eyes that are terrifying, they are red, like glowing bright red, the same as in our dream. Aarion!

I shriek digging my feet in, but he smiles revealing pointed teeth, he has fangs, frigging fangs. We are less than a metre from his side, when suddenly a sword flies down from above severing the tendrils, we are thrown back to the other side of the crater. Looking up I recognise Theo as he jump kicks Lazar in the stomach throwing him into Aarion on the other side of the portal, a roar erupts from Aarion. And what does Theo do?! He gives him the middle finger. Legend!

Theo races over to us, grabbing my hand he yells, "You need to get out of here and away from the portal." He holds his other hand out to Rae who looks exceptionally dubious.

"Rae, he is here to help, trust me."

She looks at me, hesitates, then another roar erupts from Aarion.

"THEO!!!!!!!!"

How does Aarion know him? I have no time to ponder on this as Rae grabs his hand

"Time to go." Theo winks at me.

We are just about to step out of the portal when a fist slams into Theo's face, the force pushes us all back. I roll a number of times and just manage to stop myself from touching the other side of the portal. I look up to who

attacked.
   Nix!

CHAPTER 18

<u>Danny</u>

By the time we make it back down to the caverns I am exhausted. Nix has kept a constant pace and the effects of having nearly died are starting to cause a strain. But I refuse to stop, we don't have time, Nix says the compounds systems are still holding but for how long?

Nix stops at the bottom of the stairs to the cavern, there are three tunnels that lead off, the one ahead I know is where we had entered via the portal. I move around Nix in the direction of that tunnel, but he stops me.

"They haven't gone that way," he says with closed eyes.

"How do you know, they could be waiting to go through the portal." I go to move again, as he isn't top of my list of people to simply take their word. Again, he stops me.

"I can sense they are not that way, besides it is too obvious, they would know we would check there first."

I cross my arms waiting for him to provide another answer, but he simply closes his eyes again. Probably doing that weird sensing shit Rhonda does. The seconds tick by and I am starting to lose my patience, I tap my foot nervously, realising I am leaving the fate of my friends to a man who clearly hates one of them and has no respect for the other.

"Tapping your foot like that is not going to help speed things up."

His tone is terse and really irritates me.

"Do you know where I would like to shove my foot?"

He doesn't even open his eyes, but he smirks. "Yes, I

can imagine…. I get that a lot."

Yeah, I bet he does, Mr Sunshine himself. He leans his head to one side and his brow wrinkles, then his eyes open suddenly, they are luminous, like a honey gold.

Suddenly they fade back to his usual deep brown. What the actual?

"This way."

He veers off to the right-hand tunnel at quite a speed, I will never be able to keep up with him.

"What did you sense?" I shout ahead, running at full sprint and he is a good few yards ahead. I really don't want to get lost down here.

When he doesn't answer I pick up my speed, it hurts like hell but I just picture Sky and Rae in my head. The tunnel widens and then opens up into a room similar to that which we had entered from Bree's cottage. It's a dead end!

"Great…. you …brought us to a …dead end," I wheeze out, leaning against the wall to catch my breath.

Nix moves up to the far wall, slowly rubbing his hand over it, there are two sconces that light up what is otherwise a bare room. He studies the sconces, clearly not bothered about answering me.

"Are you going to……"

"This is not a dead end," he interrupts. "I can sense them, just on the other side of here, there must be a secret doorway, the whole compound has a maze of secret passageways."

I go over to the wall, studying it for any signs of a hidden door, but that's the problem there wouldn't be any obvious signs, it's hidden!

"We must be almost directly under the great hall, I remember from the map I found when I was young that there was a secret chamber beneath the great hall, but no one has found it. It is supposed to be the original temple to the Asteria."

Suddenly the hairs on my arm raise and I feel static in my hair, turning around there is no one behind us but the feeling persists, in fact it increases.

"What the hell?"

The radio Nix has crackles. "The system is down; I can't get it back up." The security officer states.

"Shit…...everyone I think a portal is being opened beneath the grand hall, we are trying to find a way in," Nix says back into the radio, he hurriedly feels over the wall again.

A portal! That's what the static means.

"We are heading your way," Cade booms back through the radio.

"There is no time, stand back," Nix commands me.

I do as he says as his eyes light up to that luminous gold. He places his hands on the wall and the whole room starts to shake, a giant crack forms in the wall spreading out, more cracks follow just like when glass is shattering, then it just explodes out!

"Woah, dude…that's insane." Maybe I won't push him too far next time. I can only imagine what damage he could cause to my face.

A gust of wind and the sound of whirling come from the other side, what looks like a mini lightning storm is in the centre, electric purple bolts shoot out all around it, I can just make out Rae and Sky in the centre with some man.

The radio crackles with Rhonda's voice, "We ... round ... corner ...coming ...don't..."

The radio cuts out with a small pop as it smokes a little, all this electricity must have fried it.

Nix throws it to the floor. "Stay here, when I get the girls out you run back with them down that corridor, ok?"

I nod, my eyes are transfixed on the portal, it is not like the other one we went through, this is like a literal storm. Nix ducks off behind some bookcases that line the room, I move myself behind a pillar and peek out the other side. The fog of the portal is getting less transparent and I worry I will lose sight of them, moving out I almost trip over a guy on the floor.

"Shit."

He is one of the elders who attacked us, right now he looks unconscious and has an angry red mark across his throat, I kick him, but he doesn't move. Maybe he is dead?

Good.

A sudden scream draws my attention to the portal, I can make out Rae and Sky being dragged across by brilliant purple bolts of lightning.

"RAE...SKY!"

But it is lost in the wind of the portal. Looking for Nix I see him creeping closer to the edge of the portal, he crouches, leaning back ready to jump into it. But then someone drops down from the top of the portal, he has a sword and he slices through the bolts dragging Rae and Sky, then he gut kicks the other guy and moves the girls away. There is a loud roar from somewhere beyond the portal and a man yelling.

"THEO."

Is this guy who just saved Rae and Sky the same one who killed Nix's brother? I look to Nix who is frozen, rage building in his face, his eyes are luminous again and he charges for the portal, leaping through and punching the guy in the face, just as they are about to step out of the damn thing.

"Nix! What are you doing?" I yell.

Forgetting that I am supposed to stay away, disregarding that I am no match for anyone in that portal, I leap through. Staggering from the wind I less than gracefully tumble into the middle of an all-out brawl. Nix has this Theo guy pinned beneath him and is repeatedly punching him in the face.

"NIX get off him," Sky screams.

She jumps on Nix's back pulling him off Theo, her eyes are alight with energy too, electrical blue currents ripple out from her hands and surge into Nix, he convulses and falls to the floor. Sky jumps off him and whilst he is down kicks him to the chest sending him flying into me. We both crash back out of the portal and into a bookcase. The air is knocked out of me and I am half squashed beneath Nix.

Hands suddenly grab me and haul me up.

"You alright?" Anderson asks me.

"Yeah all good, just a little winded."

Rhonda helps Nix up, but he shoves her to one side and runs back into the portal.

"What the hell is going on?" she asks.

"I think Theo is in there," I offer.

"Shit. Stay here." She turns and follows Nix into the portal.

"Screw that." And again, I throw myself ungracefully back into the portal, Anderson follows suit and we grab each other to stay upright when we land. Sky positions herself in between Theo and Nix, her eyes electric blue and fists balled ready for another attack. Rae stands behind looking on with utter confusion, as dumbfounded as me that her sister is protecting a killer.

"I was right this whole time, you have been meeting with him," Nix spits at her.

"Yeah I have and you know what he has been helping me, he just saved us and you were ready to kill him." Her voice is ragged from anger.

"He is a murderer Sky; he killed my brother in cold blood and you're protecting him?!"

She falters for a second, looking back to Theo questionably. He touches her hand and then looks up at Nix

"I did not kill your brother…."

"LIES, I saw you, I saw it happen," Nix bellows.

Nix takes a step forward and Sky braces herself but then a scream erupts behind them, the elder that had been unconscious on the floor has grabbed Rae and with a smirk drags her through the other side of the portal.

"Rae …RAE," Sky screams and makes a move to get her.

"Sky no." Theo grabs her holding her in a bear hug so she can't move.

On the other side of the portal through the fog a giant man appears, covered in tattoos, he has to be at least six foot five but the scariest thing about him is his glowing red eyes.

He laughs at our clearly shocked and fearful expressions. "I have one! Now hand me the other." He eyes Sky like she is some sort of prize.

Theo thrusts Sky behind him into Anderson and me. "Get her out of here, now," Theo orders.

"No, my sister, Rae, Rae." She starts to move back again but Anderson and I grab her, by god is she strong. I don't want to leave Rae either but I have to at least get Sky to safety.

"You would defy me boy," the man bellows at Theo.

Theo smirks. "It's not the first time I have defied you. You will not touch her."

The man angrily smashes his hands against a hidden barrier, electricity pulses around his hands. "I will have her as well, but one will do for now."

A scream from Rae echoes around the portal, Sky struggles and it is taking everything we have to hold her, let alone moving her out of here.

Rhonda moves over to us and punches Sky in the jaw, knocking her clean out. "Get her out of here."

"But what about Rae," I choke out, her scream still resonating all around.

The ground beneath us starts to shake and the wind increases, the lightning zips around us, it tries to latch on to Sky, so I throw myself over her, pinning her under me. Anderson dives on top of me creating a wall between her and the tendrils of lightning trying to grab her.

Through the wind I look to where the man is, he presses his hand against the portal, it begins to swell and then he starts fading, the wind too diminishes.

"He's closing the portal," Rhonda shouts.

Nix gives one last furious look to Theo and then jumps through the portal after Rae. Then the lightning disappears and abruptly the wind stops, they are gone along with the portal. As the dust from the wind settles, I lift my head up and look around, the room is in absolute carnage. Rhonda stands unmoving staring at the spot Nix had just jumped through. I look to Theo who drags his hand through his hair in frustration. Sky moves below me, struggling to get out.

"Rae...where is Rae, get the hell off me."

Anderson and I roll off her, she jumps to her feet and runs to Theo looking around. "Where is she? Where's Rae?" Tears start streaming down her face. Theo pulls her into his chest and hugs her. What the hell? She grips him tightly crying.

"We have to get her back, we have to." She sobs.

He gently grabs her face, wiping the tears, the gesture is so intimate it ignites a well of jealousy in me.

"We will get her back, he won't hurt her, he needs her too much."

"No, you saw what Lazar did to me, he is going to cause her so much pain."

"Trust me I promise we will get her back."

He kisses the top of her head and that green monster rises in me even more, I step forward about to say something, probably something very stupid but then Rhonda is there in his face pulling Sky away.

"Trust you? You're pure evil, I don't know how you got in her head but you will stay away from her," Rhonda spits at him.

Sky pushes Rhonda back, trying to get around her and back to him.

"He hasn't gotten in my head at all, he has done nothing but help."

"You don't know him Sky, he can't be trusted." Rhonda says never taking her eyes off Theo.

Before Sky can say any more a shot is fired, a small dart-like object hits Theo in the chest followed by another, his eyes slowly roll back and he collapses to the ground motionless. Sky screams and tries to get to him.

"Get her away from him now," Bree orders.

Cade and a number of other security officers walk down to where Theo has fallen, they cuff him and then unceremoniously drag him up the stairs.

"What are you doing? He helped us." Sky's eyes begin to pulsate with energy, a wind picks up from out of nowhere and lightning sparks out of her hands, she is literally about to lose her shit. The ground shakes and the wind increases as Sky moves towards the officers dragging Theo away.

"Sky calm down," Rhonda yells at her.

But Sky is too far gone, she doesn't listen and continues towards the officers. Bree marches at an inhuman speed in front of her, clocking back her arm and for the second time in less than ten minutes Sky is knocked out. Bree catches her before she falls and injects her with something in her neck, she then motions to one of the security officers to take her. The wind and the shaking room immediately stop, the fact that Sky has just caused that is actually the last thing on my mind right. Shows how much I am getting used to all this weird magic stuff!

"What the hell are you doing?" I demand marching up to Bree, I don't care if she is old or even that she is a woman, I am about to knock the bitch out.

"It is for her own good, Theo has clearly been playing mind games with her, if she loses control of her power, she will become highly unstable." Her eyes soften a bit, clearly some regret for punching a seventeen-year-old.

Anderson steps forward, his brow is furrowed, he looks worn out as must we all.

"What do you mean by unstable?"

CHAPTER 19

<u>Rae</u>

My mind swirls with fogginess, I can't focus, can barely open my eyes and I feel insanely cold. Why can't someone put me in bed? I am clearly ill, maybe it's a fever, strange that I would get one in the summer but Mum will know what to do. I try to reach out knowing Mum can't be far, she has always been there for me when I am ill. But I feel nothing. The cold seeps deeper into me and I realise I am lying on something cold. What? I try to peel my eyes open; the image is hazy but it looks like I am on a stone floor. Weird, why am I on a stone floor? Where is Mum and Sky? A voice penetrates through my foggy brain but it sounds so far away, I struggle to hear it.

"Rae...Rae are you ok?"

"Rae speak to me."

It's a man's voice, I recognise it, Danny? I desperately try to speak but my words won't come out properly. "...anny...s...ou?"

I try to move but pain suddenly radiates from my skull right down my spine, I spasm in agony, it won't stop, I try to scream but nothing but a hoarse rasp comes out. I hear the voice again.

"Rae try to stay still, don't move it sets it off."

Through the pain, I recognise the voice, it's not Danny, it's someone else I know but I can't form his name in my head. The pain is too much, I try to do as he says making my body go rigid, a few seconds later the pain stops and I am left trembling, even more cold than I was before.

What the hell is happening to me? Why isn't someone helping me? I take a deep breath knowing panic will not help me, I force my eyes open blinking several times to rid my sight of the fogginess. When everything finally comes into focus a bit better, I am staring up at a dark jagged stone ceiling. Where the hell am I? I slowly turn my head to the side taking in my surroundings. There are metal bars not far from me, they are covered in spikes, just beyond that is a person, I assume the man who has been speaking to me. Where the hell am I, where is my Mum?

I can feel myself panicking, why am I here?

The man on the other side comes into focus, I now realise he is hung upside down and is slowly swinging side to side, I squint desperately trying to focus on his face, it takes me a while but his face slowly starts to define detail. Nix!

And then it all comes crashing back, Mum is dead and I was taken, Aarion has me. I am his prisoner! I remember the elder Reuben suddenly appearing in the portal and grabbing me, the last thing I saw before I was dragged through was Sky's panicked face. Then there had been nothing but pain, Lazar had taken a hold of me on the other side. I vaguely remember Nix jumping through the portal and then Aarion was in front of me, telling me I was his. Panic like I have never felt before ripples through me, I start to shake, tears swell in my eyes.

"Rae, please try not to panic, your movement sets it off."

His voice is so calming, a far cry from how he usually sounds which is usually a cocky jackass. What does he mean set it off? I try to speak, but it is so raspy and quite painful, I stammer out.

"Sets what ...off?"

The look of sheer concern on his face does nothing to help calm me.

"Slowly turn your head and you will see. But do it, slowly, I don't think your body can take much more."

Heeding his words, I millimetre by millimetre slowly turn my head to the other side, if I could scream I would. There is nothing to compare it to, it is not of this world, it is more like something from hell. A shiny black creature with tentacles sits on the other side of me, green slime leaks from its closed mouth with hundreds of tiny fangs protruding out, it is skeleton-like in frame. Breathing heavily and not wanting it to open its eyes which are currently shut, I follow what I can view of its tentacles, they are latched onto me, at my wrists, arms, legs and now that I am more aware, I can even feel them on my back. Looking to my wrist I can see the tentacles have tiny barbs that have pierced my skin. What the hell is this thing? The horror at knowing I'm a prisoner, trapped in this room with this thing is too much, I sob.

Wrong move! The creature's eyes suddenly open, instantly focusing on me. They are blood red, filled with anger, I want to look away but I can't, fear has me paralysed.

"Don't you do it you piece of shit," Nix bellows.

The creature turns its eyes on Nix, its mouth opens revealing row upon row of razor-sharp teeth, the smell is like rotting fish, I gag feeling vomit rise in my throat. One of its tentacles unlatches itself from my arm and shoots out across the room, through the bars and snatches Nix by the throat. Nix instantly starts convulsing and his face turns a shade of purple, he could die.

"Stop…...please stop…." I cry out hoarsely.

"Enough Dagon," a voice booms.

A low growl emanates from the creature and it slowly and reluctantly let's go of Nix, drawing its tentacle back and latching back onto my arm. I hiss with the pain of the barbs penetrating my skin.

"Not a nice feeling is it?" the voice booms again.

"Please ...please make it get off me," I sob out, gone is my courage, I just can't bear it anymore.

From out of the shadows, Aarion appears, giant in stature, huge muscles flex as he chuckles at the sight of me. "Begging, that is the first stage to bending your will. And you will. In time you will obey me of your own free will, but until then it must be forced."

Aarion crouches down in front of me, blocking my view of Nix, I reactively pull away and try to see Nix again.

"Ah how sweet, you want to see if your knight in shining armour is still with us."

Aarion inches to the side so I can see Nix, he is slowly regaining consciousness. I sigh that he is still alive.

"Oh, I wouldn't sigh with relief if I were you, I have a whole host of treats for him before I kill him." Aarion smiles, his fangs gleam even in the dull light and his eyes flare red. "But it is what I have planned for you that you should be concerned about."

I start shaking so badly with fear, I know I must have wet myself by now, but I am too cold to tell if I have.

"But for now, I think you need a little clean up. Reuben!"

The elder who had dragged me to this hell, enters, he swells with pride at being summoned and bows deeply to

Aarion.

"Take her to be cleaned and healed, then I think it is time for round two." He smiles and flicks his fingers to Dagon who instantly unlatches his tentacles.

I cry out from the pain. Aarion reaches down and strokes my head.

"You will learn the quicker you submit the less pain you will have to endure."

I try to knock his hand away but I am devoid of energy, I am struggling just to keep my eyes open.

"Don't touch her you filthy bastard," Nix spits.

Aarion laughs, standing and turning to Nix, he motions with his finger and the bars between our rooms slide open. Nix never takes his gaze off Aarion, defiant even in the face of the devil.

"The Phoenix Storm, how I have wanted to get my hands on you for some time. Your abilities have made you somewhat of a legend with my people. You have the highest kill count of all the hybrids we have faced. But now you're ours."

Reuben smirks and reaches down to grab me; I try to resist but there is nothing I can do.

Aarion cuts Nix down and with a flick of his fingers to Dagon the monster reaches his tentacles out and pulls him over to where I had just laid. He instantly spasms in pain, going rigid, the tentacles tighten causing blood to drip where the barbs penetrate his skin.

I cry out. "Please stop...please."

But Aarion just laughs. "Don't stop, make him suffer," he instructs Dagon.

Reuben starts to move off with me, I fight, turning and

struggling in any way I can.

"Nix...NIX," I scream.

I look at his tortured face, eyes wide with the horror of the pain, his focus solely on me. Reuben's hand touches my head and blackness spots my vision; I try to keep focus on Nix for as long as I can but my eyes slowly shut. My last thought is of Nix and how we are never getting out of this hell.

CHAPTER 20

<u>Sky</u>

Rae's scream echoes through my head, her pain is my pain, I can feel the cold she endures but I can't see where she is, through the darkness I bolt upright awake in an unknown room in bed. Sweating from the dream I take deep breaths steadying my heart rate. Rae, oh god she's gone, goodness knows where.

"Sky?"

I look up and see Danny sitting in a chair at the end of my bed, by the door are two security guards with weapons aimed at me, they look tense like I am some kind of rabid beast.

"Where are we?" Happy enough just to see a familiar face.

He moves slowly up from the chair and approaches, eyeing the security officers, they train a weapon on him.

"She can't go anywhere, I am just going to sit next to her," he says.

"That's far enough," one orders.

"What the hell? What is going on Danny?" I go to move and then feel a restriction, I look down and realise I am cuffed at the wrist to chains in the wall. "I'm a prisoner now!" I screech and pull against the chains.

"Sky, stop. They have been ordered to sedate you if you get out of control."

"I am chained to a sodding bed, don't talk to me about getting out of control." I can feel my rage rising, the energy stirring in my centre.

"Sky just bloody stop. Listen to me."

Danny grabs my face, not letting me look away. The power shrinks back, I don't want to hurt him, and I know I can.

"Just for once listen to me and don't talk." He nods at me.

I will give him the benefit of the doubt, just this once. I nod back.

"They don't trust you Sky, they think Theo has brainwashed you and it is making your powers unstable. If you don't learn to control them, you will become a danger to yourself and everyone around you."

"What the hell Danny, Theo hasn't brainwashed me at all. They are feeding you lies." I lower my voice. "No one here can be trusted, look at what's happened. We should never have come here." Tears well in my eyes at the thought of what Rae must be going through, I know all too well the pain they will be inflicting on her.

"I get it, I do and believe me I don't trust anyone here except Anderson. But Sky, getting friendly with a Shade?"

I pull away from him at the suggestion of Theo being a Shade. "He is not a Shade."

"Yes, he is Sky, the man who took Rae who was trying to take you, that's his father, king of the Shades."

I shake my head, nope, he is wrong, Theo would have told me something as important as that. But doubt creeps in, his eyes do illuminate to a similar purple that Lazar's did, he is covered in tattoos and has the same pale skin. But how can he be, he has never once seemed anything like a threat. They are wrong, they're liars.

Danny leans in to grab my hand and I clench onto his.

"Danny, I know you are only trying to look out for me, but trust me when I say this is not true, I know him, he is not bad."

He looks shocked and pissed at me. "You know him? Come on Sky you've only known him what, two days? How can you possibly know him?"

"I don't expect you to understand, I just want you to trust me. I can feel that he is a good person."

Danny snorts and sits back, rubbing his hands through his hair in frustration. "When it comes to you and guys, you're not exactly a shining beacon of good judgement."

I can feel my temper simmering, I desperately fight to keep it in, repeating in my head, 'this is my friend, he means well, this is my friend, he means well'. "I know the type of guys I have gone with before may not fill you with confidence but…."

"So, this isn't about a gut feeling that he is good, this is all because you have the hots for him?"

He has to be joking?

"Do you really think I would have risked my sister's life over a guy because I thought he was hot?"

I search his eyes for my usual understanding friend, but all I see is conflict and …is he jealous?

"Are you jealous of Theo?" I demand.

"What? Are you being serious?" he stammers nervously.

"Yeah I am, because if this is all over the fact that you're jealous!"

He moves in closer trying to grab my hand again but I

pull away, the hurt look on his face tells me everything I need to know. He likes me and he is letting his feelings get in the way of what is true.

"This is bigger than whether I am jealous or not Sky, the guy is a murderer, he is the Prince of Darkness, he has led countless attacks on our world."

It can't be true, Theo has protected me, even if, and it's a big if, he is Aarion's son, he stopped him from taking us. He had tried to get us out. The memory of Theo giving the enraged Aarion the finger comes to my mind.

"Maybe he is Aarion's son, but he intervened to stop him taking us, maybe he is against his Dad!"

He just looks at me disbelieving what he is hearing me say. He is never going to trust me; my own friend believes them over me.

"Are you hearing yourself Sky? His kind killed your parents, have tried to kill us all and all you're doing is grasping at straws. What the hell is it about him that you so desperately feel the need to protect him?"

I have heard enough, the rage in me is in danger of spilling over.

"And are you so desperate for him to be the bad guy because you have let your feelings for me cloud your judgement?!" I spit the words out with more venom than I intended. I have hurt him, I didn't mean to do that, but he just won't listen. He stands up, pain radiates from him. I have had a feeling for a while that he has liked me, even Rae thought so, I had hoped he would get over it. I am no good for him. If what Lazar said is true, then I have darkness in me and I could hurt those like Danny. I am on my own with this.

"You should go." I look away not wanting to see his

pained expression anymore. He doesn't move, he just stands staring at me.

"I will always be here for you Sky, I thought you would trust me by now."

"Just go." It is all I can muster in response, I don't watch him leave, I just stare at the wall letting my tears of regret spill down my face.

"They are going to execute him," he says at the door.

I turn thinking this is probably another ploy they have told him. But his face is saddened for me. The door opens and my two-armed guards usher him out.

"No, they can't, he hasn't done anything," I yell.

The guards slam the door shut, I wrench and pull at my shackles. "He is the only one who can help."

My fear at losing my only hope to find my sister swiftly turns into anger, this agency has taken everything from me, the energy burns in me, willing to be released. But before it can a dart slams into my neck followed by another to my thigh. I smell singed clothing and I briefly register that the sheets of my bed are on fire. Did I do that? I can't think straight, my vision blurs and my ears start ringing. Someone else runs into the room with an extinguisher but I can't make out who it is. I don't care anymore; all I care about is my sister and how they have taken the one other person on this planet who has been honest with me. I picture them both, memorise their faces before the darkness takes me. Hoping that I just stay asleep from this nightmare, grateful for the darts that are knocking me out and taking me from this hell.

*****

Rhonda

I pace back and forth in Cade's office, so much has gone to shit in such little time, my mind is in overdrive. How the hell are we supposed to stop what is coming?

"Rhonda would you kindly stop doing that," Bree barks.

She sits at Cade's desk, they have been reviewing the security footage to try and ascertain where Tiberius disappeared to, but there is nothing, you see him leave us and walk towards the security office, when he should have turned a corner there is nothing. Officers were sent out to check for any secret doorways but none could be found, it is like he disappeared into thin air! Which of course is impossible. But I don't care where Tiberius went, I only care that Rae has been taken, Aarion could be doing god knows what to her and Nix?! I know he is more than likely dead or at least soon to be they will have no need for him, he jumped through that portal to his inevitable death! Stupid fool. But I know if I had been closer, I would have done the same, unwilling to let Rae go through the horrors by herself.

"For the love of Asteria, stop pacing." Bree's face reddens.

"Sorry but I just don't see the point of trying to figure out where the hell Tiberius went? We have the Prince of Shades in our custody, Rae has been kidnapped by Aarion and could be just about anywhere in the Universe. Sky is quickly losing control and oh yeah my best friend just jumped through a portal to his death!"

She stays quiet, calmly watching me slowly lose it.

"Not to mention we have zero idea what the Shades are

300

up to, a town that has been overrun with them and our leaders were helping them, heck one appears to have actually been a Shade. So please excuse me for pacing a little bit and not giving a tiny rat's ass about where that piece of shit escaped to."

I have never yelled at Bree, never, I usually would not dare but I am at breaking point, my hope and bravery vanishing with every passing second.

"Don't let it swallow you up Rhonda, it could be so easy for us all to fall apart right now, but it is now we must dig deep and become stronger." She punctuates each word, not just directing it at me but to the whole room.

Anderson has barely spoken since we got here, caught up in his own thoughts. Cade jumped at the task of trying to fix the security system to protect the compound whilst his officers have segregated the remaining agents to the great hall for investigation. His priority has been to see if there are any more infiltrators. And Danny, all his concern has been for Sky, though Cade didn't like it, I knew Danny could be the only one to get through to Sky about Theo.

Just the thought of his name boils my blood, he manipulated a young girl to believe he is good? There is no end to his evil. I am just glad it was unanimous to have him executed, one less problem to worry about was the consensus. I look at the clock, in just over an hour he will be dead, at least Nix will be able to rest in peace knowing Gabe's death has been avenged.

"For now, I need to try and locate Tiberius, he has information we desperately need," Bree continues.

"What information does he have?" Anderson asks, speaking for the first time in the last hour.

"That is strictly confidential." She doesn't even look at him.

"Still keeping secrets, you know this is exactly why we are in the mess to begin with." He doesn't raise his voice but his tone is enough to get her attention.

"I don't expect you to understand but it is in our best interests to locate him." Her voice snips with dislike at being accused of keeping secrets.

"No, I don't understand, and don't even try to insinuate you're doing this in our best interest. You are simply trying to cover your own backs once the world finds out you failed on an epic level!" The disdain for Bree and the agency is more than evident.

I have never gone against Bree, trusting her with my life, but now is the time for transparency.

"Bree, everyone in this room has put their life on the line to protect those girls and our world. Now is not the time for protocol, sod clearance, what is it Tiberius knows?"

She stares a little taken aback that I would defend Anderson, I would have thought Cade would have jumped in to defend her but he simply crosses his arms and stares at her pointedly, clearly agreeing with me. She sighs and slides the chair back.

"Fine but this is to go no further than us?!"

She looks at us all. We know none of us are imposters or traitors, we each subjected ourselves to testing, everyone in this room can be trusted. We nod in return.

"How much do you know about the reason for the girls' power?" Bree begins.

"Not much, just that it was prophesied by the Asteria that two would be born with great powers and end this war," I reply.

"Yes, the Asteria did have the foresight that two would have great abilities that could one day end the war, but what has not been publicly revealed is that they could also be the world's undoing."

Cade goes to speak but Bree stops him.

"Let me finish. For the last century we have seen a growing influx of Shades, the council knew the war was coming and yet there was no sign of the two prophesized. Every agency child born was tested, we kept eyes on the human population for any indication that these two were born outside the agency, but nothing! Over the last thirty years our fears have been realised, the Shades were definitely back and the war was imminent. During our search for these two, our scientists happened across some ancient text, the reference was to the origins of both species' powers. The original form of their powers before it became watered down over hundreds of thousands of years. For a decade scientist's including Tiberius worked tirelessly to recreate a genetic structure that imbued these powers."

A ball of sick slowly rises in my stomach because I think I know what is coming.

"Test after test of trying to get this genetic structure to mould with our DNA failed."

"What were you testing it on." Anderson is stoic but I can tell he is feeling the bile rise the same as me.

Bree pauses, looking ashamed. "They were tested on unborn babies. The foetus is constantly growing and evolving, it has the ability to absorb new structures on a level a grown human or even new-born ever could. Their structure is not set until thirty-two weeks."

303

Everyone is deadly quiet, letting this information sink in, then something hits me. "Was I a bloody test subject too?"

I clench and unclench my fists, keeping my anger in, blowing up at Bree will only make her shut down and I need to know exactly what they did to these girls.

"No, the tests only started twenty years ago."

The ball in my throat eases, just slightly, I should not be relieved, but selfishly I am.

"Did Rosaline and Leon know?" I ask.

"Of course, they did, they did it for the greater good."

I can't believe that my best friends would willingly sacrifice their unborn children like this.

"How exactly were these tests performed?" Cade booms.

"We believed that in order for our power gene to ...."

"Is that what you called it? The power gene?" Anderson looks more than a little disgusted.

I am too, what the hell was I born into?

"Yes, we called it the Power Gene." She pauses to see if any of us want to say more. When we all remain quiet she continues. "In order for this gene to be absorbed correctly by the subject...."

I snort at her turn of phrase for an innocent unborn. She glares at me, but I don't care, right now I can't even look at her.

"The foetus must have the perfect DNA makeup to begin with, those within the agency of a certain age were tested and matches were found."

I remember so many times that we have all been tested, it was common protocol, we are hybrids after all. But something is nagging at me, I had known Rosaline all my life, Leon had been around for a couple of years before the girls were born, they hadn't been dating until …….

"So, are you saying that Rosaline and Leon only ended up together because they somehow made the perfect DNA match?"

"Yes Rhonda, though I have no doubt that they did love each other dearly and they loved their children." Bree stresses each word.

I just can't fathom it, there is no way I could have done something like this.

"We had found perfect DNA matches before, but there was something different in this match, both Rosaline and Leon displayed a sequence divergence, their genetic data showed a natural evolution. This is a natural occurrence and is always expected to happen and can be seen over the entire course of this planet's life, everything evolves. As such their genome was the perfect absorbent for our power gene."

She stops letting it all settle in. I need to sit, no I need to move, in fact I just need out of this room. I march to the door.

"Rhonda, you need to understand it was for the good of the world as a whole."

I stop at the door. "Really, and what about the good of two innocents? Because if Tiberius had got his way they never would have left the compound, he created them for the sole purpose of being a weapon, and now you want to find him, to what? Tell you how to control them?!!"

"Like it or not Rhonda, we are dealing with powers beyond our true understanding. Tiberius and his scientists had in-depth knowledge; we need to know how to get Sky to control her powers." Bree is defiant, obviously she doesn't see just how bad this all is.

"Why can't you just ask the other scientists?" Cade asks.

"We would if we knew where they were. After the girls were born the former council leader and Tiberius decided if the girls were to be hidden so should the data. A secret laboratory where the scientists could continue working was set up. Now only Tiberius knows where it is, and we need to find it."

I can't help but laugh, so potentially the bad guy in all this holds the answers we need?

"If Tiberius is working for the Shades, what makes you think he would tell us anything?" Anderson, ever the logical thinker has a good point.

"I genuinely don't believe he is in alliance with the Shades, call it a hunch," she says.

"Even if he is, we have ways to make him talk," Cade answers.

"Do we even want to know?" I ask.

"Nope," is all he says in response.

Which is enough to let me know that a vast amount of torture would be involved. I pinch my nose torn between wanting to run out of here and get Sky as far away as possible, and now knowing the need to find Tiberius.

"Rhonda…."

I hold up my hand to Bree urging her to just stop. "I just need a minute ok." I open the door and walk into Danny, there are fresh tear streaks down his face.

"Danny, what's wrong?"

"She didn't believe me, she wouldn't listen. Then she told me to get out. When I told her Theo was to be executed, she completely flipped out, her bed caught fire and everything. Rhonda what are we going to do?"

Shit! I had really hoped Danny would be able to get through to her, I usher him back into the room. "We will figure this out, you just have to remember she has been manipulated by a master, it may take a while to break through his lies." I try to sound confident but I feel far from it.

A siren suddenly explodes out of the speakers and Cade's radio bursts to life.

"Prisoner escaped, we don't know how but he is not in his cell," an officer yells.

I look up to Cade, knowing exactly where Theo will be heading, to Sky!

CHAPTER 21

<u>**Sky**</u>

I haven't fallen into the deep black sleep I thought I would, in fact, I am pretty sure I am barely asleep at all. You know when you're asleep but you know you're asleep and can just wake up. There is so much noise going on around me it's like World War III has broken out, I open my eyes and staring right back at me are the most beautiful purple eyes.

"Theo!"

He is alive, how can this be? Hold on maybe I am dreaming.

"You're not dreaming, I escaped," he says with a smile helping me sit up.

I notice both my guards are unconscious on the floor and I am no longer shackled, but there is also a deafening siren blasting out of the speaker in my room. A number of footsteps can be heard from the hallway getting closer.

"Time to go." Theo smiles, offering his hand.

I don't even think, despite what Danny and everyone says about him I would rather go with him than stay one more minute here.

"How are we going to get out?" It is a windowless room with one door in and out.

"Only one door that you can see."

Reading my mind.

He pulls on one of the wall sconces above the wooden

panels that line the walls, there is the sound of stone shifting and suddenly a panel swings inward.

"Quickly."

The running footsteps from the hallway are nearly outside, shouting can also be heard.

"Open that door!" I hear Rhonda yell.

I dash through the doorway, quickly followed by Theo, as the secret door clicks shut behind us, I hear the commotion of people entering on the other side. Theo moves in front of me grabbing my hand as it is pretty much totally black in the tunnel. My pulse escalates with memories of the last time I was in this tunnel. Theo squeezes my hand to reassure me.

We move quickly as it could take them no time at all to sense where we have gone.

"They won't sense you; I have placed a cloak over us, it is hiding our energy signature."

"Oh...ok, that's handy."

After a few minutes Theo slows our pace.

"Where are we going?" I whisper.

"We need to get to one of the places in the compound that has an energy centre. Like the one you came through and the one they took Rae through."

Just the mention of her name fills me with dread, we have to find her!

"We will, I promise but first we must get somewhere safe."

He stops and let's go of my hand. I reach out to get it back but my hands land on his back instead. Heat flushes my cheeks the moment I feel tense muscle, Christ even his back is ripped, then I give myself an imaginary slap round the face because he can hear me!

"Got it."

Another crunch of stone echoes and I clench my teeth that someone may have heard. Then there is light, a lot of light. I shield my eyes as we walk out into what I can only describe as Eden! A tall giant green house filled with thousands of plants, in fact it is less like a greenhouse and more like an indoor garden. There are even birds flying around and butterflies, I can also hear the rush of water like there is a waterfall.

"Wow, this is amazing!" I say

Even Theo has stopped to admire the view, green upon green of leafy plants and trees, splashed with the bright colours of tropical plants, it is a little bit of paradise.

"It certainly is." His says

He smiles at my face full of wonder and of course I blush, whenever he looks at me that way, I get a hot tingle right from my toes all the way up my back. Looking away I take in more of my surroundings, there are areas of lush green grass and I am pretty certain I can see rabbits hopping around. Why would they have this here?

"When you're stuck most of the day in a compound like that you need to experience nature, so they created this, somewhere the agents could take a break in safety."

He grabs my hand again and we move on up the path, past some trees that I have never seen before, they must be tropical in nature their leaves are huge and such a bright green. The place is a comfortable humidity, warm without being stifling, I can imagine it would be easy to sit here all day. Curl up under one of the many trees and just watch nature, there are even bees!

But then I remember where I am, STAR agency and suddenly my desire to stay in this beautiful garden evaporates.

"They are not all bad you know," Theo says. "There are many in this agency who genuinely just want to protect the world and you, like Rhonda."

"She has lied to me too many times, I can't forgive that. And you're being way too nice to the people that have branded you a murderer and the Prince of Darkness," I retort. Through our hands touching I feel him tense.

"What? What is it?" Scared to hear the answer that any of what they said may be true.

He stops taking a breath and then turns to face me, regret etched on his face. "But I am the Prince of Darkness they refer to, I am the son of Aarion, King of the Shades." He pauses allowing this to sink in.

I feel chilled to my core, they hadn't lied, Danny was right. Oh god I had had a go at him for nothing. I rip my hand from Theo's.

"You Liar!" I am so sick of everyone lying to me, I thought he was different.

"I did not lie; I just did not tell you everything about me. But listen Sky…"

"No, you listen. I trusted you, believed in you, I even stuck up for you when everyone else said all those things. And for what, they were right. You're just evil." Even saying the word evil feels wrong, it doesn't fit with all he has done, in fact it is at complete odds. The words Danny said pass through my head; 'he manipulated you'.

"I did not manipulate you. I have not been the Prince of

Darkness for a very long time. A while ago I discovered something that changed everything, I opposed my father's plans and as such was labelled a deserter. Since then I have done everything in my power to thwart his plans, he no longer sees me as his son."

When I don't speak he continues.

"I have done some horrible things in my past, things I am ashamed of and will spend the rest of my existence trying to amend...."

"Stop, you can't amend murder, they are dead, there is nothing you can do that will correct that!" I think of the pain and loss Nix must have gone through when his brother was killed, weirdly I no longer blame him for his reactions. Apparently, he was right on the money there.

"I did not kill Gabriel; I can see how it must have looked but I was not the one to murder him."

"So, who did, Nix said he saw you do it and so did Rhonda!" Two witnesses against one.

"It was my father." He genuinely looks like he is telling the truth.

I am not getting that warning feeling that he is lying. But he is a Shade and apparently a pretty badass deadly one.

He moves closer to me and even though I know I should move away I don't. He tentatively lifts his hand to my face, gently cupping my cheek. His touch is electric and instantly heat blooms in my stomach, I should not be feeling this way with him.

The side of his mouth twitches with a smile and then becomes serious.

"Sky ... I would never hurt you; I am not the person I used to be, I may never be good, but I will spend a lifetime trying."

I can't explain it, I should run from him screaming but I can't, because I know in my heart he is good, he has changed. I can trust him. There is no sense or reason to this, just pure gut instinct and wherever he goes, I must follow, not for me but for Rae. The moment is destroyed by the sound of a gun and a bullet whistles across, exploding the beautiful plant just to the side of me. With lightning speed Theo moves us behind a tree.

"Over there," someone yells.

Shouts from other officers come from all angles, we are cornered.

"No, we're not." Theo grabs my hand; he forces us into the bushes and keeping low he pulls me along.

The sound of the waterfall gets louder, drowning out the sound of the officers. We pause, Theo getting me to crouch. Through the lush foliage I can see the waterfall ahead of us, I have no idea what his plan is though. Are we going to hide behind the rocks?

"No, the waterfall is another energy source, the system is still down so I can guide you to create a portal." He stills as a pair of boots come into view right in front of our exit.

"No I don't see them, anyone else?" Whoever he is he must be pretty massive because his voice is so booming.

Theo looks back at me and lifts his finger to his lips in a shhh motion, then sparks ignite on his fingers, he leans forward through the foliage and grips the guy's ankle. Electricity pulses from him into the man. Within seconds he hits the ground twitching. I recognise him as the one who had shot Theo with the dart, I do feel for him a little as he is only doing his job but at the same time it feels like great pay back!

"Move now."

We sprint across the open space to the waterfall; he grabs my hand and stretches it out towards the water. Static builds in my chest, my body humming with power, it's an intoxicating feeling.

"Send your power out to the water," he says as we get to the bottom of the waterfall.

The energy balled in my chest releases down my arm in a surge of lightning that hits the centre of the water pool. I can see the water starting to churn, purple lightning bolts flicker up and around. I am creating a portal all on my own! He takes my hand helping me up onto the edge of the rocky waterfall. Again, the portal is mesmerizing and totally different from the last time, it is like a whirlpool of purple water.

Shots ricochet off the rock as officers come running towards us.

"Stop shooting you idiots!" Rhonda's voice screams.

They lower their weapons. There must be at least fifteen of them and this time I doubt the guns are filled with darts.

"We have our orders, shoot to kill," one of them says to Rhonda as she storms through their line.

"Theo, yes but not Sky you dumbass!"

Instinctively I move directly in front of Theo shielding him from their guns, the look Rhonda gives me is of sympathy.

She slowly approaches hands up. "Sky you can't trust him, whatever he has told you is a lie, he is not the good guy."

Who the hell is she to call anyone a liar, she has lied to

us our whole lives, god knows what else she is keeping from us? Danny, Anderson and Bree come rushing through.

"Listen to her Sky, you need to stay here, your powers are unstable and could do some serious damage," Bree barks

I laugh, it's a little hysterical and I can feel Theo tense beside me, is he worried I will lose it too?

"So you can keep me drugged and locked up until I am of use to you?" I can't stop laughing, do any of them think for a second I will stay?

Danny looks at me pleadingly. "Please Sky, there are people who care about you here."

I know he cares, but it is not enough, my sister comes first and I know this is the best way to rescue her.

I look to Anderson, the man I barely know but who has put his life on the line time and time again for what he believed to be right. His face is stoic and unreadable, he looks at Theo and then back at me, it is not filled with hate or anger at Theo, in fact he doesn't even look concerned. He simply mouths 'Go' and winks.

It is all I need, I don't even think, I just act, using my hips I push us back into the swirling pool, Theo's arms tighten around me as we plunge through the whirlwind vortex, the world above disappearing as the fissures of lightning stretch across sealing the entrance to the portal.

I have no idea where I am going, or if Theo's intentions are for the good of Rae and I, but I know one thing, for the first time in the last few days I finally feel in control.

THE END

SNEAK PEEK

BOOK TWO: POWERBORN 'The Alliance'

I am running through a dark alleyway, it is raining and thunder strikes overhead, my path illuminates with lightning, casting eerie shadows ahead. The air is charged and I know Sky must be close, I can feel it, her power is like a beacon to me, the lightning above is not from the weather, it is coming from her. The end of the alleyway is ahead and I pause peeking out round the side for anyone, the coast is clear, I dash across the deserted Highstreet now thoroughly soaked through from the rain. I need to stay out of sight, so I slip into another alleyway full of bins, hoping that my presence has so far gone unnoticed. She must not see me coming, she must not sense my presence. I pause as I focus on the cloak I have placed over my powers; I should be invisible to her. I continue, pulled on by the sense of her growing power, trusting that our bond is leading me in the right direction. The alleyway comes to a dead end, there are a number of skip sized bins next to the wall that I scale with ease, I take the wall up onto the roof of the terraced house, keeping low and close to the chimneys I peer over the edge. The houses look onto the local park, which has never looked so different. The once green grass and tall leafy trees are gone, burnt to a crisp, the playground now nothing but twisted metal and rubble from being blown apart, and in the centre is Sky. Electricity swirls around her, shooting out from her hands and across the ground. Large bolts ripple across the sky lighting up the area for miles. What is she doing? I move carefully from my vantage point to a lower roof, keeping to the shadows, strange that I have not seen any Shades so far. Across from Sky the bulking mass of Aarion stalks across the park, he is alone, which is worrying, is an army of shades suddenly going to appear out of nowhere. Sky doesn't look phased by Aarions arrival, in fact it looks like she has been expecting him, she smiles at him. What! And then she does the unbelievable, she bows to him and then clicks her fingers. Behind her electricity whirls in blue and purple, spinning into a portal, how is she opening one by herself? Through the portal Theo appears, then another shade and another, as the portal widens many more shades can be seen. I need to stop this, now. I look back to Sky but she has disappeared, I move my position to try and locate her in the mass of shades but she is not there.

"Hello Sister!" Her voice sounds above me.

I look up and there she is, hovering, elevated in the air by lightning bolts. She looks like a god.

"What have you done Sky?"

She smiles at me, there is sadness to it.

"What I had to."

She unleashes a blast and next thing I know I am falling.

ACKNOWLEDGMENTS

This book has been a labour of love and I could not have achieved this without the support of my family and friends.
Thank you especially to Lance for your constant encouragement and faith in me pursuing my creative side.
Thanks to my sister Chloe for inspiring me to write characters I know!
Thank you to my friends Kate, Rachel, Emily and Rosie for taking the time to read my book and give me feedback. To Simon O'neill O'Kill for your editing and proofreading. And to Alix Kelman for her incredible creation of the book cover.
Last but not least I want to thank the dozens of authors who inspired me to just start writing, to create my own story and to trust that someone out there in the world will want to read it.

To my readers, thank you so much

Leila xoxo

www.leilakotori.com

POWERBORN

Printed in Great Britain
by Amazon